COLD REVENGE

ELLIE KLINE SERIES: BOOK SEVEN

MARY STONE

DONNA BERDEL

Mary Stone

To my husband.

Thank you for taking care of our home and its many inhabitants while I follow this dream of mine.

Donna Berdel

First, a big thank you to Mary Stone for taking a chance on me by collaborating on this story. I'm honored and indebted!And, of course, to my husband. Thank you for being you. You're my rock.

DESCRIPTION

Revenge is a dish best served cold...

Since she was fifteen years old, one man has hovered in the background of Charleston Cold Case Detective Ellie Kline's life, like a sinister ghost watching from the shadows. She nearly caught him once. Instead, she maimed him. Badly. As a result, Dr. Lawrence Kingsley retreated underground to lick his wounds and transform into a new façade of evil.

Ellie always knew that, sooner or later, the murderous psychiatrist would reappear. That time has come.

When his former assistant goes missing from federal protection, Ellie races to Oregon in a desperate attempt to locate Kingsley before the killer can spill more blood. Will Ellie track him down in time, or will The Master once again declare victory in his game of life and death?

Just when you think you're safe from the evils of the world, *Cold Revenge*, the seventh book of the Ellie Kline

Series, will remind you of just how flimsy the locks on your doors really are.

1

Maribel Green snuck a hunted glance over her shoulder, checking to make sure none of her coworkers in the Arlington, Virginia United States Marshals' office were watching before slouching low into her government-issued desk chair. With her heart clamped in an invisible vice, she tapped at her phone, but her hands shook so much that she hit the wrong app. Facebook popped open, filling her screen with a political rant by a woman she'd gone to high school with and had never spoken a single word to since.

"Dammit." She flinched as the whispered curse came out louder than expected. After a frantic look toward her boss's office to make sure he hadn't noticed her outburst, Maribel closed her eyes and inhaled through her nose the way every yoga instructor over the last ten years had taught her.

One one-thousand, two one-thousand, three one-thousand, four one-thousand, five...

At the last one thousand, she released the air through her mouth. It took Mirabel ten repetitions before her hands ceased the worst of the trembling. This time, she managed to tap the correct icon. The encrypted messaging app she'd been instructed to download popped open, displaying a single new message. Mirabel opened it, and a link appeared. She held her breath as she clicked.

Please, please, please...

As promised, a video popped up, and Mirabel struggled to recognize anything in the dimly lit room. Her pulse threatened to sputter out. Where? Where were they?

Just as her hand started trembling again, the lighting improved, and she spotted the two small forms huddled together on a weathered cot in the far-right corner. The video zoomed in, showing the zip ties binding their wrists and ankles and the blindfolds swallowing half their faces. After squinting long enough to ensure their chests were rising and falling, Mirabel nearly sagged onto the floor in relief.

Her babies. Her babies were still alive.

As Mirabel reached a shaky finger to touch little Ava's face through the screen, her phone buzzed. She jumped, making her chair lurch forward while she swallowed a startled scream. A new message appeared, catapulting her heart into her throat.

As you can see, the little darlings are still fine...for now. How long that lasts is up to you.

She muffled an escaping sob with her hand. She needed to pull it together. Focus. Remain calm. Hysteria would only serve to get her children killed.

On the bright side, the kidnapper didn't have any new instructions for her, which was one of the things she'd feared. That happened too often, she'd learned in her role with the Marshals. A kidnapper started by demanding one thing before asking for a second and a third.

For now, it appeared that her children's kidnapper merely

wanted to remind her what was at stake if she failed to meet his demands.

Merely.

A hysterical laugh bubbled up Mirabel's throat as the absurdity of the situation hit her. She clamped her lips together to hold it in while her hands clenched into fists. She worked for the U.S. Marshals Service, for heaven's sake. Why was she following the instructions of some lowlife scumbag who'd kidnapped her kids and held them hostage when help was only steps away?

All she had to do was march around the corner to her boss's office and tell him what was happening. Within seconds, Seth Conway, the Assistant Director of the U.S.M.S. Witness Security Program, would spur the marshals into action. Mirabel didn't have to do this alone.

She was halfway out of her chair before fear shattered her newfound resolve like a hammer splintering her office's glass wall. She sank back into her seat as the kidnapper's message from earlier that morning flitted through her head.

Be warned. I'm listening to every word you say. I watch every move you make. I'll know the second you mess up, and poor Liam and Ava will be the ones to pay the price.

Mirabel knew he was telling the truth about monitoring her because she'd already tested him once. In a panic, she'd started to dial Seth's number, but a new message popped up before she could finish.

I see what you're doing.

Mirabel shivered. That was all the kidnapper had said, but it was enough to convince her. If he wasn't lying about his ability to monitor her every move, then she had no choice but to believe him when he said he'd take any of her mistakes out on her children.

Her sweet, precious babies, all bound up like criminals in that dark room. How terrified must they be? Mirabel opened the video again. Her spine straightened, even as her stomach turned.

She didn't want to steal the highly classified information the kidnapper demanded, but she would. In Mirabel's mind, a choice between handing over names of people in the WITSEC program and forfeiting her children's lives was no choice at all.

Now, she just needed to wait for the right time.

Mirabel pretended to be engrossed in a memo on her monitor while the minutes ticked by. After what felt like hours, a flicker of motion in the hallway caught her eye through the glass partition. Right on time, her boss walked past her office on his way to the conference room for a scheduled meeting.

This was it.

Mirabel watched the time on her monitor like a hawk. When exactly five minutes had passed, she gathered a stack of folders as cover, stood up from her chair on trembling legs, and headed toward her boss's empty office. She kept her head down and exhaled a sigh when she reached his desk without interruption. Her gaze fell on Seth's computer.

I can't do this. I can't.

Before she realized it, she'd stumbled back a step. She tightened her fists and fought against the instincts urging her to turn and flee.

If she did that, Liam and Ava were as good as dead.

That was all the reminder Mirabel needed. Skirting the edge of her boss's desk, she sank into his chair and clicked the mouse. She entered the passcodes stored in her head from all the years of working with him. A few clicks led her to the file she needed.

WITSEC

There they were. The real names of the people currently

in the federal witness security program. Their aliases and contact information. All she had to do was write them down.

Just three of them, she reminded herself.

Three names in exchange for her two beautiful children.

What else could she do?

Mirabel reached for her pen to jot the information onto the paper she'd brought along with her, but her hand refused to budge. She wasted precious seconds reminding herself that the majority of people on that list were criminals. Scumbags who had only escaped federal prison by cutting a deal and ratting out someone who was even more awful. The most terrible of bad guys.

Not innocents, like her babies.

With a trembling hand, her pen scratched across the notepad as she jotted down the information the kidnapper had requested on the three names. When she finished, she glanced at the page, startled to find that the cursive didn't look familiar. No tidy, flowing letters. Instead, her handwriting looked like the wobbly attempts of a second grader.

She shook her head to clear her scattered mind. Forget the cursive. What mattered was that she'd retrieved all the information he'd demanded. All she had to do now was get out of there without being caught.

Mirabel logged out of the computer, replaced the mouse where she'd found it, and pushed to her feet. With all the calm she could muster, she called on her dwindling reserve of self-control to force her legs to walk out of the office, instead of the full-out sprint her nerves demanded. Once she arrived at her desk without incident, she collapsed into her chair, gripped the edge of her desk until her knuckles turned white, and waited for her pulse to stop its frantic drumbeat in her ears. Everything would be okay. The hardest part was over, and no one was the wiser.

Yet.

When her heart no longer threatened to punch its way out of her chest, she tapped out a text: *Got the info you requested. Can we meet now?*

Mirabel's eyes never left her phone as she waited for a response.

Wait for GPS coordinates. Don't do anything foolish in the meantime.

Before she could set her phone back down, an image popped up, a close-up of her babies' sweet, sweet faces as they slept.

A reminder of everything at stake.

Goose bumps erupted all over Mirabel's skin, and she rubbed her arms to chase them away. She didn't know how she would make it through the rest of the workday without having a mental breakdown, but she needed to figure it out, and fast.

The rest of the day dragged by. Mirabel checked the time so often that the numbers swam before her eyes, dissolving into meaningless symbols. Even the tiniest, unexpected noise caused her to jump in her chair. She stared sightlessly at the file open on her monitor, unable to focus on anything other than the names on the paper she'd tucked into her pocket. That, and her children.

Thunk!

Mirabel yelped and jerked in her chair, causing an unpleasant screeching noise. She swiveled to discover her boss looming in her doorway with his fist still mid-air from where he'd rapped on her window. Deep creases lined his broad forehead.

Oh god. Did he know she'd accessed his computer? Her legs quivered while her brain performed frantic calculations of her odds of darting past him and making it to her car.

"You okay in here? You've barely poked your head out all day." Seth's gravelly baritone sounded the same as always.

Mirabel's chest eased a little. "I'm fine, thanks. Just not feeling one hundred percent."

Her boss's too-sharp gray eyes inspected her. "You look pale, like you're coming down with something. That stomach flu has been going around, so if you're not feeling better tonight, take tomorrow off."

Tomorrow off.

Yes, that was precisely what she needed. After this, Mirabel wasn't sure she'd ever be able to let her kids leave her sight again.

She forced her lips into a semblance of a smile. "Thank you, I'll do that."

"Good." He jerked his head toward the hall. "Why don't you go ahead and leave a few minutes early?"

Before she could respond, Mirabel's phone buzzed in her lap. She knew without looking who it was, and the smile froze on her face, though she forced her voice to remain calm. "Yes, I think I'll do that. I'm pretty beat."

Please, leave already.

"Feel better." Seth nodded, and to her immense relief, turned and headed back down the hall. She waited until he disappeared from sight to open the new message.

I was worried you were being foolish, but you kept your mouth shut, good girl.

How? How could this stranger know that? Either he had a bug in her office, or he could hear via her cell phone.

The how didn't matter right then, though. All that mattered was what she needed to do next.

Bring the information, drive straight to the coordinates below, and wait. It would be unfortunate if you made any mistakes now, when you're so close to being reunited with your children again.

A pin appeared, providing blessed directions to a spot on the map a little over thirty miles away. She hurried into her coat, snatched up her purse, and rushed into the hallway.

Taking in a calming breath, she forced herself to slow to a brisk walk. She couldn't let her actions be memorable. Nothing to see here, folks.

Almost there, almost there.

The chant accompanied her down the hallway, into the elevator and out through the lobby area. She exited the building into a world freshly blanketed in a dusting of white. Frigid gusts of wind chafed at her already winter-dry cheeks, and she welcomed the awakening slap it provided.

Only last week, the temperatures had been unseasonably warm for December, sunny and in the low seventies. Mirabel had begrudgingly given in to her kids' whining and taken them on a bike ride. Guilt swelled in her throat at the way she'd initially resisted. At the time, she'd been tired from a long week at work.

She shivered and quickened her pace to the parking garage. The beep-beep of her remote echoed through the deserted building, and lights flashed, leading her to the white Buick Enclave. She flung open the door, lunged into the seat, and shoved the key in the ignition.

Once Liam and Ava were home safe and sound, she'd take them wherever they wanted to go. They could build a snow-man. Make hot cocoa and watch holiday movies. Mirabel vowed never to take them for granted again.

BEEP!

Mirabel yelped and slammed her foot down on the brake so hard that her head whipped forward an instant before the back of her skull smacked the headrest. She winced, rubbing her neck while her heart continued to race. A glance in the rearview mirror reflected the silver SUV she'd come within inches of backing into, along with a woman Mirabel didn't recognize flipping her off.

Mirabel weakly fluttered her fingers at the pissed-off driver. "Sorry."

Her hands tightened their grip around the wheel before she relaxed, releasing an unsteady breath. So stupid. Now wasn't the time to let her focus wander, not when she was so close to having her babies back safely in her arms.

Once the SUV cleared the path, Mirabel scanned both ways before easing her foot onto the gas. She exited the parking garage and followed the directions dictated by her GPS.

The first thirty minutes were excruciating as traffic moved at a crawl. Apparently, she wasn't the only one off work early. She switched on the radio, scrolled to a classical station she normally found soothing, but punched it off again a minute later. Each note was like a hammer on her taut nerves.

She finally cleared the D.C. traffic when the GPS navigated her off the highway and onto back roads. Soon, she was winding her way down unfamiliar streets. White flakes fluttered onto her windshield like ash, and when Mirabel passed a car smashed into a fence on the shoulder, she eased her foot off the accelerator.

Another ten minutes passed before the GPS guided her down a deserted road that Mirabel was sure she'd never been on before. The longer she drove, the more the acid ate at her stomach, burning as it attempted to rise up her esophagus. The sun was getting close to sinking from the sky, and she hadn't passed another car in a while.

"Turn left."

Mirabel did as the robotic voice instructed, then breathed a sigh when she was informed that she was only point two miles from her destination.

"Thank God."

Mirabel squinted through the falling snow, attempting to spot a building or structure of some kind.

Her phone pinged. *Pull to the side of the road.*

Not even bothering to be surprised that the villainous man knew her exact location, Mirabel did as she was told. She shifted into park and craned her neck to inspect her surroundings. She didn't like what she saw.

No one else was around. No other cars, no anything, except what appeared to be a deep ravine to her right. Beyond the ravine, day slowly gave way to night, and despite her nerves, Mirabel couldn't help but admire the riot of reds and oranges streaking across the sky, courtesy of the cloud-camouflaged sun.

A shrill ring interrupted Mirabel's trance, and she yelped before realizing it was her phone. The panic subsided, and her lip curled as anger fired within her every cell. Nine years. That was how long she'd been working for the Marshals. Nine years of her dealing with some of the worst of society and yet arrogantly believing she could continue unscathed indefinitely.

A mentor had once given Mirabel some serious advice. "Those of us who work in law enforcement all pay a price eventually, one way or another." At the time, Mirabel had merely smiled and dismissed his claim.

Not her.

She was careful. She ate healthy, meditated, did yoga. Kept her personal information under lock and key. Didn't post photos of her children anywhere on the internet. She did everything she'd convinced herself would protect her and her family from the ugly side of her job. Only now did she fully understand her mentor's warning.

Slipping the Sig P365 from her purse, she checked that the magazine was full before placing the gun in her coat pocket. She'd never killed anything before, but she'd kill this man if needed. Gladly.

Mirabel's skin buzzed with the need to do something. She shifted her weight in the seat and reached for the door handle before switching gears at the last second and wiping at the growing cloud of moisture fogging up her driver's side window. The text had instructed her to wait in the car, so that was what she'd do. Wait, even if her body was desperate to move.

She was close to crawling out of her own skin when she spotted headlights in the distance. They glided toward her like a beast in the night: slow, calculated, predatory. The sedan slowed as it approached and pulled up beside her.

Her phone pinged. *Show me your hands.*

Mirabel dug her nails into her palms before doing what he said. Had he seen the gun somehow, or was he just being extra cautious?

When the driver stepped out, she took in every detail she could see. Around six feet tall with broad shoulders, the man wore dark jeans and a plain black sweatshirt. A ski mask prevented Mirabel from further observation.

Without so much as a glance her way, the man headed for the back of his car. There was an audible click, and then the trunk flew open.

Mirabel gasped. Had that monster shoved her babies in the trunk? What if they couldn't breathe in there? A knot clogged Mirabel's throat as she smashed her face to the window in an attempt to get a better view.

The man pulled her children from the trunk, one at a time, and gripped them each by an elbow.

Horrible, but they were standing. Her babies were okay.

A strangled sob escaped Mirabel's lips as she fumbled for the handle, threw open the door, and jumped out. "Liam! Ava!"

"Mommy!"

Two little bodies propelled their way to her at a dead sprint. They launched themselves into her arms with such force that Mirabel staggered backward under their combined weight. She regained her balance and squeezed them tight, relishing the sweet feeling of their warmth pressed up next to her.

She laughed and sobbed and inhaled the sweet scent of their apple blossom shampoo. She was filled with a wave of maternal love so fierce she had to force her arms to release the pair because she never wanted to let them go.

There would be time when they got home for her to smother them with kisses and love and check to make sure they hadn't been harmed in any way. Right now, she needed to get them all to safety.

With that in mind, she hurried to open the back door and guide their shivering bodies inside. First Ava, then Liam. Before she could close the door, the driver appeared at her side, his gloved hand clamping down on her arm.

"The list?"

With fingers that felt numb, Mirabel pulled the folded paper from her pocket. Her fingers brushed the steel of the gun, but from the way he squeezed her bicep, she knew she wouldn't be able to pull it out, let alone lift it high enough to aim at anything important.

She just needed to give him what he wanted and go. She'd let Seth and the others track him down afterward. Maybe...

A part of her, a very cowardly part of her, knew that she'd never say a single word about this day to anyone. She didn't want to be targeted again.

Lord, please forgive me for what I'm about to do and protect those three people on the list.

She extended the paper toward the man. She was so distracted by the way he whipped his hand out to grab it that she never saw his other fist coming. Pain exploded in her cheek, and Mirabel flew backward before crashing to the ground.

The toe of a boot connected with her temple, and her

world dimmed even further as a loud ringing filled her ears. And pain, there was so much pain. Her face, but also her lungs. It was like someone had parked a car on her chest.

Mirabel gasped, and air wheezed down her throat. As awareness slowly returned, cries and screaming prickled her consciousness. She frowned, wincing as the motion made fresh pain explode in the side of her face. As her mind desperately tried to piece together the events of the last few minutes, her body jerked, then lifted. The screaming grew more distinct.

Her kids. Ava and Liam.

Her eyelids flew open, her gaze landing on the man in the ski mask. Her memory came crashing back, and Mirabel began to writhe in his grip. She flung an elbow into his abdomen, but either he was too strong or she was too weak for it to make an impact.

"I gave you the names! Please, put me down!"

A low chuckle was her only answer. The amused sound increased her panic by several degrees.

"You don't have to do this." She pushed at his shoulders, tried raking her fingers in his eyes. In response, he clamped her so tight against his chest, she couldn't move. Could barely speak. "I won't talk. I won't say a—"

Without warning, the man threw her inside the open driver's door, and the sudden jolt of her head filled her vision with flashing, agonizing light. She screamed, and bile rose in her throat as darkness threatened to consume her once again. She gritted her teeth against the pain and nausea.

No. Must stay awake. Liam. Ava. Need me.

Focusing on her children's sobs, Mirabel fought to remain conscious. This might be their only chance to escape. She felt for the gun in her pocket but couldn't seem to find it. Where had it gone?

"Shhh, babies. It's going to be okay. Mommy's here now."

At the sound of her voice, the children's sobs subsided into whimpers. There. She'd be okay once she caught her breath and her head stopped spinning. As soon as her vision cleared, she'd fight back. Grab her babies and make a run for it.

She thrashed at a new pressure against her chest, but when her hands flew up to fight, all she grabbed was a thick fabric strap. Her seat belt. Why had this horrible man fastened her seat belt?

A blurry figure filled her vision, and she tried to slap the dark demon away. It didn't go. Instead, it reached past her, doing something to the gearshift before turning the steering wheel in a clockwise rotation. While her mind was still trying to make sense of what was happening, a hand fell above her right knee, fingers biting into her muscle.

"What—?"

The Enclave roared as her foot pressed onto the gas pedal. The awful reality hit Mirabel when the SUV launched forward, taking a hard right turn. The man hung on to the door, his foul presence remaining at her side... pressing...pressing...

No. No! This can't be happening.

She pumped the brake with her other foot, but she was too late. It was done.

As the man jumped away and the Enclave's nose dipped down, Mirabel remembered her third-grade teacher sharing Newton's law. "An object in motion stays in motion..."

Her body went weightless. The first few moments when the heavy SUV caught air were peaceful, like floating in a hot air balloon. The children must have found it peaceful as well because neither of them said a word.

"...unless acted upon by an unbalanced force."

The front end crashed against the rocky crevice, cata-pulting the vehicle into the first of many somersaults.

The last thing Mirabel heard before her forehead cracked the windshield was the high-pitched sounds of her children. *"Mommy!"*

"Mommy's here," she whispered as the SUV tumbled two-hundred feet down the rocky ravine. She reached back between the seats, longing to touch them one last time. "Mommy's here."

—————

2

Ellie Kline set the last take-out container of Pad Thai shrimp on the table next to Jillian, the cardboard hot on her fingers, before scooting into a chair beside her. "That's all of it, dig in."

"Don't have to tell me twice." Jillian grabbed the yellow curry chicken and scooped a healthy serving onto her plate before passing the food to Jacob Garcia. Jacob was Ellie's former partner at the Charleston Police Department, but he'd grown into Jillian's real-life partner. The two had been dating for months.

Ellie grinned at the lovebirds, so glad that her two best friends had found happiness together. The grin widened when her stomach rumbled in response to the delicious spicy-sweet aroma wafting her way. She pressed her hand to her belly to shut the beast up.

The growling was so loud that Jillian paused with her fork halfway to her mouth and snickered. "You know, if you ate once in a while, maybe your stomach would be less vocal."

Jacob snorted as he helped himself to a serving of Pad

Thai "So, what you're saying is, Ellie should start eating every half hour instead of every hour?"

Ellie shrugged, unbothered by their good-natured teasing. "Sounds like a solid plan to me." She liked food. She especially liked food when it was shared around her dining room table with her closest friends.

"I still think it feels a little weird eating out of cardboard boxes while sitting at this fancy table with that even fancier light overhead." Jacob gestured to the elegant crystal chandelier that glittered like diamonds above the exquisite dark dining set. "Shouldn't we be serving the food out of china or something?"

Ellie waited until she swallowed a bite of sweet, pan-fried noodles before responding to her former partner's joke. "The rule is, whoever uses it, washes it. Oh, and by the way, my mother insists that the family china be washed by hand."

At the mention of Helen, Ellie's perfectly-put-together mother and more-than-a-little intimidating matron of the elite Charleston, South Carolina Kline family, Jacob lifted his hands in surrender. "On second thought, take-out containers are perfect, *Eleanor*."

The way he said Ellie's given name sounded suspiciously like her mother.

Jillian Reed rolled her eyes at the man she was dating before breaking into an indulgent laugh. Across the table, Clay Lockwood broke into a faint smile. Proof that even special agents with the FBI had at least some sense of humor.

Ellie surveyed them, a warm glow filling her. All her favorite people, living here in one place. Ellie could barely remember what it used to feel like, back when she'd lived alone in this giant four-bedroom luxury apartment in the building her parents purchased when she insisted on moving out of their family home.

That was before she'd met Jillian Reed in the basement of

the Charleston Police Department. Ellie and the petite blonde evidence clerk had become fast friends, so the natural thing to do when Jillian's landlord objected to her big goofy mutt, Sam, living in her old building was for Ellie to invite her friend to move in.

Clay cleared his throat, drawing Ellie's attention across the table to the handsome, dark-haired Texan cowboy she'd met while working a trafficking case. The FBI agent had charmed her almost immediately with his easy-going nature and lack of arrogance. Clay's eyes met hers, and the flash of yearning she detected in their brown depths sent an electric current racing across Ellie's skin.

She shifted in the chair and dropped her eyes to her plate. Having Clay Lockwood as a temporary roommate was... complicated. As much as she liked him, Ellie still hadn't completely forgiven him for his role in setting Katarina Volkov free, and worse, letting the vile woman take her innocent daughter with her. Even under the protection and guidance of WITSEC marshals, and even though Katarina would have to undergo extensive therapy and parenting training, it just felt wrong.

Very wrong.

But that was how law enforcement sometimes worked, she knew. You tossed the smaller fish back in the pond in order to catch the larger ones. Plus, setting Katarina free wasn't Clay's doing, she knew. The orders had come straight from the Attorney General, whose only concern was the information Katarina could give him. If Clay hadn't been involved in convincing her to turn state's evidence, someone else would have.

But still...he could have fought it harder. Done something more. Not tossed that little girl to that wolf. What he could have done, she still didn't know. She just knew little Harmony had been living with the treacherous woman for two months now, and Ellie could only pray that the sweet girl was safe.

Not that anyone had done anything to keep Katarina safe when she'd been Harmony's age, Ellie knew. Katarina, named Marcella at the time, had been thrown to the biggest wolf of them all...Lawrence Kingsley. There was a part of Ellie that felt terribly sorry for Katarina. Maybe being with her daughter could make a difference.

A hand came down on Ellie's shoulder, and she jerked her attention back to the present. Jillian gave her a little squeeze before dropping her hand away. "You okay?"

Ellie stabbed her fork into a bite of food. "Of course. My mind just wandered a bit." She glanced over at Clay to find his gaze on her. It was time to let it all go, she knew. The past couldn't be changed. She smiled at the agent. Relief flooded her when he smiled back.

He was important to her, and she needed to get down off her high horse and realize that everyone was just doing the best they could with the shitty circumstances they'd been handed.

Ellie was deeply glad he was here...for several reasons. His company, sure, but also because she felt safe around him. Ellie appreciated both him and Jacob taking up residence in her home after a stalker planted a bomb in her Audi.

The stalker hadn't planned on one thing, though. Ellie had been out of town on a case, so Jillian was the one using her car. The chicken Ellie chewed turned to ash as she remembered how close her friend had come to dying in the explosion. If it hadn't been for Ellie's custom keyless ignition, the paramedics would have been scraping Jillian off the concrete, one tiny piece at a time.

Ellie grabbed her glass of water and guzzled it down, trying to wash away the bile burning her throat.

Clay wrinkled his brow at her before launching into a

discussion of his recent Florida trafficking case. Almost like he'd recognized that she'd needed a distraction. Yet another reason she was glad he was here...he knew her well.

He was in the middle of sharing that six more of the children illegally adopted by a smarmy attorney in Florida had been located when a loud buzz cut Clay off mid-sentence. All four of them searched for the culprit, which turned out to be Ellie's phone, dancing its way across the table. "Oops, sorry."

Ellie grabbed the device with the intention of dismissing the call but frowned when the notifications caught her eye. Six missed calls, all from the same unknown number. The hairs on the back of her neck prickled. Wasn't 503 a Portland area code?

"It's probably nothing, but I'd better take this just in case." She shoved her chair back and jumped to her feet. "Hello, Detective Ellie Kline."

"Ellie!" Her name burst through the speaker, forcing her to pull the phone away several inches. "Oh, thank god, you finally answered! Where have you been? I've been calling you for hours!" The words came out in a frenzied rush, but even though his voice was higher-pitched and much louder than she'd ever heard him speak, Ellie recognized the caller instantly.

She hurried around the corner and into her bedroom, shutting the door so as not to disturb her friends. "Gabe? Is that you?"

"Yes, and I've been trying to reach you for the last few hours. I'm sorry to disturb you, but I'm freaking out here. I think I'm in trouble, and I need your help."

Despite the pleasant temperature inside her apartment, Ellie shivered. The fact that the usually soft-spoken Gabe Fisher was calling her in an obvious panic did not bode well.

Once the assistant to the notorious sociopath Dr. Lawrence Kingsley, Gabe Fisher had risked his life to help

Ellie and Jillian escape the murderer's clutches by shooting Kingsley's partner-in-crime...the former Charleston PD psychologist, Dr. Earnest Powell. As a result of his heroic actions, Gabe had likely propelled himself to the top of Kingsley's personal most wanted list, leading Ellie to help him enter into the U.S.M.S. WITSEC program.

The marshals had whisked Gabe away—apparently to Portland she'd just learned—under a new identity, issuing him strict instructions to keep him safe. One of those rules was no contact with people from his former life.

Ellie hoped that Gabe was overreacting. For his sake.

"Slow down and tell me what's going on. You know you're putting yourself in danger by breaking protocol."

"It's an emergency. I promise I wouldn't be calling you otherwise."

An odd wheezing emitted from Ellie's speaker. It took her a second to comprehend the noise. "Are you hyperventilating?" Gabe choked out an indecipherable reply that Ellie accepted as confirmation. "Okay. I'm here now, so why don't you take some deep, slow breaths to calm down, and then tell me what's going on."

"O-okay."

While Gabe worked to control his obvious panic, Ellie leaned on her antique dresser, battling her own rising sense of unease. Her mind refused to help. Instead, it insisted on dredging up vivid memories of exactly why Gabe was in WITSEC.

Ellie remembered the knots in her gut when she'd learned Kingsley had kidnapped Jillian, using the file clerk as bait to lure Ellie to his lair.

Ellie's Audi Q3 bumped down the dirt driveway off Clements Ferry Road, teeth clenched as the Master's voice guided her back to the warehouse where his sick obsession with her first started when she was only fifteen years old. The rusted-out, sagging metal struc-

ture loomed on the hill, conjuring reminders of the time she'd spent trapped inside.

As she approached the building, a chill swept over her. The Master is only a man, she reminded herself before pressing on. She had no choice but to continue. That monster had Jillian.

When she first stepped into the shadowy interior, she was as good as blind. The only light flickered from a single, bare bulb. She waited for her eyes to adjust while, from within the darkness, a steady drip-drip of water pinged the floor. Over time, shadows formed into murky objects, so she eased forward, her hand hovering near her holster. A metal table solidified in her path first, then a human-shaped figure.

That was how Ellie discovered her best friend. Unconscious. Her head listing to one side, and her mouth slack.

But the rope cinched around Jillian's neck was the detail that struck true fear into Ellie's heart. That, and the audible click of the complicated pulley mechanism the Master had created, which tightened the rope every thirty seconds.

Goose bumps flared at the unwanted memory. Ellie rubbed her hands up and down her arms, soothing the prickly flesh. The truth proved more difficult to banish. If she hadn't shown up to rescue Jillian, her friend would have slowly strangled to death.

The high-pitched rasp of Gabe's breathing softened and slowed, alerting Ellie that he'd be ready to talk soon. She listened with half an ear while her mind wandered to the other person who'd nearly killed her. A man she'd trusted with all her secrets…Dr. Powell.

During Ellie's attempt to rescue Jillian, she'd believed the middle-aged and very kind Dr. Powell was an ally. If it hadn't been for Gabe rushing in to shoot the doctor as Powell pretended to help Ellie free her friend, both Ellie and Jillian would be six feet under right now. The mild-mannered doctor had fooled them all, working out of the Charleston

PD office as the resident police psychologist for years. No one had been the wiser.

Proof that evil came camouflaged in a variety of ways.

Ellie's hand curled around the dresser's edge at the memory of all those times she'd spent in Dr. Powell's office, revealing her innermost thoughts and fears. Never once suspecting that he was part of the nightmare of her past or that he passed every bit of private information she shared straight to Kingsley.

Gabe was the reason Dr. Powell was dead, and Ellie was free. Kingsley would never forgive his former assistant for that. Or forget.

Ellie straightened from the dresser and began circling her room, her tension mounting with each passing moment it took for Gabe to calm enough to explain.

"I went to the mailbox this afternoon, and I found a box." Gabe whispered as if he was worried the boogeyman might be lurking right around the corner, eavesdropping. "It was from him. Kingsley."

Although she'd already suspected it to be the case, Ellie's stomach still tightened when she heard the name. If Gabe was right, that meant Kingsley was back in action. "Are you sure?"

"The address was in his handwriting. I worked with him long enough to recognize it immediately. And…there was a bird inside."

When no further explanation came, Ellie's gaze returned to her dresser, as if an answer might materialize, genie-like, from one of her perfume bottles lining the top. "A bird? I'm sorry, I'm not following you."

"I started bird-watching as a hobby, something to pass the time. I was even considering joining the local Audubon society until I opened the box." Gabe broke off, his breath a harsh rasp in Ellie's ear. "The bird was dead. Its eyes stabbed out and throat sliced."

"Kingsley." His name was like knives leaving Ellie's mouth.

"Yes. He *knows*, Ellie. I don't know how, but he does. My new identity and where I live, even my new hobby. For all I know, he's watching me as we speak, getting ready to grab me any second and punish me for turning on him."

Ellie chewed her lower lip. Gabe was right. There was a chance Kingsley planned to grab him any second now, but somehow, she doubted it. A quick capture wasn't exactly Kingsley's style.

"I don't think so. There's a distinct possibility that he's holed up somewhere miles away from you, recovering from his injuries. He could have easily sent a lackey to do this kind of dirty work. Plus, we both know how much Kingsley enjoys playing his twisted little games. It's likely that he's content deriving pleasure from toying with you."

She didn't add, *for now*. Gabe was worked up enough without her fanning the flames of his fear.

Gabe, though, knew Kingsley well. He said the words for her. "For now."

Ellie pressed the heel of her hand to her forehead, trying to think this all the way through. "Walk me through your steps these past couple of weeks. Who have you had contact with? In-person and electronically."

Seconds ticked by before Gabe replied. "No one. I go to a coffee house to order and say thank you to the barista, check out books at the local library, bird-watching, but that's, uh, that's about it. It's not like I moved here to join clubs and make new friends."

There was an unusual cadence to his speech that struck Ellie as odd. A little hiccup, followed by a rise in pitch. She frowned, then shrugged the oddity off as nerves. Or something to delve into further when Gabe's alarm bells weren't ringing so loud.

"I'm not accusing you of anything, Gabe." She kept her voice slow and even. "These are questions that need to be asked."

"You think I wanted to give Kingsley the chance to find me? I know I didn't recognize how truly horrifying he was when I first worked for him, but I promise, I'm not stupid." Gabe's tone softened this time, to the point that he almost sounded sad. "How do you think he found me?"

Ellie was already racking her brain over the same question. If Gabe was telling the truth—and she had no reason to suspect he wasn't—then how had Kingsley tracked him down? That was a mystery that needed quick solving.

"I'm not sure, but trust me, I'll do everything in my power to find out."

"I know you will."

His simple declaration of confidence tugged at Ellie's heart. The hand pressed to her forehead fell away, and she straightened her spine. She would get to the bottom of this. She'd been the one to arrange for Gabe to go into WITSEC, which made her responsible for what happened to him. Dammed if she'd let Kingsley hurt another person on her watch.

"For now, stay put. Forget your lattes, books, forget going for a walk. Stay locked inside and keep your eyes peeled. I'll call you back as soon as we have a plan. If anything else happens, no matter how small it might seem, call me immediately. Me. No one else."

"Don't worry. It's not like I'm talking to anyone else, so you're the only one I can call." Gabe gave a nervous little laugh. "If there's any way you could please pick up quicker next time, though, I'd really appreciate it."

Ellie shot a guilty look into her mirror. She looked pale.

Heck, she felt pale.

"Sorry about that. I turned my ringer off before a work meeting, and I must have forgotten to turn it back on. I promise to answer right away next time."

After a few more encouraging words, Ellie hung up, her mind spinning as it struggled to process what Gabe had told her. She needed a plan. Quickly. Lucky for her, she had her own planning committee conveniently seated at the dinner table down the hall.

Despite the seriousness of Gabe's call, Ellie found herself smiling a little bit as she rushed from her bedroom. If she knew that trio as well as she suspected she did, they were sitting on pins and needles, trading ideas on who was important enough to pull Ellie away from her food. All three of them, nosy as hell when it came to her life.

Their interest grew once they'd started sharing Ellie's apartment, a roommate situation she owed to the bomb that destroyed her Audi. Ellie had hired private security, but both Jacob and Clay insisted on staying on as additional protection. That worked perfectly for Ellie. If anything happened to Jillian because of her, Ellie would never forgive herself.

Jacob and Jillian had used the time together to grow even closer as a couple, whereas Ellie and Clay? Well, she wasn't sure exactly where they stood. Ellie sighed as she retraced her steps to rejoin her friends in the dining room. That one weekend they'd shared the same bed had been wonderful, but ever since they'd returned from their trip to Florida, their relationship had grown increasingly strained.

Living together in the FBI ACTeam building hadn't helped, but the real kicker was discovering Clay had not only agreed but actively participated in convincing Katarina to trade a prison sentence for entry into the WITSEC program. Even now, Ellie's blood boiled, thinking about how Katarina had escaped the consequences of her crimes, but at the time?

Oof. Her blowup at Clay had served as the proverbial straw that broke the camel's back. Only in this case, that last straw propelled Ellie and Clay back into the friend zone.

Ellie paused before she rounded the corner, twirling a red curl around her finger. Sometimes when he didn't think she'd notice, she caught Clay staring at her with intense hunger and longing in his dark eyes, only to turn away the moment he spied her watching. She was pretty sure he wanted more than friendship, and some days, so did she. But any time she considered making the first move to tell him as much, something inside her shied away.

No, not something. *Someone.* Nick Greene, to be precise. Her complete failure to maintain a relationship with her ex-boyfriend had taught her a hard lesson: romantic relationships and detective careers didn't mix. Not for her, anyway.

Lifting her chin and pulling her shoulders back, Ellie entered the dining room and paused behind her abandoned chair. Forks dropped to plates. Chatter ceased. Three pairs of eyes focused on her.

"So?" Jillian swept a stray tendril of blonde hair behind her ear, worry furrowing her brow. Ellie's roommate and coworker spent enough time with her to read the unnatural stiffness in Ellie's posture.

"That was Gabe Fisher. He got a package in the mail today, in Kingsley's handwriting. Addressed to his new alias."

Jacob swore under his breath while Clay nodded. "We were afraid this might happen," Clay said.

"Sure, but this quick?" Jacob's head whipped toward the special agent, making his K-9 partner release a low, worried whine from his spot on the dog bed. "Shh, it's okay, Duke."

Clay shrugged. "The Marshals are excellent at their jobs, but they can only protect those people who follow the rules precisely." He met Ellie's gaze. "Did he say he followed the rules?"

Ellie thought about the change in Gabe's tone. "He said he did, but…" She lifted a shoulder. "It's possible he slipped."

Clay looked grim. "From what I understand, it happens more often than not. Plus, Kingsley has the kind of resources that most people can only dream of, and when it comes to Gabe, he's highly motivated to seek revenge."

Clay's calm demeanor washed over the table. Not for the first time, Ellie found herself grateful for the FBI agent's quiet confidence, a trait she attributed to his work on the bureau's anti-trafficking coordination team.

Clay's ACTeam role was what drew them together in the first place. Fortis assigned Ellie to help the agent with a cold case involving a runaway named Charity, which led to a wild chase to capture a serial killer and ended with a dark web auction organized by Katarina Volkov herself.

Jillian pushed the remnants of her chicken curry around her plate, trailing yellow streaks across the white paper. The grooves above her nose grew more prominent, a sure sign that she was deep in thought. "You know, one of my old friends from college is in the Marshals' Washington office. Her name is Mirabel Green. We don't keep in close contact or anything, but we do touch base once every year or so. You want me to reach out to her and ask if she might be able to help?"

Ellie considered Jillian's offer for a moment before shaking her head. "Thank you, but let's hold off on that for now. It's good to know you have a contact in case we do end up needing an insider we can trust."

Clay patted his mouth with a napkin. "Speaking of the Marshals, did you tell Gabe to call the marshal handling his case?"

"No, not yet. I wanted to check in with you first and make sure that was the best plan. Do you think it's safe?" Ellie sipped her water, hating that she even had to ask that question. Leaks in any organization were possible. So were traitors. Ellie knew that to be true personally.

Clay tapped a finger to his chin as he mulled it over. "What proof do we have that there is a leak or a mole inside the U.S.M.S.?"

Jillian exchanged a glance with Jacob, her mouth twisting. "Do we need more of a reason beyond the fact that Kingsley knows Gabe's whereabouts?"

"I don't think that's enough of a reason to jump to any conclusions. With Kingsley's network, there's no telling how he got the information." Ellie rubbed her aching temples. "We know that he's had moles in the Charleston police department, though, so who's to say the informant isn't from an outside agency? Or a computer hacker?"

"I agree. And even if there is a leak somewhere, the chance that Gabe's personal marshal is involved is slim. In my mind, that play would be way too risky and obvious." Clay lifted his eyebrows at Ellie. His subtle way of asking if she agreed.

Ellie nodded. "Right, and for better or worse, the local marshals are Gabe's best shot at protection for now." She picked up her phone and redialed the last number, hitting a button to switch the call to speaker.

The phone only rang once before Gabe picked up. "Ellie?"

"Yeah. Listen, I need you to call your marshal as soon as we hang up and tell him what happened."

"Okay, I can do that." Gabe's ragged intake of breath filled the dining room. "Does that mean I have to move again?"

Ellie sought Clay's gaze across the table. She caught the inclination of his head, which confirmed her own instincts. "I'm afraid so. It's not safe for you to stay there, now that he knows where you are. We need to set you up with a new name and house as soon as we possibly can."

Gabe cleared his throat. "What if I don't want to? What if

I'm okay taking my chances here?"

The sudden increase in Gabe's volume made Ellie frown.

Clay leaned forward, a growing storm clouding his eyes. "Pardon my French, but why the ever-loving hell would you want to stay there, knowing that Kingsley has your location locked and loaded?" The FBI agent's voice was soft. Dangerously so.

Silence followed, broken only by Sam's whimper as she twitched on her dog bed next to Duke, chasing imaginary bunnies in her dreams.

Ellie fisted her hands tightly in her lap as her suspicions grew. "Gabe? Is there something you need to tell us?"

Clay obviously had the same suspicions. "Now isn't the time to hold anything back. Not if you'd like to keep on breathing."

At Clay's sharp reminder of what was at stake, Gabe let out a low moan. "I met someone, okay? I know, I was stupid and didn't follow the rules. I'd say I'm sorry, but that would be a lie. He's decent and smart, and the thought of picking up and leaving and never seeing him again breaks my heart."

Clay and Jacob groaned in unison. Ellie dropped her face into her hands. *Oh Gabe, what did you do?* She felt bad for him, but at the same time, she wondered how he could be so reckless.

Clay pinched the bridge of his nose. "Am I dreaming, or did you tell Ellie a few minutes ago that you hadn't met anyone?"

"I said that because I didn't want to move, but now I guess it's happening anyway." Gabe sighed over the line. "It's not my fault that Kingsley found me, so how is it fair that I have to upend my life all over again?"

Clay dragged a hand through his short, dark hair and waited for Gabe to reach the inevitable conclusion. They all waited.

Gabe's sigh lasted longer this time. "Right. Life isn't fair. I should know this better than anyone."

Ellie's heart twinged. "I'm sorry, Gabe, because you're right. It's not fair. We understand that, but unfortunately, the facts don't factor fairness into consideration. Your safety has to come first. Now, walk us through your movements over the past few weeks again, and please, don't leave anything out this time. We can't keep you safe unless you're completely honest."

The next few minutes were spent listening to Gabe recite his movements and periodically responding to questions that Ellie, Clay, or Jacob decided to ask. By the time they finished this round of inquiries, Ellie felt confident that Gabe had shared everything he remembered.

"Thank you, Gabe. That was very helpful. Now, listen closely. As soon as I hang up, call your marshal like we discussed. Then, once you hang up with them, I need you to remove the SIM card and battery from your phone. From now on, only contact me with a burner phone." Ellie paused to give Gabe a chance to process her instructions. "Did you catch all that or should I go through it again?"

"No, I understand. Call the Marshals, then remove the SIM card and battery." He sounded on the verge of tears.

Once they said their goodbyes and she ended the call, Ellie leaned back into her chair with a loud exhale that transitioned into a groan.

Jillian studied her. "So, now what?"

"Now, I ask Fortis for permission to fly to Portland. If Kingsley is monitoring Gabe, that means he might be lurking somewhere nearby, and I want to be there if he is." Ellie inhaled deeply before meeting each of her friends' eyes in turn. "I need to be the one to take that bastard down, once and for all."

3

I paced the length of the cabin that Creighton Holt had so kindly offered up to me, checking my phone for the tenth time in the last thirty minutes. My screen remained infuriatingly blank. No new messages.

I kicked the wall made from knotty pine and growled, listening as the guttural sound bounced around the cozy space. It should have been me tucking my package into Gabe's mailbox. After the way the ungrateful little shit had turned on me, I deserved to witness in person his pretty face crumple once he realized I'd tracked him down.

"It's too soon. You'll get your chance soon enough."

My whispered reassurance took the edge off my rage. Living alone in the middle of Creighton's vast acreage, a compound used to deprogram cult members, had led to many conversations with myself.

I huffed. Also Gabe's fault. If he'd remained loyal the way I deserved, he'd be here with me. By my side. Instead, he'd flipped sides, throwing away my years of nurturing to flock to that redheaded bitch's side.

Ellie Kline.

My newly crease-free eyes narrowed, and my collagen-enhanced upper lip curled into a snarl. Fire raced through my veins while my muscles clenched in helpless rage.

I consoled myself by walking over to the full-length mirror affixed to the back of the door. A golden-skinned, dark-haired stranger stared back. The new me, or should I say, Abel del Rey from Costa Rica?

That was the name etched across my new passport. Even after all these weeks I'd had to adjust to my new face, I still experienced a momentary disconnect between the image my eyes processed versus the expected one stored in my brain. I reached up and patted my cheek, firmer now, thanks to implants. I ran my fingers through my newly thickened hair. Turned sideways to admire my youthful profile and my tanned skin, brown now, thanks to a daily pill created by Dr. Sandoval.

"See that, Ellie Kline? You think you hurt me by cutting up my face, but I'm like a bone. Try to break me, and I'll only grow back stronger. Look at me!" I stepped back and spread my arms wide, beaming at my reflection. "You did me a favor. Not only am I twenty years younger, but I'm unrecognizable. All the better to creep up on you when you least expect it and make you pay for everything."

An unwelcome memory burst into my head. A reminder of the searing agony I'd felt when that bitch bashed my face in, and the way I'd had to flee the United States like a mouse chased by a cat. Me, the Master, flee! Like I was no better than terrified prey.

My reflection changed, the new mouth curling into a sneer. Oh yes, she would pay dearly for that outrage.

Luckily, I'd headed straight to Dr. Sandoval, and after countless painful surgeries, that genius of a man had reconstructed my old face into this brand new, youthful version. I'd been so weak during my long recovery period, completely reliant on the beautiful assistant Dr. Sandoval had assigned to cater to my every need. My long, difficult journey had paid off, though, because here I was, better than ever. More than ready to exact my revenge on those who'd been foolish enough to cross me.

Like Ellie Kline.

Planting my hands on the mirror, I kissed the image before stepping away. "You'll have your turn, Ellie, don't worry. But you'll need to be patient. First, we have to take care of the ungrateful one in our midst."

I was busy admiring the deep bronze of my skin when a ringing interrupted me. I snatched the phone from my pocket and spotted the embedded link. A video.

Giddiness bubbled up my throat like champagne when Gabe appeared in the frame, grainy but clear enough. Perching on the edge of a brown La-Z-Boy recliner, I watched my clueless ex-assistant's dark curls bounce while he pranced out to his mailbox like he didn't have a care in the world. When he withdrew the contents, I pressed my hands together with glee.

Here it comes…

The camera showed Gabe scanning the mail, sliding one envelope beneath the next. When he came to a small package, he went perfectly, deliciously still. Like a beautiful statue, planted right there on the sidewalk.

"Surprise," I whispered.

I zoomed in, not wanting to miss his expression, and oh, what a treat it was. Those sweet, full lips fell open, and his puppy-dog brown eyes turned round with fear. His fear was a virtual feast. The exact sustenance I needed right now to feed my poor, deprived soul.

I watched, licking my lips while his beautiful face transitioned through a number of emotions before settling on horror.

"Boo."

As if my softly whispered word had trumpeted in his ear, Gabe jumped and dropped the box. I smiled. The way his hands trembled was gravy topping an already decadent meal.

My heart nearly overflowed when he stumbled back a step. Threatened to explode with joy when his head jerked this way and that, frantic in his search to locate the danger.

"Look all you want. You won't find me."

As if hearing me speak, Gabe whirled before picking up the box and darting into the house. The door slammed behind him, followed by the blinds blinking shut, one by one.

I clapped as if just witnessing the finale of the finest ballet. The visual of his panic had been the perfect balm for my dark mood. "Oh, that was delightful. You can run, dearest Gabe…"

I replayed the entire video from start to finish. This time, I could almost taste Gabe's fear. I wanted to savor the exquisite flavor. I wondered what it would smell like.

My gaze swept the chest of drawers towering next to the mirror and landed on a candle. I lifted the wax square to my nose and inhaled. Ah, vanilla spice. My former assistant looked so innocent that I could imagine his terror smelling equally as sweet.

Replacing the candle, I reached for my phone, intending to hit play for a third time. Before I could tap the little triangle, though, my phone burst into sound. I glanced at the number to identify who was calling.

Milos.

My initial spurt of annoyance at the interruption mellowed. Ah, Milos. At first, I'd been pessimistic about how my friend Creighton's referral would work out. Creighton was a humanitarian who dedicated his life to deprogramming cult members. I dedicated mine to inflicting pain. Or, as I'd once joked to myself: Creighton returned people to their families, whereas I returned them to their creator.

I needn't have worried. Creighton's referral had far surpassed my exacting expectations, and as a result, I owed him a debt of gratitude.

My finger hovered over the button. I was tempted to reject the call, but the video had lulled me into a generous mood, so I accepted instead. My new assistant had done an excellent job. He deserved the reward of hearing my voice. "Well done, Milos. Superb job finding those addresses so quickly. I trust the marshals are none the wiser about the source of the leak?"

"Thank you, sir, and no. I've been listening in to the police dispatcher, and our little secretary and her brats haven't been found yet. And even once they do find her car, they won't suspect anything. I made sure of it. They'll think Mirabel took a curve too fast on slick roads and blame the death of her and her two kids on a tragic accident."

"A tragic accident, yes, I like the sound of that." I rose and strolled back over to the mirror, smiling at my reflection. "As long as there are no nasty surprises. I would hate for anyone to figure out that Mirabel was our source. It might ruin my game." My tone dropped a little in warning.

"No, sir, there won't be. There's no reason for them to connect Gabe to Mirabel."

Milos spoke in a rush, and I pictured perspiration stains growing on the tall, sepulchral man's shirt. Good. A little fear served as a great motivator in times such as these.

"Excellent. Now, the marshals will most likely be moving Gabe to a new safe house at any time. Did you complete the rest of my task as instructed?"

"Yes, sir. I was able to override the security system as well as the security cameras and access Gabe's house. I planted several tracking devices. One in his shoe underneath the insert, one in his duffel bag through a small slit in an outer pocket, another in the jacket he wears most often, and one in his wallet. All inactivated for now, just like you asked."

Yes, perfect. Everything was going according to plan. The marshals were predictable.

I'd waited a couple months before making my move, waiting for Gabe and his marshal to put down their guard and settle in. Easy enough. And now, before they moved Gabe again, I also knew what they'd do.

In an abundance of caution, they would go over all his belongings with a bug detector, but I was too smart for them. The device could only locate activated bugs. All we had to do was wait for them to finish their scan, and then, presto! We'd activate the tracking devices, which would lead us right to Gabe's new location.

You can't hide for long, darling boy. And even if you do, that's okay. The harder the hunt, the sweeter the kill.

In the privacy of my room, I performed an impromptu dance. This day was looking up more and more every minute. "You've made me very happy, Milos."

"Thank you, sir. That means a lot."

The eagerness in his voice added extra energy to my step. But it was the last thing he said that had me wanting to skip across the room in sheer delight. "Oh, and I almost forgot to tell you. Gabe has a boyfriend."

I froze mid-twirl and stared at the phone. Surely my luck couldn't be this good? "Are you positive?"

"They met up at the coffee shop, and I saw them hold hands under the table when they didn't think anyone was looking."

"Oh, Milos, this is such exciting news." I clapped my

hands again, and the stranger in the mirror did the same. The dark eyes reflecting back at me glowed with a deepening satisfaction. "The universe dropped a gift into our laps, and we don't dare squander it. I think it's time we sent our dear Gabe another message."

4

On Tuesday morning, Ellie hovered near the lobby doors of the Charleston Police Department and kept her attention trained on the entrance. She'd hustled out of bed early and grabbed her coffee to go in hopes of intercepting Lead Homicide Detective Harold Fortis the moment he arrived.

The front door swung open, and her boss swept inside. Except for the smattering of gray among his dark curls, Detective Fortis hadn't changed much since Ellie had started working under him. Tall and solidly built, he exuded an aura of capability, and Ellie swore those golden eyes never missed anything.

Like now, for instance. With a second nature that came with years of training, the forty-something detective's gaze swept left, then right, before landing on Ellie. His mouth drooped a little when she pushed away from the wall. By the time Ellie blinked, his expression had rearranged itself back to neutral. The head detective didn't break stride, just jerked his head in the direction of his office.

Ellie rushed to follow him. She knew that was the only invitation she'd get.

The elevator ride to the second floor was silent. Once the doors dinged open, Ellie trailed her boss into the large communal space labeled Violent Crimes, an area that always smelled faintly of coffee and cake. Fortis led her past the seven spaced-out desks to his glass-walled office located along the far wall.

"Shut the door behind you."

Ellie did as her boss commanded before heading for one of the two chairs opposite his desk.

Fortis sank into his own chair with a creak of old metal parts and steepled his fingers atop the scarred surface. "What can I do for you today, Kline?"

Ellie knew better than to jump right in and ask for a favor. She had to ease her way into her boss's good graces. "First off, I figured now was a good time to catch you up on my last case."

Fortis grunted, which Ellie took as a prompt to continue.

"Remember the cold case I closed last week?"

Fortis wrinkled his nose. "You mean the one with the homeless guy found bludgeoned to death in the dumpster six years ago?"

Ellie shook her head. She'd forgotten that she'd cleared that case within the past two weeks too. "The other one. The case with that eighteen-year-old who was found strangled in a storage unit." Fortis nodded, so she continued. "The homeless case didn't make any waves, but I've had reporters loitering outside my apartment off and on over the eighteen-year-old."

Fortis perked up at that, leaning forward onto his desk with the beginnings of a hopeful grin tugging at the corners of his mouth. "Good news, I hope?"

Ellie allowed herself a smile in return. For Fortis, it would be great news. The head detective loved any press that made him and his department look good. Which was exactly why Ellie had decided to lead their impromptu meeting this particular way.

"Good news. As it turns out, John Doe's dad has come up in the world over the last fifteen years. He's now sitting on the board of a big Texas gas company, and he reached out personally to tell me how grateful he was to finally be able to lay his son to rest."

"How grateful?"

If Fortis were a dog, he'd be salivating right now, over the juicy bone Ellie had waved beneath his nose. Not that she blamed him. Being head of Violent Crimes came with a lot of pressure and often involved dealing with bad press. It made sense that he was eager for any good press he could get.

She slid a printed confirmation across the desk to him. "Very grateful, to the tune of a half a million dollar donation to our police foundation."

Fortis's golden eyes widened before his mouth cracked into one of his rare grins. "Nicely done, Detective."

Ellie shrugged. She didn't bust her butt on cold cases to garner the department large cash donations or for the glory that often accompanied them. The most rewarding thing in the world to Ellie was the relief in the faces of the loved ones of the deceased when she was able to finally provide them with closure. The ability to help end their suffering was a precious gift. One she didn't take lightly. No monetary reward or ego stroke could come close to the high that suffused Ellie from that.

"How many cold cases have you solved already? Let's see, there were those women from the Ghana trip, Valerie Price. All of Matt Loomis's victims." Fortis grimaced when he mentioned the long-distance trucker's name, as if merely uttering it out loud left a bad taste in his mouth.

Ellie could relate. The long-distance trucker had claimed that he'd murdered upward of ninety women over several decades, leaving a trail of bodies strewn along highways spanning the entire country.

Her boss drummed his fingers on the desk while he tried to come up with the rest. "That messed up Tucker Penland case. And then…Katarina."

At the mention of the woman's name, Ellie stiffened. "Katarina's case doesn't really count, though. It's not like justice was served."

Katarina Volkov had been Kingsley's protégé and partner in crime. The cunning woman had led Ellie on several wild chases, eluding her more than once before Ellie finally managed to catch up to her in Fayetteville, North Carolina. But only because Ellie caught a break.

She and Clay had discovered that the daughter Katarina believed to have died at birth was alive and well and living with a young couple after being traded from family to family in an adoption trafficking ring.

When she and Clay had realized that Katarina had uncovered the same secret, it turned into a race to see who would reach Harmony first. Ellie recalled her fierce battle with the other woman, and the painful bruises she'd carried for weeks afterward. With a little luck and skill, she'd managed to subdue Katarina and bring her to justice.

Only justice had never been served.

Ellie's lips tightened as the shock of Katarina's fate washed over her anew. Instead of living out the remainder of her years behind bars like she deserved, Katarina had taken a deal. The beautiful, clever criminal had turned state's evidence in exchange for entry into WITSEC. Now, she was off living under a new name, in a new location, with no consequences for all the terrible acts she'd committed. That didn't sit well with Ellie.

In all fairness, Katarina's situation was complicated. Her infant daughter had been kidnapped and sold to the highest bidder. No mother deserved that fate. Despite her feelings about Katarina, the person, Ellie's heart warmed a little for Katarina, the mother. A mother who, somewhere out there, had finally been reunited with her daughter.

For better or worse.

Ellie prayed it was for the better...for them both, but especially for the innocent child.

As far as Ellie knew, Katarina was the only other person besides herself to escape Kingsley's clutches, but that was the end of their similarities. Ellie had only been held captive by the sociopath for a short time, whereas Kingsley had snatched Katarina as a ten-year-old and raised her as his own.

Ellie didn't want to think of how she might have turned out if their situations had been reversed. Nothing excused Katarina's crimes, but there was room in Ellie's heart for compassion, for the innocent little girl Katarina had once been.

When Ellie looked up from her lap, Fortis studied her with an impatient frown. The expression surprised her into blurting out a startled, "What?"

Her boss snorted. "Don't *what* me. I know what you're doing, and you need to stop. A win is a win. Accept it and move on." His gaze fell to the haphazard stack of files on the left side of his desk. His deep sigh spoke volumes. "Now, if that's all you needed..."

Ellie twisted in her chair. "Um, actually, there was one other thing I wanted to talk to you about."

Fortis dragged a hand through his dark curls before rubbing his temple. Ellie was tempted to offer him some ibuprofen but kept her mouth shut. "Of course there is.

Hurry it up, then. I've got a shitload of files to get through before my meeting at noon."

Not the warmest invitation, but it would have to do. "I got a call last night from Gabe Fisher."

Her boss's head whipped back up from the file he'd opened. "And you didn't lead with this, why?"

Ellie shrugged, not about to tell him that she'd intentionally buttered him up first.

Fortis blew out an exasperated breath. "Continue."

"He got a package in the mail yesterday. From Kingsley."

Her boss went still. "He's sure it was Kingsley?"

Ellie nodded and explained more about the package and its grisly contents. "He recognized the handwriting. Plus, it's exactly the kind of sick thing Kingsley would do. Gabe betrayed him. No way a sociopath like Kingsley would let that go."

"So, that maniac kicks off a game of cat and mouse to torture the poor bastard." Fortis's jaw clenched. "You're right. It does sound like Kingsley."

Ellie released a silent sigh of relief. Step one of convincing Fortis that Kingsley was involved had proven easier than expected. Now all she needed to do was sell him on the rest of her plan. "Right. Which is why I need to go to Portland. If Kingsley left any clues behind, I'm the best person to find them."

Across the desk, Fortis's expression didn't change. The man had the kind of poker face that came with years on the job. Ellie might as well have been trying to read a rock, for all the emotion she was getting. Her shoulders drooped anyway. He was going to forbid her to go. She could feel it.

Ellie's jaw gaped open when a huge grin softened his harsh features.

"I already spoke to Clay this morning. He's going to be

leading the Kingsley Task Force. Take a wild guess who the first person he asked to be assigned to his team was?"

What? How? What?

Ellie's jaw snapped shut with an audible click. Conflicting emotions raged inside her while her mind whirled to process this shocking information. Clay was leading a task force on Kingsley? And he hadn't told her? The man was living in her house for crying out loud. How dare he keep such crucial information from her?

But even as she ground her molars together, her body vibrated with excitement. A Kingsley Task Force! That was so much better than an authorized trip to Portland to investigate on her own. More than she'd ever dreamed of, if she were being honest. A task force meant the kind of additional resources and manpower that Ellie would never be able to access solo.

Her eyes narrowed. Oh, she still had a few choice words to share with Mr. FBI Agent Clay Lockwood. But for now, she shook off her irritation and beamed at her boss. "A Kingsley Task Force, even better."

Fortis wagged his finger at her. "Remember, the task force isn't about Gabe or his safety. That's what the Marshals are for, so let them do their jobs. The last thing they need is you to prance up there and start interfering, and the last thing I want to do is field annoyed phone calls from the U.S.M.S."

Prance? Please. She didn't prance. Ellie wanted to stick out her tongue, but for once, she curbed her impulses. No sense giving her often grumpy boss any reason to change his mind. "No annoyed phone calls. Got it."

The dark brow Fortis raised looked skeptical. Ellie batted her eyes in an effort to look innocent, which only caused Fortis to rub the back of his neck and groan. "Look, the main reason I approved you for this task force is because I want

Charleston PD to get credit when you bring this son of a bitch in. You got that?"

"Yes, sir." Ellie jumped to her feet. She wasn't about to argue. Fortis was entitled to his motives, and Ellie was entitled to hers. Forget credit. All Ellie cared about was catching the evil bastard and making him pay for all the pain he'd inflicted. "Thank you, sir, you won't regret this."

As she turned to race out of the office before he could change his mind, Fortis raised a beefy palm. Ellie stopped, her heart hammering. *Now what? No way he could have changed his mind already.*

"Until the task force is complete and ready to go, I have another cold case for you to work on." Fortis dug through the files on his desk, pulled one out, and slid it across the wooden surface.

Ellie grabbed the folder. The name scrawled across the top jumped out and prickled her memory.

Danielle Snyder.

Ellie remembered the case well.

Danielle had gone missing at a party years ago and was currently presumed dead. Witness interviews said that the sixteen-year-old had discovered her boyfriend cheating and run. She was never seen alive again.

Ellie frowned. She didn't understand. Fortis had tossed this case to the bottom of the list months ago. "I thought you said this case wasn't high priority enough for me to investigate?"

Fortis nodded toward the folder she was holding. "It is now that her dad got a phone call from someone claiming to be his long-lost daughter."

Ellie twisted a loose red curl around her finger, frowning at the manila file. "But why? I don't get how a single phone call changes things. Can't one of the other detectives work it?"

She knew Danielle's dad was Charles Snyder, a local celebrity game show host, but she still didn't understand. Any case not related to Kingsley was a distraction right now.

Ellie jumped when Fortis banged his fist against his desk. "They could," he growled, "if I told them to work it, but I didn't. I told you, and I expect you to follow orders. Are we clear?"

Oopsies. Fortis's jaw twitched, so Ellie nodded and edged her way to the door. Any more pushing, and her boss might very well explode. "Very clear, sir."

Once she'd responded with as much gusto as a new marine recruit, Ellie whirled and fled. No way was she going to give her boss a chance to rethink his decision to name her as part of the new task force.

5

The bell rang, sending his classmates rushing for the door.

Gabe grabbed his backpack off the floor and pulled out his Walkman. Once his headphones were on and he pushed play, he headed out into the hallway, safe inside his little music bubble.

He allowed the noisy stream of students to carry him down the hallway and out the front door, darting to the left after he cleared the stairs, to where his ancient blue ten-speed with a crack in the seat waited. The armpits of his light gray shirt were already dark with sweat. Another sweltering Florida day.

Gabe unlocked the bike and hopped on, pedaling home as fast as he could, hoping to catch a breeze.

By the time he reached his house, sweat dripped down his back. He hopped off and wheeled the bike to its storage place in the back-yard. Desperate for an ice-cold glass of lemonade, or maybe one of those strawberry popsicles if his mom hadn't finished them off while he was at school. Man, he really hoped not, because now that he was thinking about them, he'd kicked off a serious craving.

He hurried to the back door and flung it open, and then froze. The raised voices hit him like a surprise attack, making Gabe tense up and want to curl into a protective ball. Although the fight *shouldn't be surprising. Not by now. His parents fought like clock-work every time they were high. And they were high almost as often as they were sober these days.*

Cringing, Gabe toed off his shoes. He crept his way across the kitchen to the freezer.

"I should've known better than to marry a loser like you! Rent's due, and they're gonna kick us out, and then what?"

Gabe turned up the volume on his Walkman to drown out the screech of his mom's voice. He had no interest in the specifics of their argument of the day. All he wanted was a cold drink and a Popsicle.

He blew out a relieved breath when he reached the fridge without drawing his parents' attention. Carefully, he eased open the door and began reaching for the top shelf where his mom stored the lemonade.

It took him a second to comprehend what his eyes were seeing.

A head.

There was a severed human head sitting on the top shelf where the lemonade should have been.

Gabe yanked his hand away, missing touching a dead cheek by mere inches. His heart raced in his chest as he stood glued to the yellowed linoleum, the Walkman clattering to the floor. The front of his shorts turned warm and wet, clinging to his thighs like a second skin. A puddle formed between his bare feet.

As Gabe stumbled back a step, the head's eyes popped open. Emerald green irises tracked his movements. Familiar eyes. Ellie's eyes.

Gabe screamed. He tried to run, but the floor sucked at his feet like wet cement, holding him in place.

The severed head's jaw unhinged, and a laugh exploded from the red mouth. Ellie's laugh, only more sinister, with a hissing that slithered over and then coiled around him like a poisonous snake. Saliva strings flew out and stuck to his face, pulling him toward the pitch-black cavernous space between her gaping teeth.

"No, stop! Why are you doing this to me? Please, stop!" Gabe's begging made no impact. The laughter and giggling and cackling grew in pitch until it completely engulfed him, twisting and pulling as Gabe yanked at his useless legs to escape.

In desperation, Gabe shut his eyes and covered his ears with his hands. The laughter ceased. Hope fluttered to life in his chest.

"You're next! You're next! You're NEXT!" The head shrieked, so gleeful, it tumbled from the shelf.

Hands came down on his shoulders...shaking him, harder and harder...

"Gabe, wake up!"

Gabe jumped, and his eyes flew open. Frank Otto of the United States Marshal Service stood peering down at him, his big hand latched to Gabe's shoulder.

"Are you okay?" The marshal stepped back, frowning. "I heard you yelling. Nightmare?"

Gabe blinked several times and gave an involuntary shudder. A dream. That had all been a dream. There were no severed heads in his fridge. No Ellie screaming that he was next.

He rubbed his eyes with the palms of his hands. "Yeah, I'm fine. Can't even remember what the dream was about now." A complete lie, but Gabe didn't want to talk about it.

"We got word from the higher-ups. We'll be transferring to the new safe house in an hour. Go get dressed and grab your things so we can be ready." Frank turned to head out of the bedroom and give Gabe some privacy. He paused in the doorway. "Oh, and you'll need to hand over your phone before we leave here."

Once the door shut, Gabe lifted his shirt to wipe his sweat-drenched face. The dream's vibrancy faded, leaving behind a steady trickle of dread. What he needed was a quick shower to wash the sweat and lingering sense of doom away.

Fifteen minutes later, Gabe was clean and dressed in jeans

and a fresh t-shirt. The sweat was gone, swept down the drain along with his shampoo and body wash, but the *drip-drip-drip* of uneasiness down his spine remained disturbingly insistent. Probably because Ellie's shriek kept echoing in his head.

You're next!

He shivered before turning his attention to packing his scant belongings into a navy-blue duffle bag. It was a dream, nothing more. His conscience's way of reminding him that he should have gone to the authorities about Kingsley sooner. Maybe if he had, he could have saved more lives. Maybe if he had, the police would have captured Kingsley by now, and Gabe wouldn't be on the run.

He looked down to find his hands in a death grip, squeezing the life out of a sweatshirt he'd folded. Reminiscing over Kingsley was probably the worst way to try to push past his anxiety. Better to focus on the good in his life. Like Rob.

Rob's lopsided grin and twinkling blue eyes filled Gabe's head, helping his hands release the garment and return to packing. He'd run into Rob at the coffee shop one morning, and the two of them had started bantering while waiting on their lattes. Before long, Gabe and the handsome librarian were laughing and sharing stories like a couple of childhood friends. Talking to Rob had been so easy, even during that first meeting.

Gabe frowned at the sweatpants he was in the process of folding. Maybe too easy?

He didn't like the direction his thoughts were going, but he couldn't stop them from wandering down that dark trail. Someone had ratted him out, and Rob was the only person in Portland Gabe talked to, with the exception of Frank. What if Rob had been sent to the coffee shop by Kingsley?

Had he really been so gullible? So stupid? So...lonely?

Gabe shoved the remainder of his clothes into the bag, followed by his toiletries. No, that was absurd. No one could fake the warmth that filled Rob's eyes whenever he looked at Gabe. Or the passion in his voice. Rob loved him, and Gabe felt the same way about Rob.

It had been so perfect.

Gabe's fists clenched, and a low moan escaped his lips. And now he had to leave Rob behind in Portland, without so much as a word of goodbye. How could Gabe possibly do that to him?

Gabe stuffed the last item into his bag and zipped it closed with a determined tug. He couldn't. No, he refused. There had to be a way to tell Rob where he was going, but how? Face-to-face was out of the question, and a phone call was only slightly less risky. A letter, maybe?

He had to find a way. He just had to.

He looked at the device, turning it over and over in his hands. Maybe there was a way...

After wasting time waffling over what to do, Gabe peeked under the rickety bed with the loose spring that poked him whenever he rolled to the right, before peering into the drawers of the garage-sale dresser that was missing two of its knobs.

Once he was satisfied he hadn't missed any of his meager possessions, Gabe hustled into the living area to meet Frank with only two minutes to spare. "Ready."

Frank held up a hand while he pressed a radio to his ear. "Yeah, copy that. Just tell me when." When he finished, he turned to Gabe. "Sit tight for now. The team is still finishing up their sweep, and given the circumstances, we want to be extra careful that no one's watching the transfer."

Gabe nodded and sank onto the vomit green couch behind him. "Hey, tell them not to hurry on my account. Extra careful sounds great to me."

Frank's mouth twitched up on one side, which for the serious marshal was the equivalent of a full-blown grin. "Figured it might."

"Do you know where I'm being transferred to yet?"

The marshal's expression returned to its usual deadpan state. "I'm afraid I'm not at liberty to reveal that information quite yet."

Gabe slumped. "Extra careful, I understand."

"I'm glad to hear that. I've never lost a witness under my watch, and I'm guessing we're both equally invested in keeping it that way." This time, Gabe detected a softening around the federal agent's eyes before his radio squawked and snagged his attention. After listening for a moment, Frank gestured at Gabe. "It's time."

Gabe slung his bag over his shoulder and followed the marshal into the entryway. Before they made it to the door, Frank turned and held out his hand. "Almost forgot. Phone."

Gabe's nerves jangled wildly as he dug his phone out of his pocket and dropped the device into Frank's outstretched palm. Gabe held his breath, and even his heart seemed to temporarily cease beating while he waited for the marshal's reaction. If the other man checked for the SIM card, Gabe was destined for a long night of interrogation.

Gabe's legs went weak with relief when Frank popped the battery off the back of the phone and then chucked both parts into a sack that dangled from his arm. Safe. For now.

The marshal pulled a Cubs cap from the same bag and handed it to Gabe. "Put this on."

Gabe smashed the baseball hat over his curls.

Frank perused him from head to toe and gave a satisfied grunt before opening the front door.

Gabe paused to take one last look around. He wouldn't miss this place much. The furnishings were neither stylish nor particularly comfortable, and the interior always smelled faintly of mildew, no matter how many times Gabe cleaned. No, the real loss was his coffee shop…and Rob.

Maybe.

He thought of what he'd just done, hoping he hadn't made a terrible mistake.

Gabe trailed Frank to one of the two domestic SUVs idling at the curb, the thrum of their engines interrupting an otherwise quiet evening. Frank led the way to the second SUV, opening the door and ushering Gabe into a back seat that smelled like a combination of pine air freshener and old burgers.

It wasn't until the doors locked around them and the driver accelerated after the lead vehicle that Gabe realized how taut his muscles had been. The smaller the house shrank in the rearview mirror, the more he relaxed into the leather upholstery. The dark tint on the windows made him feel like he was tucked away in the safety of a hidden cocoon.

"Sorry for all this." Frank waved his hand around the SUV's interior. "Since we don't have any leads on how Kingsley tracked you down, we're operating under an abundance of caution." Frank pinned Gabe with his dark, probing gaze, making Gabe flinch. He knew what was coming next. "Are you sure you haven't been in contact with anyone lately? It's important you're upfront with us. Otherwise, we can't protect you effectively."

"I know, but there's no one." Gabe shoved his crossed fingers beneath his thigh. No one except Ellie, who he'd only contacted after he'd received Kingsley's letter.

And Rob.

Like a sudden rainstorm, uncertainty washed over him, making Gabe fidget in his seat. Had he been too quick to dismiss Rob as the potential leak? Gabe knew his feelings for the Portland librarian were real, but how could he be sure that Rob truly loved him in return? Gabe had yearned for a boyfriend so badly, and Kingsley knew that. Was it really that unlikely the doctor would plant a hot guy like Rob to weasel his way under Gabe's defenses?

The driver navigated the SUV onto the freeway, keeping a few car lengths behind the first one. For the next three hours, Gabe stared out the side window. A single question tumbled over and over again, trapped in the relentless spin cycle of his mind.

Was Rob the culprit or not?

Gabe didn't notice that the SUV had stopped until Frank snapped his fingers in front of his face. "Hey, anyone awake in there? We're here."

Gabe jolted upright and looked around. The tidy brick house they'd pulled in front of was bathed in light from several strategic fixtures. Neatly tended shrubs lined the narrow brick walkway to the front door.

After waiting on the porch while the agents from the lead SUV inspected the interior, the tall one who reminded Gabe of a bulldog on stilts poked his head out. "All clear."

Frank jerked his head at the door, indicating that Gabe should go first.

He stepped inside a neat entryway that opened to an expansive living area with high ceilings. The walls glowed a cheerful pale yellow. An open kitchen beckoned to the left, at least twice the size of the last one.

Gabe brightened for the first time since he'd left on the trip at the sight. "Granite counters? Double ovens? Damn. This whole time, all I had to do to get a nicer place was blow my cover? Now you tell me."

The bulldog-faced marshal with the sagging jowls snickered in appreciation at Gabe's jest. Even Frank's upper lip twitched.

His spirits bolstered, Gabe headed off in the opposite direction and inspected the three bedrooms. The master had a large en suite bathroom with an oversized tub and separate shower. A quick bounce on the king bed revealed no broken springs and a pillow-top mattress.

By the time he returned to the living room, Gabe felt at ease for the first moments since Kingsley's letter. He plopped onto a cream and blue pin-striped couch that didn't make him wonder if the fabric had ever been cleaned and punched a button on the remote he nabbed off the glass coffee table. The sixty-plus inch TV blinked on.

Gabe flipped through the channels, pausing a few seconds on each in search of something lighthearted. A comedy, or maybe a rom-com. He passed up a news station before the images on the screen penetrated.

No. That couldn't be.

Gabe squeezed his knees together, his heart lurching into his throat. No. He must have been hallucinating. He'd spent most of the night tossing and turning, and between that and his stress, it only made sense that his mind was playing tricks on him. Still, his hand trembled as he hit the arrow button, backing up to the channel he'd skipped over too quickly.

A male reporter stood in front of a stately stone building, the familiar look of which had caught Gabe's eye. The Portland Public Library.

Whooshing rushed through Gabe's ears, drowning out the reporter's voice. His attention was glued to the headline scrolling across the page. Rob had told him that the headline was called a chyron because Rob knew so many little things like that.

Rob.

Portland librarian discovered dead at work in what local authorities are calling the most gruesome murder they've seen in years.

A high-pitched whimpering cut through the static in Gabe's head, the kind of terrible cry a wounded animal made. He slapped his hands over his ears, desperate to block out the sound, but that didn't help. Gabe could still hear the pitiful moans. If anything, the wailing grew louder.

His hands fell uselessly to his sides. Footsteps pounded on the wooden floors, but Gabe still didn't comprehend where the whimpering came from until Frank's hand dropped onto his shoulder.

"You okay? What's wrong?" Frank and the bulldog marshal ran around, checking every corner of the room before returning their attention to Gabe.

"I need to borrow your phone." When Frank hesitated, Gabe pressed his palms together. "Please. Just for a minute. It's important, I swear."

The bulldog shrugged at Frank. After one last hesitation, the agent handed his phone to Gabe. "Don't make me regret this."

Gabe snatched the phone and navigated directly to YouTube, not even bothering with trying other news channels. He knew that the very first thing people did during a tragic situation these days wasn't to help...it was to pull out their phones.

With trembling fingers, he typed *Portland librarian murdered* into the search window and prayed as the live streams popped up. With his stomach churning, he clicked on the top result. Hit play.

A man's body filled the screen. All splayed out behind yellow crime scene tape, surrounded by puddles of a red substance he instantly recognized as blood. Too much of it. Both on the floor and staining the grisly wounds carved into the victim's chest. Some monster had used a sharp object to leave a message in his flesh, which the YouTuber helpfully zoomed in on.

I'm watching.

Gabe's eyes burned with tears. His throat clogged.

Although the victim's shirt was in tatters, enough fabric was left for Gabe to recognize the unique pink-on-gray design.

His stomach revolted, and the phone clattered to the floor as Gabe raced to the bathroom. He closed the door, barely making it to the toilet before he puked up everything he'd eaten that day. He heaved until not even yellow bile was left to expel.

A sharp rap bounced off the door. "Hey, you okay in there? What's going on? Talk to me."

But Gabe ignored Frank's command. He rose, flushed the toilet. Washed his mouth out at the sink. Weary to his very core, he unlocked the door. His bleary gaze skimmed Frank's before he brushed past the marshal and into the master bedroom. He eased the door closed on the man's startled expression and turned the lock. Then he collapsed face-first onto the bed and sobbed.

Gabe's last coherent thought before he passed out centered on the SIM card he'd stashed in his pocket and whether or not he should slide the tiny bit of plastic into his new phone. Just in case. On the off chance that a different librarian in Rob's pink and gray shirt had been murdered and Rob was fine, curled up by his fireplace at home.

But Gabe knew better. He drifted off with certainty ringing through his head like a death knoll.

His boyfriend, his Rob, was dead. Murdered to punish Gabe. Carved up to send him a message. A message that Gabe had received, loud and clear.

Somewhere out there, Kingsley was watching, and he wanted Gabe to know that he'd stop at nothing to ensure that Gabe suffered and spent the rest of his days suffering.

Rest of my days.

Even in this new place, Gabe didn't know how many of those he had left.

6

FBI Agent Clay Lockwood whistled as he shouldered his way into the front door of the Charleston police department, balancing a tray of steaming lattes in his right hand. If he were the singing type, he'd be belting out a tune right now. Maybe some Luke Bryan, or a little Queen.

No one who watched him saunter into the building with the extra spring in his step would guess that he'd been up since four that morning. Clay's muscles practically hummed with energy, and it wasn't from mainlining caffeine.

No, he had the new Kingsley Task Force to thank for that. Approval from the SAC in the Charleston FBI field office had arrived at the butt crack of dawn, yanking him out of a deep sleep and the warm, cozy bed he currently inhabited in one of Ellie's spare bedrooms. For once, he hadn't bemoaned the lost REM cycles. Not today.

He nodded at the uniformed patrol officer he passed on his way to the elevator and stabbed the button. His whistling gave way to a grin as he pictured the look on Ellie's face when he told her about the task force. Fortis had already given him the okay to add her. Now, Clay needed to track her down and break the good news.

The elevator doors dinged before they slid open. Clay stepped inside and studied the buttons, debating between 2 and B. Ellie's permanent desk was on the second floor with the rest of the detectives, but lately, she'd taken to spending more time in the basement, the very place where she'd begun her detective career.

Back then, camping out in the bowels of the PD building had been practical since Ellie worked exclusively on the cold cases stored down there. Now, though, Clay knew that Ellie's motives involved not wanting to leave Jillian alone for long stretches of time. Not that he blamed her. The evidence clerk's close call with the car bomb had all of them on edge.

In the end, Clay bet on Jillian and hit B. While the rickety old service elevator lurched and creaked its way down a floor, he dug his phone out of his pocket to check the screen. No new messages. Ellie hadn't replied to either of his texts yet. A prickle of foreboding stung the back of his neck, but Clay shrugged the feeling away.

At Ellie's request, their relationship had been relegated to the back burner ever since they'd returned from a work trip to Miami. Clay couldn't make the memories of that weekend disappear so easily. Hectic days of hunting for clues in a child trafficking ring melded into balmy nights spent tangled together between the sheets.

The temporary setback didn't matter, though. At least, not to Clay. He'd waited a long time between their very first kiss and their first night together. He could wait again now. Not that keeping his distance was easy. Especially on days like today, when he wanted to celebrate by picking up Ellie and swinging her around until her red hair flew behind her like a comet and she was breathless with laughter.

The elevator opened, and Clay stepped out, giving his

head a rueful shake. Time to calm his jets and chill the hell out. As much as he'd happily announce his feelings for Ellie to the entire Charleston PD, he knew she wasn't ready. And wouldn't be until they hunted Kingsley down like the vermin he was and eliminated the bastard's particular brand of plague from the planet.

That was one of the reasons Clay was falling for her. She was the kind of woman who'd do anything to keep the people around her safe, even if that meant sacrificing her own happiness in the process.

Clay could relate. There was no mountain he wouldn't move to protect Ellie. From Kingsley or anyone who tried to harm so much as a single, copper curl on her head.

The click of his boots on the cement floor echoed down the damp, narrow corridor as he rounded the corner. He kept walking until he reached the metal door. He rapped three times.

"Who is it?" Jillian's bubbly voice floated through the door.

"It's Clay."

Two seconds later, the door clicked open. Clay entered the cave-like room and performed a quick scan before spotting Jillian. "Ellie here somewhere?"

Jillian's blonde ponytail swung back and forth as she shook her head and pointed toward the ceiling. "Nope, she's still with Fortis."

Clay deflated. Hell. He knew what that meant: Fortis had stolen his thunder about the task force and told Ellie first.

The ancient door clicked, and Ellie bounced in, carrying a file under her arm. Pink tinted her cheeks, and her emerald eyes sparkled until her gaze landed on Clay. Upon spotting him, her full mouth thinned, and her eyes narrowed. She shot him a laser-cold look that he swore penetrated all the way down to his bones.

He stifled a groan. With the way Ellie was spitting fire at him, not a doubt in his head remained that Fortis had ruined Clay's surprise. Damn. He should have known better. Ellie detested being surprised. He'd wanted to make sure everything was signed off on before he got her hopes up, but that strategy appeared to have backfired, catching him right in the ass.

Clay hoisted the tray as a peace offering. "Coffee?"

"Thanks." Ellie reached for a paper cup and sipped the steaming liquid, closing her eyes and sighing. "This hits the spot."

Before Clay could release the pent-up air in his lungs, Ellie's green eyes flew open and speared him with a frigid glare. Her free hand latched onto her hip. Yeah, no, he wasn't out of the doghouse yet.

He set the tray on Jillian's desk next to a unicorn statue and held up his hands, palms facing out. "Whoa, hold up. I take it that Fortis told you the news?"

Ellie tossed her head, sending a tendril of red hair to tumble free of the French braid she favored at work. "He did and imagine my surprise. A Kingsley task force set up by the very FBI agent who's currently living in my home. Yet the first I heard of it was this morning in my boss's office. He was the one who told me that you'd picked me to be on your team. What I don't understand is why you couldn't have told me yourself?"

"Didn't you get my texts this morning? That's exactly what I planned to do, only Fortis went running his mouth off first."

She harrumphed. "Last I checked, I didn't live with Fortis. Why couldn't you tell me a week ago? Or even over the dinner table last night?"

Even mad, Ellie was beautiful. Or maybe the anger flushing her fair cheeks a rosy pink made her even more dazzling. Clay couldn't let on that her appearance distracted him, though. Ellie would tie his balls in a knot if he gave the slightest indication of where his focus had temporarily gone.

"I know, and I'm sorry. I was worried about getting your hopes up before I had approval from my SAC, and that didn't come until four this morning. And then I wasn't sure that Fortis would give the okay to add you to the team until I talked to him after that."

Some of the ice melted from Ellie's eyes as she stood there, biting her lower lip.

Relief eased the cramped sensation in Clay's chest. Reassured, Clay took a chance and stepped closer. "Look, I know how important getting Kingsley is to you, and I knew you'd move heaven and hell to get on that task force once you knew it existed. That's why I wanted to tie everything up first. I wanted to spare you the agony of any wait time."

After a few tense seconds ticked by, Ellie's entire body seemed to relax. "Fine." She shot him the stink eye, but he saw the humor behind the gesture. "I still don't like it, but I understand why you decided to handle it that way."

It wasn't the warm endorsement that Clay might have hoped for, but he'd take it for now. "Good, I'm glad we got that cleared up."

Ellie studied him over the top of her coffee cup as she took a long sip. "Can you fill me in on the specifics?"

"Not much to tell. Not yet. The idea came to me in the middle of the night, and I'm barely into the planning stage now. I want this task force to be different and integrate bureaus from every region of the U.S. That way, if Kingsley shows up on the West Coast, for example, we'll have someone nearby who is up to speed on the case."

Ellie seemed impressed. "That's actually a very good idea."

He blew on his knuckles. "I have my moments." Ready to

change the subject, he nodded at the file under her arm. "So, what's that?"

Surprise flashed across Ellie's face, like she'd forgotten it was even there. Her mouth turned down at the corners as she pulled the file free. "That is the new cold case Fortis assigned me after he welcomed me onto the task force. Danielle Snyder." Two furrows formed between her copper brows. "I don't get why this is suddenly a priority."

Clay was pretty sure he'd never heard that name before, but Jillian's head popped out from behind her monitor, where she'd been pretending not to eavesdrop on their conversation. "Danielle Snyder? Just a second, I'll grab her box. Poor thing. Sixteen is too young."

Jillian hopped up from her chair and headed straight for the door that led to the labyrinth of white evidence boxes. Her fingers pinged against the buttons as she entered her code, followed by the door clicking open. She vanished into the room and reappeared within seconds, carrying a box holding who knew what.

Clay shot her a teasing grin. "Hey, you're good. Ever consider a career in the FBI?"

Jillian snickered. "Thanks, but no thanks. I'm perfectly content here." She placed the box on the empty desk that used to serve as Ellie's.

Clay eyed the neat letters on the label. *Danielle Snyder.* Beneath that, it simply said *Missing Person.*

Clay wondered if the box had been misfiled. "Missing person?"

Ellie brushed past him to pull the lid off. "Maybe not anymore. Danielle's dad got a call from someone claiming to be her."

Clay let out a low whistle. "Wow. After how many years?" He crossed the short distance to the table and stood next to

Ellie while she reached inside and carefully extracted the contents.

"Fifteen." After she removed a folder and performed a quick review of the written report within, Ellie reached back inside the box. This time, she extracted a sealed plastic bag containing a small rectangular object. Cell phone, Clay noted.

Another dive into the box produced a plastic bag holding a second phone. "According to the evidence log, this one," Ellie pointed to the bag on the right, "belonged to Dani. The other one was her friend Roxanne's, who was found murdered the same night Dani went missing."

Jillian, who'd resettled behind her desk, bounced back up to her feet. "Roxanne Freeling, right? I'll go grab that box for you too."

She reappeared with Roxanne's evidence and plunked the box down next to Danielle's. Working as a team, Jillian and Ellie extracted the contents and spread them out across the table. Clay examined the clues right along with them. Not that there was much to go on. A green jacket once belonging to Danielle filled another evidence bag, and Roxanne's box contained an autopsy report and crime scene photos.

"Those were found by the scene?" Clay pointed at an image of a set of footprints encased in a soft, grainy-looking substance. Sand, he guessed.

Ellie nodded. "Yeah, by the swing set where Roxanne was killed." She rearranged the photos so that they could better view all the details. "Prevailing theory is that she tried to run and ended up falling and hitting her head on the retaining wall."

Clay leaned in, narrowing his eyes on a different picture. "And those prints indicate a struggle?"

Ellie pulled that picture close, tilting her head as she studied the image. "Exactly. Forensics suggests that's where

Dani struggled with their attacker, and see here?" She dragged yet another photo over to him. "Single tracks, but deeper than the earlier ones."

"Which suggests that the kidnapper was carrying additional weight in the form of Danielle."

After one last glance at the image of those shoe prints carving out little valleys in the sand, Clay straightened. Jillian and Ellie continued going through the reports and inspecting each piece of evidence while his mind drifted to a different day and location. A different little girl who went missing.

Clay covered his ears with his hands, trying to block out the ragged gasps of his mother's sobs. A loud crunch interrupted, followed by the guttural string of curses his father yelled. Clay flinched and glanced up to find his father's left fist, buried deep in the hole he'd just punched into the wall. Little flecks of white plaster sprinkled the carpet, like a dusting of new snow.

That vile, acrid taste rose in Clay's throat. The way it had been every day since his sister disappeared.

The detectives murmured some soothing words to his parents, but Clay knew they were meaningless. From his spot where he curled in a chair in the far corner of the room, he glared at the two men. When were they going to do something to help actually find her?

The taller detective rubbed his neck and whispered to his partner. As he turned his head, his gaze fell on Clay.

His stomach filled with dread, and he immediately dropped his head and curled into a tighter ball. No more questions. They'd already asked so many. The same ones, over and over again.

"Did you have a good relationship with your sister?"

"Did you two ever fight?"

"When did you last see her, and what did you two talk about?"

"When did you realize she was gone?"

Clay squeezed his eyes shut. Why couldn't they leave him

alone? But as the backs of his eyes burned and the sour taste grew stronger, he answered his own question.

The cops were obviously just as convinced of Clay's guilt in his sister's disappearance as Clay was.

Clay jumped when a hand landed on his arm, yanking him back into the present. The memory vanished, replaced with the image of Ellie peering up at him with a worried expression wrinkling her forehead and a question in her eyes.

"You okay?" The question came from Jillian, making Clay realize that he must have really been zoning out.

He forced a lighthearted chuckle he didn't feel. "I'm fine. Tired after my early morning. Guess I'd better start pounding more caffeine."

Grateful for the excuse to escape their concerned gazes, Clay turned away under the guise of grabbing his coffee and taking a long, drawn-out sip. The warm, bitter liquid grounded him in the here and now. He wasn't a little boy anymore, and this case wasn't about his sister. Danielle Snyder deserved his full attention.

He tilted his head back, drained the cup, and then returned to the other table. "So, what did you two come up with while I was nodding off on my feet?"

The skeptical look Ellie flashed him let Clay know that she wasn't fully buying his story, so his shoulders eased when she turned back to the scattered evidence.

"Not much. Mostly speculating on what might have happened. Did the killer move Dani to murder her at some other location? Or did he kidnap her, and she's still out there somewhere?" Ellie tapped a finger on a photo of a teenage girl with thick, dirty blonde hair that fell in waves past her shoulders, wearing a wide smile and a plaid flannel.

"And if she was kidnapped, to what end? Did she suffer,

and is she still suffering now? Why would she reach out to her father after all this time?"

The photo of the smiling teen blurred around the edges. In Clay's head, it rearranged itself into an image of a different girl. A younger one with bright blue eyes and a mischievous smile. His heart twisted when he realized that his memory was so old that he'd have no idea what his sister would look like now if she were still alive. Would he recognize her if he passed her on the street? Or would they walk right by each other like two strangers, neither of them the wiser?

Caraleigh, what happened to you? Are you still out there somewhere?

A cough interrupted his pointless musing. When Clay blinked back to awareness, both women stared at him with identical concerned expressions. Not that he blamed them. If one of them were acting the way he had over the last ten minutes, Clay would be worried too.

His gaze wandered back to Danielle's smiling face. Almost immediately, he averted his eyes and tugged at his collar. The underground space with low ceilings and no windows was starting to feel cramped and airless, like a trap. "I need to head back to the field office and get started on assembling the task force. See you two back at the apartment."

Without waiting for a reply, Clay pivoted on one booted heel and strode straight for the door. He figured the second he escaped the room and into the corridor, that sensation of being locked into a dark cell would subside, and it did. In its place, an icy finger shivered across his back, like a spectral presence trailed him as the evidence room door clanked shut.

"I'm sorry, Caraleigh."

His whisper floated down the narrow hallway and vanished, swallowed by the repetitive click of his boots.

He shivered before clenching his jaw. It was too late for Caraleigh, but Danielle was a different story. Maybe if he helped Ellie find Danielle, it would ease some of the guilt he'd carried with him all these years, like an extra thirty pounds strapped to his chest.

Maybe if he helped find Danielle, he'd be one step closer to forgiving himself for losing his baby sister.

7

K atarina whipped a dust cloth across the gleaming surface of the wooden dining table before turning to inspect the rest of the room. It didn't take long for her to admit the truth: nothing needed attention.

And she was bored to death.

The house was small, almost cabin-like, with an open living and dining area featuring rustic wooden panels and comfortable plaid upholstery in shades of cream and hunter green. She carried her cloth down the short hall and into the master bedroom, scowling at the blue and white checked comforter she'd already straightened that morning and the wicker laundry basket, empty from when she'd folded and put away the clothes last night.

"Just call me Cinder-fucking-ella," she muttered.

Maybe she'd be lucky, and a handsome prince would find her here and whisk the daily grind of housekeeping away. He'd slip a glass slipper onto her foot and...

And what?

Watch it crack under her every step?

Send sharp splinters into her soles. Slash her Achilles?

No thank you.

Who in the hell wore a glass slipper anyway? That was a sure ticket to the emergency room.

She just needed to keep busy. That was all.

After delivering a swift kick to the laundry basket with her fuzzy slipper and savoring a moment of satisfaction as it cartwheeled across the hardwood floor, Katarina brightened. Harmony's room! Surely there was something for her to tidy in there.

Katarina pivoted and made her way to Harmony's doorway before she flinched, remembering. She corrected herself. No, not Harmony. *Bethany.*

They were Bethany and Katrina now.

Mother and daughter.

The notion warmed Katarina's heart. When she'd been told her baby had died right after birth, Katarina had been devastated. And six years later, when she'd discovered that Kingsley had lied and placed her newborn baby into adoption, she'd been overcome by a murderous rage, coupled with determination.

Katarina had vowed that nothing would stop her from reuniting with her daughter, and nothing had. Her dream of them sharing a normal life together had come true.

As normal as a life could be within the WITSEC program.

Katarina surveilled her daughter's tidy room and flopped onto her back on the moss green comforter with a groan. Yes, Bethany and Katrina. A normal mother and daughter, living together in this little house, in the middle of Nowhere, Wyoming. A place where Katarina was convinced she would die of boredom before the year was out.

She stared up at the wooden beams that crossed the ceiling, deliberately slowing her breathing to calm the claustrophobic feel of the walls closing in. If Kingsley were here to witness Katarina's sad little attempt at domestication, he'd laugh his head off and tell her, *I told you so. You and I aren't meant for a mundane life, Katarina. We're not like everyone else. We need to hurt people to feel alive.*

"No!" Katarina's denial echoed in the tiny room. Great, now she was arguing with ghosts from her past. Out loud, no less. Kingsley was the whole reason she was stuck in the boondocks in the first place. And if she planned on keeping that son of a bitch confined to the past instead of haunting her future, then she'd better quit whining and accept her new reality here in Wyoming. "I do want a normal life. I finally have Har-*Bethany* back, and things are perfect. I just need a little time to get used to this life."

Katarina wasn't sure if she truly believed what she was saying or if she was trying to convince herself. Either way, she felt a little better. Across the country, millions of women stayed home with the kids and took care of the house. If they could do it without smashing their heads against the wall to relieve the boredom, she could too.

A little boredom was a small price to pay for a normal life.

Katarina stretched her arms over her head and contemplated what she could do to fill the time. What she needed was a hobby. Knitting? She snickered at the image of her sitting in a rocking chair, patiently hooking a pair of those oversized needles through colorful yarn.

Please.

She was far more likely to stab someone with a needle than craft some silly blanket that would end up in the corner of someone's closet. Who wanted a blanket full of holes, anyway? Not Katarina. She required a hobby that raised her pulse above dead to entertain herself. An activity with a little violence to take the edge off. Like hunting.

She pushed up to her elbows, brightening. Now, that might work. The Feds wouldn't allow her to have a gun, but what about a bow and arrow? She was picturing herself spearing a chattering, annoying squirrel from fifty feet away when a rustle trickled in through the window.

She went completely still, straining to hear over the sudden frantic drumming of her pulse. She was probably imagining things. This wasn't the first time since entering WITSEC that her imagination had conjured up an unsettling noise.

Crunch!

No, she hadn't imagined that.

A shiver raced over her. On cat-like feet, Katarina eased off the bed and crept toward the window, pausing only to listen and grab one of the solid buffalo-shaped bookends she'd picked up for her daughter in town. When she reached the window, she edged the heavy green curtains aside, peering through the sliver of an opening.

At first, all she saw were trees. Trees and rolling hills, and in the distance, a view of the Grand Tetons. Apart from the insistent chirping of a bird, the yard remained silent.

Crunch!

Katarina flinched, whipping her head to face the direction of the noise. She caught a flash of movement behind a tree. Her breath caught in her lungs and then released again when she identified the source. A damned buck, nibbling on a wild plant.

Her panic subsided, leaving Katarina feeling foolish and more than a little annoyed. With her free hand, she rapped on the window. "Get out of here! Go find dinner somewhere else!"

At her knock, the buck's head whipped up, but the stupid thing didn't budge. That was how low Katarina had fallen. Once upon a time, not even that long ago, she'd been an apex predator. Now, she couldn't even scare off a prey animal.

Her fist tightened, and she banged on the window again, hard enough this time to make it rattle. "Get out of here!"

This time, the deer whirled and fled, leaping away on long legs. When he disappeared from sight, she let the curtains fall closed and headed from the room, her back stiff and her teeth clenched. She needed to get a grip on herself and figure out how to settle into this new life. For her, and for Harm—no, *Bethany*. If she didn't, then Kingsley would win. And Katarina had no intention of letting the man who'd first abducted her and then her daughter win, or proving him right when it came to her.

She could make this regular life thing work. She simply needed a way to stay busy. Striding into the hallway, she whipped open a closet and pulled out the broom before heading into the kitchen. After hitting a button on her phone, music filled the tiny space. Soon, she lost herself in the rhythm of a hip hop beat and the methodical sweep of the broom across the wooden floor.

Her mind drifted and filled with memories of more exciting times. Of the satisfying crunch a nose made beneath her fist or the way a knife felt, sinking deep into human flesh. Of the thrill that came along with deceiving someone and leading them straight into a trap.

When she realized the direction her thoughts had taken, Katarina froze. "Stop it. You're a mother now."

But a glance around the empty house only made her frustration grow. Bethany spent most of the day at school. What was Katarina supposed to do in the meantime? Spend long hours watching soap operas and cooking shows and sweeping up floors that didn't need cleaning?

Or...even more laughable...get a job.

Though the clock was ticking until she'd need to get one of those.

"Argh!" Katarina's hands clenched hard around the

broom, and she brought it down over her raised knee. "Ouch!"

The stupid thing didn't even break. Katarina flung the broom across the room and hopped around on one leg, cursing and clutching her throbbing thigh. By the time she realized how ridiculous she must look, her breath came in ragged pants. Great. Not only was she bored senseless, she was weak and out of shape too.

Her hands flew to her sides and squeezed the flesh hanging over her pants. There, see that? Rolls! She even had rolls now! Not a lot, but still. Any amount of fat around her midsection was noticeable compared to the washboard abs she'd once sported.

Katarina had always busted her butt to ensure her body stayed fit and honed, in keeping with the weapon it was. Now even that part of her life was changing, and she hated the shift. She detested everything about this stupid house and new existence.

A sharp pain stabbed her rib cage when she remembered. Bethany. She hated everything except Bethany. Duh.

After stomping over to the sink for a glass of water, Katarina sipped the tepid liquid and gazed out the front window. In her view, a middle-aged man walked his scruffy dog down the road. Maybe only sixty feet separated her sink from the walkway. So close.

As Katarina continued sipping from the glass, she allowed her mind to drift away. To ponder the what-ifs.

What if, for example, Katarina set down her glass, selected a butcher knife from the wooden block, and strolled over to the front door?

What if she opened the door, balanced her hand on her hip, and tilted her body in an inviting way, showcasing her curves to their advantage?

What if she called out to him? In her sweetest, most help-less voice.

"Excuse me, sir, could you come help me for a minute? I'm cooking, and I need a strong pair of hands to pry a jar open for me. I promise I'll make it worth your while."

The man turned toward her voice until he located her, his uncertain gaze becoming more confident as he eyed her up and down. "Sure, happy to help." In reality, he was sizing her up as prey, convinced that Katarina was too stupid to grasp what he had in mind.

But she knew. She allowed her smile to widen as he dragged the scruffy dog toward her. Drawing closer. And closer. The nearer he came, the more Katarina's skin tingled. She fluffed her hair back with her right hand, even as she kept her left hidden behind her back, the knife clutched in her fist. Anticipating the perfect moment to deliver his surprise as she opened the door wider, beckoning him inside.

That's it. Come to me. Come inside and play a little while.

Katarina blinked away the fantasy to find herself standing in the open doorway. No man or scruffy dog approached her porch. Instead, they were disappearing farther down the road. She swallowed hard, pulled her left hand out from behind her back, and inched her gaze down to the glimmer of a long piece of metal. With a yelp, she uncurled her fingers. The knife clattered to the floor.

She backed away, shaking her head. "This isn't working. I can't be cooped up in here all day." A glance at the clock told her she still had an hour until she needed to pick up Harmony—no, dammit, Bethany!—from school.

Screw this. Katarina grabbed her coat off the hook by the front door, shouldered her purse, and fled to the car. She reversed out of the driveway and drove aimlessly down the streets without any goal in mind other than to get the hell out of that house. A few weeks of housework was all it took for Katarina to start losing her mind. That had to be some kind of record.

After ten minutes of cruising, a sign caught her attention. An old-school cheesy neon one that proclaimed BEER, with an arrow pointing at a dingy-looking wooden structure with darkened windows. Another sign flashed above the first one: Bob's Bar.

On impulse, she whipped the car into the parking lot with a squeal of tires and parked out front. Most of the spots were empty, but a handful of dusty trucks and Subarus filled a few of the spaces. Katarina passed them by on her way to the front door.

Just one drink. That was all she needed to take the edge off. Then, she'd drive to the school and wait in the mile-long pick-up line to get Bethany like a good little mom. Maybe she could take Harmony Christmas tree shopping after—no, no, no! Fuck! *Bethany, dammit!* She could take *Bethany* Christmas tree shopping, buy some ornaments, and pick up some hot chocolate to drink while the two of them decorated the tree back home. The way families did.

She entered the bar to Bono serenading the patrons with his smarmy lyrics and debated turning right back around and leaving. Please. Easy for him to croon about a beautiful day while wallowing in his millions. Take away his money and stick him in Katarina's monotonous Wyoming existence? She bet that obnoxious joy petered out in a month, tops.

Whatever. The music would change soon enough, and it wasn't like she had anything better to do. Squinting in the dim lighting, Katarina's nose wrinkled at the pungent, sweet odor that assaulted her. Stale beer, most likely. She shrugged and headed straight to the back. She'd smelled far worse.

Stopping in front of a sixty-ish, gray-ponytailed bartender who tended a long bar wallpapered with faded band flyers, she gave him a once-over before discretely scanning the business's other occupants. Her inspection didn't take long. Besides a cluster of four men laughing at a table in the far corner, the only other day drinkers were an elderly couple who sipped domestic beers and watched sports on one of the two TVs.

A poster advertising holiday happy hour specials hung over the taps, reminding Katarina that this would be her first-ever Christmas with her daughter. Her heart swelled in her chest but doubt soon pricked holes in her elation.

Since when did she know the first damn thing about celebrating the holidays, with a freaking eight-year-old, no less? She needed to make sure everything was perfect, but how? It wasn't like Katarina and Kingsley had sat around the Christmas tree, singing carols and stringing colorful lights. And she'd rather not dwell on her foster families before that.

"Whaddaya having?" The bartender stood in front of her with his round stomach bulging beneath a black t-shirt, staring from beneath a pair of arched, bushy gray eyebrows.

Katarina's gaze wandered back to the poster, and the doubts multiplied.

You and me, we're a family now, Katarina. No one else could possibly understand us.

She'd planned on ordering a beer, but the unwelcome intrusion of Kingsley's voice changed her mind at the last second. "I'll take a gin and tonic." Banishing the psychiatrist from her head required stronger measures.

The bartender went to work, mixing her choice into a squat glass and topping the combination off with a twist of lime. He slid the drink across the bar to her. "That'll be five dollars."

Katarina handed him six and then spun sideways on her stool to discourage any additional conversation. She sipped at the drink, the first she'd had in months. The more she sipped, the more her anxiety melted away.

A new song kicked off on the ancient jukebox. Some twangy tune by a country singer, moping about his ex-girl-friend and his pickup truck. A howl of laughter from the corner drowned out the chorus, and Katarina spun in that direction in time to catch one of the four men eying her.

He was attractive, with tanned skin instead of the pasty winter pale most everyone else sported in this god-awful December hell. His wavy brown hair looked soft and thick while a hint of stubble on a squared jaw promised a hint of pain. Broad shoulders filled out his flannel shirt nicely.

The man flashed her a cheeky grin, lifting his drink in an informal salute. Katarina snorted and turned away. She knew the type. A bad boy wannabe who fed his ego by charming his way into women's beds.

Katarina had every intention of ignoring him, but there wasn't much else to look at in the little bar, so her gaze kept sliding that way. Assessing. It was astonishing how much a person could learn about a stranger through simple observa-tion. For example, Katarina would bet money that the cocky drink-saluting man was the ringleader of his little group of rowdies. The way the other men instantly quieted down whenever he'd lift a hand or shake his head was the giveaway. He both commanded and expected attention.

She also predicted that he'd swagger up and hit on her any minute now. She wasn't disappointed. Right on cue, he sauntered over and dropped onto the stool next to hers, straddling the cushion and leaning his elbows over the backrest.

"Another Jack and Coke?"

The man winked at the bartender as an answer before turning to Katarina. His grin revealed a chipped upper tooth.

"That, and another of whatever this little lady just guzzled down."

With a start, Katarina glanced at her empty glass. How had she finished the first one so quickly? Not that it mattered. She pushed the glass away and faced her would-be drink buyer with an arched eyebrow. "No, thanks. If this little lady wants another drink, she'll buy one herself."

The man's blue eyes narrowed for a split-second before his grin widened. "Feisty. Good to know. How about I buy you a drink another time instead?"

Katarina pretended to consider his offer before shaking her head. "Sorry, but I don't think so." She bent over to rummage in her purse, hiding a smile. If she knew one thing about men like him, it was that they always wanted what they couldn't have.

Sure enough, when she rose from her seat, the man slid a cream business card in front of her. "Here's my name and number, in case you change your mind."

Almost too predictable. And probably far too wholesome for Katarina, despite the bad boy vibe he exuded.

Taking pity on his hopeful expression, she leaned in, curling one hand over his shoulder as she whispered into his ear. "Trust me, I'm doing you a favor. You don't want to get to know me."

The man reared his head back and laughed. He didn't notice how serious she was. "Why not?"

Still leaning on his shoulder, Katarina placed her other hand on his leg right above his knee, smiling as her fingers inched their way up his jean-clad thigh. She made eye contact with him at the exact moment her hand curved around his balls and squeezed, wanting to savor the change in his expression.

Except, nothing happened. The man didn't so much as flinch. Katarina squeezed harder. Still not a peep.

Interesting.

Katarina tilted her head, considering him with new eyes as a genuine smile curved her lips. "Because people around me get hurt."

Never breaking eye contact, the man grabbed her hand and pressed it even harder against the growing bulge in his pants. "Perfect, darlin', cause I like pain."

A shiver raced across Katarina's skin. She wet her suddenly dry lips with the tip of her tongue, relishing the way his gaze followed. Maybe she'd been a little too quick to turn him down. She swiveled her head, locating the restroom sign that beckoned to a dark hallway a few feet away. Did she dare? He exuded that adventurous-type vibe. The kind of man who'd be up for joining her on a quick trip to the ladies' room.

Music burst from her purse, intruding on her plan. "Hold that thought."

She dug her phone out, staring blankly at the alarm notification until she remembered. Shit! Time to pick up Harmony—*Bethany!*—from school.

She shook her head. What kind of terrible mother was she to forget about her kid so quickly? Over a stranger with a high pain tolerance that she'd met in a bar?

While the man watched, Katarina gathered her things. Time to leave. "Bye now."

She had every intention of heading straight for her car, but on impulse, pivoted back to the man. She intended the kiss to be nothing. A simple brushing of her lips against his. She'd underestimated his reflexes.

Quick as a snake, the stranger's hands whipped out, pulling her close as his mouth moved over hers. He tasted of Coke and spice, a delicious combination that made Katarina's body tingle all over. His teeth sank into her bottom lip, an unexpected pinch that sent flames racing along her nerves.

Her phone blared its second reminder, insisting that she go. With effort, Katarina pushed away, surprised to note the fuzziness in her head. Damn. She'd seriously underestimated the stranger. Either that, or she'd miscalculated how much she missed being with a man.

Katarina didn't bother saying goodbye. After patting him on his tanned cheek, she turned and strolled across the bar, sensing his gaze on her the entire way to the door. It took her every moment of the drive to the school to shift her focus back to the afternoon she'd planned for her and her daughter.

Christmas trees and hot chocolate and Bethany.

That was her future.

Not some player who hung out in dive bars in rural Wyoming. No matter how good of a kisser he was.

But as she pulled into the pick-up line, Katarina's gaze fell onto the business card she'd tossed into the center compartment. Clayne Miller of Miller Distributing. She reached down to rip it into shreds but hesitated as she ran her fingers over the glossy surface.

She ended up tucking the card into her glove box instead.

Clever girls knew when to keep their options open. Lucky for Katarina, she considered herself to be an exceptionally clever girl indeed.

8

The sudden burst of pain stole Jillian's breath as she pushed into a sitting position on the edge of her bed. She dug her fingers into the mattress, waiting for the burning sensation that shot into her leg to subside. Every morning, the same thing. Ever since Ellie's car had exploded.

Not that Jillian was complaining, because she was lucky. She knew that. A few scrapes and an occasionally stiff back were a small price to pay, compared to the carnage Kingsley had intended when he'd planted the bomb.

As she dangled her legs off the mattress and waited for the pain to recede, her eyes gradually grew accustomed to the darkness of the early hour. Once she was ready, Jillian eased to a standing position. Her toes curled into the plush rug that protected her feet from the chilly wooden floorboards.

Creak.

She cringed. Stupid mattress, always making noise at the most inopportune moments. The covers behind her rustled. Jillian glanced over her shoulder at the bulky shape sprawled across the other half of the bed, and her heart softened.

Jacob Garcia rolled onto his back, but his eyes remained closed. Once the slow, rhythmic rise and fall of his chest reassured her that he was still asleep, Jillian grabbed the work clothes she'd laid on her dresser the night before and crept into the adjoining bathroom to shower.

After she finished dressing in a pair of gray pants and a navy-blue polo, Jillian brushed tinted moisturizer onto her face, applied her favorite matte red lipstick, and once she pulled her blonde hair back into a low ponytail, pronounced herself ready to go. She worked as the evidence clerk in the Charleston PD basement, not the Ritz. No need for her to get all fancied up when the only thing to impress down there were rows of evidence boxes.

Shoes in hand, Jillian left the bedroom and padded toward the kitchen. She zoomed directly to the fancy coffee maker on the counter, where a pot half-full of the dark brown ambrosia beckoned. After filling her oversized *I'm a Badass* mug—complete with an illustration of a donkey—to the top, she turned, inhaled the delicious fragrance, and sighed. Coffee. The most wondrous liquid elixir known to womankind. In Jillian's opinion, whoever invented coffee hadn't received nearly enough credit.

She set the mug on the kitchen table and plunked into the chair next to where Ellie sat, already dressed and hunkered down over an open file. After her first sip, Jillian sighed again. "Have you ever wondered how we have all these national days—National Donut Day, Hug Day, Take Your Aardvark to Work Day—and yet we don't have a National Coffee Day?"

Ellie lifted her head from the notebook she'd been staring into like the pages contained the answer to the meaning of life and wrinkled her nose. "There's a Take Your Aardvark to Work Day?"

Jillian shrugged, swallowing another life-giving sip of the

warm liquid. "I don't know, but I wouldn't be surprised if there was."

Her friend's mouth curved up briefly before she returned her attention to the papers spread out before her.

"The Danielle Snyder case?" At Ellie's nod, Jillian clucked her tongue in sympathy. "Would it help to go over the details out loud?"

Ellie rubbed the back of her neck. "That would be great, actually. If you're sure you don't mind."

Jillian snorted and rolled her eyes. "When have I ever minded you sharing your cases with me?"

If anything, Ellie talking through cases with her tended to be the highlight of Jillian's workday. Sure, Jillian enjoyed working as the evidence clerk at the Charleston PD, deriving a great deal of satisfaction from creating an orderly system in that file wasteland of a basement. But even satisfied girls needed a fresh challenge every now and then.

Ellie shuffled the papers around on the table. "Okay, so you already know the night Dani Snyder disappeared. She went to a party with her best friend, Roxanne, right?"

Familiar with her friend's process of asking rhetorical questions as she worked things out, Jillian didn't bother to answer. She sipped her coffee and waited.

"According to witnesses, Dani ran out of the party early after catching her boyfriend making out with another girl, crying. Roxanne followed her, and that's the last time the two girls were ever seen alive."

"Yikes. That's terrible." Jillian hadn't meant to comment yet. The words had just sort of slipped out. She took another sip of coffee to shut herself up.

Ellie nodded and brought her own mug to her lips. She took two long swigs of the brew before continuing. "Roxanne's body was found at a nearby park, near the swing set. Blood found on the retaining wall turned out to be hers. The medical examiner found bruises on her upper arms, consistent with an assailant grabbing her and Roxanne trying to pull away. The shoe patterns in the sand leading to the girl's body also indicated a struggle, so the theory is that Roxanne tried to run, fell, and hit her head. She died of a traumatic brain injury." Twin furrows formed over Ellie's nose. "No DNA linking Dani to the scene, but the detectives recovered her phone and jacket."

Jillian flinched. Poor Roxanne. And Dani. She bet whatever whisked the latter girl away from her best friend's dead body wasn't good.

Also, poor Ellie. Jillian studied her roommate, searching for signs of strain within the heart-shaped face. The circumstances of Dani's disappearance mirrored Ellie's own kidnapping, in that both girls vanished after running away from a party. Until she solved the case, that similarity would eat at Ellie. Like a bone cancer.

Jillian worried the overlap would also spur her friend to work herself to the point of exhaustion.

After a minute passed by where Ellie brooded into her mug without a peep, Jillian figured it was safe to ask a question. "Any other evidence at the scene?"

Her friend twirled a copper curl around her finger. One of the cute little habits that Jillian caught her friend performing whenever a puzzle piece refused to snap into place. Although, cute really wasn't the best way to describe Ellie. More like beautiful. Or stunning.

"Not much." Ellie pulled her finger down, stretching the curl straight before letting it spring back up. Only to recapture that same tendril around her finger yet again.

Twirl, release. Twirl, release. Jillian wondered if someone could hypnotize themselves by watching that copper curl coil and uncoil, over and over again.

"They found three sets of footprints, sizes eight, nine, and thirteen. The larger prints were shallow heading toward the swings and got deeper on the way out, probably because he was carrying Dani by then. Those same prints led to Roxanne's body, where they stopped and shortened to show only the front half of the tread."

At that last detail, confusion clouded Jillian's mind. "Wait, don't tell me, let me see if I can figure it…" She gasped. "Oh! I get it! The attacker crouched down by the body to get a closer look?"

Ellie glanced up from the file to flash Jillian a quick smile. "Smarty pants. That's exactly what they believe happened."

Jillian lifted her nearly empty mug. "I'm telling you, it's the coffee. Studies show caffeine improves your brain function."

A gloomy sigh escaped her friend's lips. "I should probably drink up then because this case looks like it's going to be pretty damn tough."

"You say that every time when you start a new case but look at how many you've closed. You're a rock star. In fact, forget National Coffee Day. What we really need is an Ellie Kline Day."

That last comment coaxed a snicker out of Ellie. "Now, that would definitely endear me to the other detectives back at the station." When she looked at Jillian, though, her green eyes glowed with appreciation. "Thank you for the vote of confidence. I need it more than you can imagine."

Jillian inclined her head in her interpretation of a regal nod. "Hey, that's what I live for: drinking coffee and giving my best friend pep talks."

Her black Lab mix chose that moment to trot over, plopping her furry butt on Jillian's bare foot, and gazing up at her with reproachful brown eyes. "And yes, I live for giving Sam ear rubs too, my bad."

The dog's ecstatic groans filled the room as Jillian

scratched that hard-to-reach spot behind the mutt's drooping ears.

"How do you predict Jacob's going to feel when he finds out Sam made the list of things his girlfriend lives for and he didn't?" Ellie teased.

Jillian fake gasped. "You wouldn't dare." She bobbed her eyebrows and gave her friend a sinister grin. "Mostly because I have way too much dirt on you."

"Sad, but true." Ellie turned back to the notebook, her shoulders slumping again.

"Anything else?"

"No. That's the problem. That's really all there is to know. The most likely scenario is that Dani was taken alive, possibly to sell into a sex or human trafficking ring. I'm betting Roxanne would have met the same fate if not for hitting her head."

"That's really not much to go on, is it?" Jillian swirled the coffee in her cup.

"Not so much. I have to meet with Charles Snyder this afternoon, and it's not like I have any good news for him."

That name pinged around in Jillian's head before landing. Her eyes widened. "Not the same Charles Snyder who hosts *Do You Feel Lucky?*"

"Yep, that's Dani's dad. My theory is that after all this time, the call is a fake. So, I'm not particularly excited about this visit."

"Oof, I'm sorry." Jillian now better understood her typically optimistic friend's slumped posture. This was why Jillian was happy to remain tucked away in the basement. It took a special kind of person to deal with grieving families in a sensitive way, and Jillian knew herself well enough to know she didn't qualify. Even now, her cheeks burned with helpless anger. "Also, what kind of an asshole prank calls a devastated father and pretends to be his kidnapped daughter? After all these years?"

"The worst kind of asshole." Ellie rested her chin in her palm and blew out a breath. "And I can only come up with two reasons to bother. Either the caller wanted to inflict pain, or they want money."

Jillian mulled over the two options. Pain or money. Great.

She rested her chin in her own hand, suddenly feeling depressed too. "Okay, but why him? And why now? Surely there are more recent targets to go after for ransom money, if that's what they're after."

"One would think, yeah."

After Ellie responded, both of them stared off into space as they struggled to connect the dots. The time-lapse was the weirdest part, as far as Jillian was concerned. Especially if money was the kidnapper's goal.

"So maybe the caller is someone looking to hurt Dani's dad." But why? Jillian could maybe understand if the man had been a prosecutor or a corporate raider. Who would hold that kind of a grudge against a game show host, though? An idea struck, and Jillian bolted upright in her chair. "Do you know if there were any disgruntled game show contestants? Could someone have gotten pissed about not winning the big prize and decided to get revenge?"

"I'm looking into that, but so far, nothing."

Jillian returned to swirling her coffee and frowned. "I mean, far-fetched as it sounds, isn't it possible the caller really is his daughter?"

"I mean, that would be great, wouldn't it? And you know as well as I do that anything's possible." Ellie rose from the table and stretched her back. The frown crept over her face again. "I've come to realize that if something in a case seems too easy, there's usually a reason for it. And in this instance, Dani Snyder being alive feels way too easy."

9

Later that morning, Ellie's GPS navigated her Ford Explorer northbound up US-26 to Goose Creek. Chase, her security detail for the day, had been less than thrilled when she informed him that she planned on driving her own car by herself, but Ellie had insisted.

The whole point of funding private security out of her own pocket was to ensure that she called the shots. The rearview mirror confirmed that Chase still shadowed her by a few car lengths in his own SUV and that his expression had yet to lose that "sucked on a lemon" look.

Ellie wondered if the disgruntled guard would feel better or worse if she told him that the heads-up regarding her plans had been a gift because she'd been "this close" to sneaking out. She wiggled her fingers at the disgruntled guard, then refocused on the road.

Around twenty minutes later, the robotic GPS voice announced that she had arrived at Charles Snyder's address. Ellie turned up a long circular driveway constructed from interlocking layers of red brick and concrete. The house was a stately brick affair featuring four elegant white pillars, and based on the sheer size of the structure, Ellie suspected at least double that number of bedrooms.

"Guess the game show business is doing okay."

Ellie scowled as the sound of her own voice accompanied her up the elegant brick path to the oversized double front doors. She didn't usually talk to herself on her way to interview victims, but something about this case plucked at her already taut nerves.

Ellie still suspected that Mr. Snyder's caller was a fake, without coming any closer to answering the pivotal mystery of *why now?* Puzzles without logical solutions tended to mean Ellie was missing crucial pieces, which wasn't a feeling she particularly enjoyed.

When she reached the porch, Ellie grabbed hold of the ornate bronze ring and knocked twice. The door swung open, revealing a petite middle-aged woman wearing creased black slacks paired with a black polo shirt featuring an immaculate white collar. The woman smoothed her perfectly tamed ponytail and offered Ellie a polite smile. "Hello, may I help you?"

Ellie flashed her badge. "Detective Ellie Kline with the Charleston Police Department. I called ahead to let Mr. Snyder know I was coming."

"Detective Kline, yes, he's been expecting you. I'm Mary, the housekeeper. Please, come in."

The woman moved aside, pulling the door open wide. Ellie entered a large foyer with a white and gray marble floor. Two elegant curved staircases swept up to the second floor from opposite sides, but Mary led her between them and down a wide hallway, her short legs covering the ground with such miraculous speed that Ellie almost broke into a trot to keep up.

Mary paused outside an opening on the left and held out a hand with no-nonsense short nails, gesturing her inside.

"Please, make yourself comfortable in the parlor while I fetch Mr. Snyder."

"Thank you."

Ellie meandered into the elegant room. A beautiful white piano resided in the far corner, its polished wood gleaming in the sunlight streaming in from an enormous picture window. A custom, hand-carved mantelpiece framed a fireplace that appeared large enough to serve as a small-car garage. A trio of plump red and white couches created a cozy sitting area, and the entire room exuded the sweet scent of fresh flowers.

On the wall near the fireplace hung a color portrait. The teenage girl in the picture looked a couple years shy of sixteen, but Ellie still recognized Dani Snyder's wide smile and heart-shaped face instantly. She started toward the picture when footsteps echoed behind her.

Ellie turned as Mary led an attractive middle-aged man with a full head of salt-and-pepper hair into the room.

"Detective Kline, thank you so much for coming."

Charles Snyder's gray slacks and navy button-down were immaculate and an expensive cut, as was his hair. His house and furnishings practically screamed understated wealth, and according to Ellie's research, the ratings for the game show he hosted had hit an all-time high. Despite all of that, his smile looked sad. Or maybe Ellie was projecting, based on what she knew about his daughter's case.

Charles Snyder approached and shook her hand with a firm but kind grip before motioning her to the couch. "Please, have a seat. Can I get you something to drink?" In real life, his voice was much softer than the booming baritone he was known for, one that had blared from her television speakers on more than one occasion. She found that surprising for some reason.

Ellie shook her head, perching on the edge of the couch. "No, thank you."

Mr. Snyder turned toward the door. "Mary, can you please bring us some muffins, coffee, and juice?" After making his request, Charles Snyder eased himself onto the couch opposite Ellie. "Thank you for driving out here. You said you had some questions for me about the phone call?"

"Right." While Ellie collected her thoughts, her gaze wandered back over to the piano. "Do you play?"

Mr. Snyder stared at the instrument like he was waiting for a song to burst from the polished keys. "No. Dani did. It hasn't been played since she disappeared. I held on to it this whole time, just in case…"

He didn't finish the sentence. He didn't have to. Ellie's brain completed the ending as if he'd kept right on speaking.

Just in case Dani comes home.

Before Ellie's eyes, the piano changed from a beautiful instrument to a lonely one. She cleared her throat. "Why don't you start by telling me about Elaine."

The older man's eyebrows shot up. "My ex-wife, Elaine?" When Ellie nodded, he stroked his chin. "There's not that much to tell. We've been divorced for a long time now. She remarried years ago."

Ellie jotted down a note on her pad. "Do you know her new address?"

"Sorry, no. I've had no reason to know it, as we haven't spoken in years. Her new last name is Morris, though, if that helps."

Ellie scrawled the name *Morris* on the page before glancing up. "Does Elaine know about the phone call yet?"

Mr. Snyder shook his head, averting his gaze. Almost like he was embarrassed. "I didn't tell her, if that's what you're asking. Since I'm not really sure what's going on and I don't have her information anyway…" He lifted his hands and lowered them again. "Was that wrong? Should I have told her already?"

The slight waver to his deep baritone pricked at Ellie's heart. "No, Mr. Snyder, you did nothing wrong." She made her own voice soft. Gentle. "There's no guidebook that comes with this type of situation."

Charles Snyder closed his eyes and exhaled, clearly relieved to be excused of blame.

"I know this might be hard to talk about, but would it be okay to go through Dani's case again?"

He nodded. "Sure, we can do that."

Ellie glanced at her notes. "Let's start off by going over the other kids at the party. I'd especially like to fill in any details we might have missed about Dani's boyfriend."

Five minutes of talking with Charles Snyder failed to reveal any new details, beyond him admitting that the investigation had stretched on for several years before the lead detectives finally shelved Dani's file in cold cases. Their discussion did manage to fill Ellie with guilt, though. Her heart hurt in the face of the father's obvious pain.

"To be completely honest with you, I gave up on finding Dani alive years ago. A parent is never supposed to give up hope, but I did. The not knowing ended up being worse than anything, so in my head, I buried my daughter, put her to rest. Is that terrible?" He folded in on himself, suddenly appearing older and frailer than he had when they'd first met.

Ellie's chest ached. Losing a child had to be the worst experience in the world. "Mr. Snyder, the only terrible thing is the person who stole your daughter from you. No one should be judging you for how you grieve, not even you."

A throat cleared behind Ellie. "Here we are. Muffins, coffee, and orange juice."

Mary wheeled an old-fashioned cart into the room at

breakneck speed and parked it between Ellie and her employer. After the housekeeper poured both of them a glass of juice without so much as spilling a drop, she stepped back. "Do you need anything else?"

"That'll be all, Mary, thank you."

Once the door clicked shut behind the housekeeper, Charles finally met Ellie's eyes. "Thank you for that kindness earlier."

"Of course." Ellie took a sip of juice before continuing. "Now, can you tell me about that call? Do you remember what the caller said?"

"Not like I could possibly forget it." Mr. Snyder eased his glass back onto the tray. "I picked up the phone with my usual greeting. 'Hello, this is Charles Snyder, may I help you?' And a strange woman's voice replied. She said, 'Daddy? Is that you? It's me, Dani. I'm alive, and I need to see you.'"

He ducked his head and shuddered, bracing his palms on his thighs. "Sorry, I think I'm still in shock."

"No apologies necessary. Take your time."

His Adam's apple bobbed as he swallowed hard. Once. Twice. "That was it. She hung up after that."

Ellie frowned down at the words she'd written. Not a whole lot to go on. She'd hoped for more. "Is there anything else you can tell me about the call? Her voice, any background noise? Accent?"

He brightened. "No accent, but she spoke quickly, and she sounded out of breath, like she'd been running or something. Does that help?"

"Every little detail helps over time." Not really the truth, but not an all-out lie either. Ellie didn't have the heart to tell him otherwise. That she had no idea how the detail he'd provided would help solve Dani's case. "Anything else?"

"I tried to call her back right afterward, but no one answered." Several seconds ticked by. When he spoke again,

Ellie strained to hear him. "Do you...do you suppose there's any chance it might have been my baby?"

Ellie twined a stray strand of hair around her finger. This part was so tricky. On the one hand, she hated to give victims' families an inflated sense of hope, especially when the odds rarely favored them. On the other hand, crushing a grieving parent's hope altogether felt cruel. Experience had taught her that striking a balance between the two extremes required both skill and a delicate touch. But even then, there were no guarantees.

After a brief deliberation, Ellie settled on a variation of what she'd said to Jillian earlier. "There's always a chance, Mr. Snyder, even if after this many years out, it's more likely that someone is playing a prank. Stranger things have happened. Without more to go on, though, it's really difficult for me to speculate."

"I understand, and I appreciate your honesty."

Ellie didn't doubt the older man's understanding. She imagined he read between the lines all too well, an insightfulness forged by living through hell. To experience all of this —a daughter going missing, followed by the ups and downs of an investigation that dragged on and on but ultimately led nowhere—changed a person. Forever.

The same way that Ellie's own kidnapping had forever altered her.

Fifteen. That was her age when she'd snuck out of the house to meet a boy at the movies. At least that's where she thought she was going. Her crush had switched up the plan, though. He'd driven them both to a party, and once there, attempted to pressure Ellie into sex. Disgusted, she'd fled the party on foot.

What a perfect target she must have presented, lost in her own teenage drama as she wandered those deserted, late-night streets alone.

One stupid mistake that triggered a cascade of events, leading to Ellie's kidnapping by Kingsley. She lived with that knowledge every day, along with the guilt.

Ellie's throat burned. She'd trade her entire inheritance for a chance to alter the past, but this was the real world. Magical wish-granting genies only existed in fairy tales.

She lifted her chest, forcing herself to draw strength from the words a wise man had once spoken.

"As a kidnapping victim yourself, you're one of the few people who truly understands."

Chief Marcus Johnson. The police officer on duty who'd rescued her that fateful night, after Ellie escaped the warehouse where Kingsley held her captive and stumbled in front of Johnson's car.

More than a decade after her kidnapping, Chief Johnson uttered those words to Ellie when she marched into his office to request an end to her mandated psychologist appointments. He'd also said that her empathy made her a better detective.

Now, whenever guilt reared its ugly head, Ellie strived to remind herself of that simple truth: that the darkest moments in a person's life often yielded the greatest strengths.

Charles Snyder cleared his throat. Heat shot into Ellie's cheeks when she realized how long she'd gone without speaking.

Too bad one of her tragedy-inspired strengths didn't include a cure for daydreaming.

"Sorry, my brain goes into overdrive sometimes when I'm in the middle of a case. I'll need the phone number of the caller, so our tech team can try to trace the number."

Mr. Snyder recited the number without hesitation. "I memorized it, in case she calls back."

Ellie wrote the number down. She hesitated, doodling

blue squiggles around her notes while framing her next question. This man had been through so much. The last thing she wanted to do was cause him more pain by pressing too hard. "Did the person on the phone sound like she could be an older version of Dani?"

Charles Snyder's shoulders drooped. "I don't know. It's been so long since I heard her voice in person..." When he looked up at Ellie, his brown eyes glistened. "Honestly, I know this is a long shot. That more likely than not, it's some sicko playing a trick on me. But I knew I couldn't live with myself if I didn't follow up."

"And that's why I'm here, Mr. Snyder. To follow up. No one would expect you to do anything else." Her chest blazed with a familiar sensation. Determination. Ellie would leave no stone unturned to solve this mystery. One way or another. Charles Snyder deserved that much, at least. "Now, let me show you how to record the phone call, in case she calls back."

Ellie rose and sat beside him on the couch, spending the next several minutes showing him how to record a call and educating him on how to handle a number of possible scenarios. "So, what do you do if the woman calls back and claims it's an emergency or says she's in danger and needs money to escape and get back to you?"

Mr. Snyder recited the script they'd rehearsed without hesitation. "I tell her to give me the information on where to send the money but say that I invested in a retail property, so I'm a little cash-strapped at the moment and need a day or two to get the funds together. Then I call you."

"And if you can't get ahold of me right away?"

"Then I call Clay Lockwood with the FBI."

Satisfied that he had the script down, Ellie nodded. "Perfect."

Acting on impulse, she reached down and curled her

hand over his, causing his startled gaze to fly to hers. "I want you to know that I'm going to track down every lead I find. I promise that I'll do everything I can to bring Dani home to you, no matter how this plays out."

He layered his free hand on top of hers and squeezed. "Thank you. Closure of any kind at this point would be... thank you."

After one last squeeze, he scooted back and stared out the window, which Ellie took as her cue to wrap things up. "I think that's all for now. Thank you for your time."

Charles blinked up at her, almost like he'd forgotten she was there. "Oh, right. Thank you for coming."

Good manners had him pushing to his feet. Ellie waved him back down. "No, please don't get up. I can show myself out." She hustled to the parlor door, pausing to look over her shoulder. "Remember, call me the moment you hear back from the caller. And don't forget to record."

Mr. Snyder nodded once before turning away. Ellie left him alone in the room, gazing at the empty piano as though one day, Dani might appear. Right there on the bench.

Ellie hurried toward the front door, faster on her way out than even the efficient Mary. She didn't realize how overwhelming the atmosphere of sorrow was inside the huge, empty house until she burst outside, and the weak winter sun warmed her chilled skin.

10

Shortly after the private jet cruised down the long runway and glided to a stop, I collected my suitcase and headed the short distance through the small terminal and out to the sidewalk. I rolled my bag to the designated pick-up spot where Milos waited, his lanky, scarecrow-like frame leaning on the passenger door of a sleek black sedan.

He straightened when he spotted me. "Mr. del Ray, so nice to see you. How was your trip?"

"Wonderful, thank you." I couldn't begin to describe how delightful it was, strolling among all those people, secure in the knowledge that not a soul would recognize me as Lawrence Kingsley. Not even my own mother.

My grin slid away as I realized that wasn't completely true. Somehow, some way, my bedbound mother had recognized me when I'd paid her a little visit in her retirement home in Florida. A mother's intuition, maybe? I didn't know. Didn't care.

I'd made sure that she'd never be able to share my little secret with anyone else. I hoped she wasn't nagging the devil to death down in her fiery home.

A part of me wished I could share those joys with Milos, but alas. No one beyond my plastic surgery team in Costa Rica knew about my face remodel. For safety's sake, I intended to keep that information under wraps.

For now, anyway.

Milos took my bag, allowing me to settle into the supple back seat and inhale that new leather smell while he tucked my bag into the trunk. I twitched with impatience as I waited for him to climb behind the wheel. I had an important question that needed answering, and I didn't like to wait.

Finally, Milos slid into the driver's seat. Before I could pounce, he spoke first. We hadn't been working together long enough for him to know that he was breaking a sacred rule, so I let it go and focused on the information. "The Vancouver warehouse is rented and ready to go. I scouted the area, and as far as I can tell, there's nothing going on there, no activity at all."

A delicious warmth curled inside me at his words, like the steam from a cup of hot chocolate. My plan was coming together perfectly. "Which means no one to spy on us or accidentally venture where they shouldn't."

Milos glanced into the rearview mirror and smiled at me. A shark's smile, cold-eyed and sharp-toothed. I liked that. Creighton had done well by recommending him.

At first, I'd wondered if Creighton could really be associated with the blood thirsty type of associate I needed, and it had taken several tests before I'd deemed Milos worthy of assisting me with my plans.

I studied the back of his dark head as he steered the sedan into traffic. When I'd approached Creighton for a referral, I'd requested a man of action. A person of unquestionable loyalty, who was comfortable with battle and taking one life to protect another. Hacking skill preferred, if possible.

Creighton had nodded and told me that he might know a

man who checked all those boxes. At best, I figured his recommendation would be competent, and if I were very lucky, comfortable working in gray areas. Since the jobs I required veered more into pitch-black territory, I hadn't been all that optimistic.

A person couldn't be too careful nowadays, after all. Law enforcement types infiltrated the tightest organizations, planting themselves in the midst before ratting the people they were supposed to be loyal to out.

I refused to let that happen to me.

Knowing that anyone wearing a badge couldn't go as far as committing a crime even while undercover, I began to plan how best to test Milos's loyalty.

To my eternal delight, Milos had proven to be a perfect match for my needs in terms of skill set and character from day one when I'd put him to test on the spot.

While Creighton shared a story about a teenage boy he'd rescued from a religious cult back in Tennessee, I studied the newcomer over a bowl of homemade stew. The gaunt, quiet stranger crammed into the chair opposite me—introduced to me as Milos, no last name—wasn't what I'd expected. He didn't say much, but those calculating eyes of his swept the room, assessing every detail.

Creighton finished his story, then stretched. "Why don't you two take a walk and talk privately, decide if you're compatible? I have some paperwork to finish up anyway."

Suited me. My compatibility test required whisking Milos away from prying eyes. "Sounds good to me. How about you, Milos? Up for a stroll?"

Milos inclined his bald head. "Whatever works best for you, Mr. del Rey."

Mr. del Rey. I liked that. A formality that conveyed the perfect touch of deference.

Of course, the real test was yet to come.

I rose to my feet. "Shall we?"

We stepped outside into the crisp Rocky Mountain air. Milos trailed a respectful two feet behind me as I led us toward one of the less-used hiking paths that crisscrossed Creighton's compound. Neither of us spoke as we passed beneath canopies of towering pines, allowing us to enjoy the wind that whistled between the branches and trills from nearby birds.

After twenty minutes, I stopped in a small clearing. Now for the first part of the test.

"Because I have some rather...unusual job requirements, I'll need you to perform a task for me before you start. To ensure that we're a good fit."

I turned to examine Milos's reaction and tilted my head back in surprise. The man was taller than I'd anticipated, towering over me by several inches. An odd-looking sort, all sharp angles, gawky limbs, and shrew eyes dominating a pale face. Even padded with a winter jacket, he resembled a cadaver.

Milos nodded. "No problem, Mr. del Rey. What's the task?"

"The task is to capture an animal, take it live to your cabin, and get creative. All while keeping Creighton in the dark."

I'd planned my wording well. If Milos freaked and tattled to Creighton, what terrible thing could he accuse me of? "Get creative" was open for interpretation.

Any lingering concern vanished when Milos licked his thin lips and smiled. "Yes, sir. I'll start right away."

The squirrel he'd disassembled bit by bit over the next two days was utter perfection. Staked to the dresser by a hunting knife, the shivering little animal sported round, bloody holes where his eyes used to be, and a stump instead of a tail. The gleam in Milos's eyes as he inspected his work sealed the deal. We shook hands, and soon after, I sent him on his next mission to ensure his trust.

A sweet little family.

He hadn't hesitated. In fact, Milos had seemed more than a bit disappointed that the family I chose consisted of only a wife and husband along with their three-year-old daughter. And he seemed even more disappointed that I didn't allow him more time with the girl.

I was ecstatic and sent him on yet another mission...

Gabe.

I shook my head, tickled anew by my stroke of luck. How else could I describe being gifted an assistant so well versed in torture? Endless possibilities stretched before me. Countless ways to make my enemies pay.

Contemplating the buffet of options now pumped my heart full of pure bliss, and I could almost feel my neurons gobbling up extra doses of serotonin. My stomach growled, as if jealous to be excluded from the party. "Pull off at the nearest place with food so I can grab a snack." Planning satisfying torture methods required a surprising amount of calories.

"Of course, Mr. del Ray." Milos signaled and guided the car onto the next off-ramp. As we idled at the light, he pointed at the far right corner. "That place okay, or too crowded?"

I followed the direction of his finger to a little A-framed structure surrounded by a packed parking lot. A sign announced The Vancouver Grind, Best Coffee and Muffins in Vancouver. "No, it's perfect."

Milos pulled into the parking lot, gliding around for a minute in search of a spot. One opened up a few yards ahead. Before the car even had a chance to straighten up after backing out, Milos hit the gas. He zoomed the sedan into the open spot, cutting off a white Ford Escape that had been waiting on the opposite side.

A horn blared, but Milos ignored the commotion. He took his time, backing up and straightening our car like nothing fazed him. But when the angry driver gave up, I noticed a gleam in his eyes as he watched them drive away.

Milos caught me looking and flashed another one of his predatory grins. "Sorry. It amuses me sometimes to watch people rage ineffectually when they don't get what they want."

I pressed my fingertips together and smiled. Creighton really had outdone himself with his recommendation. "No apologies necessary."

"Would you like me to run in for you?"

I unsnapped my seat belt. "No, I'll go in too."

There was something exhilarating about walking among so many people and knowing not a single one of them would match my new face with the one on the FBI's Most Wanted list. Simpletons, all of them. They almost made it too easy.

I also enjoyed the admiring looks my new face elicited from women. Even now, as I strolled up to the coffee shop door, a pair of middle-aged moms in yoga pants and fleece sweatshirts shot me appreciative glances before giggling into each other's ears. A little too old for my tastes, but I might have made an exception had we not been in the middle of a crowded venue in broad daylight.

Fifteen minutes later, we were back on the highway. I brushed the last of the apple-cinnamon muffin crumbs off my lap and dabbed at my mouth with a napkin. "Any new developments with Gabe's little friend? Or little dead friend, I guess I should say."

I clucked my tongue. Dear silly Gabe. Had he really believed he could hide a boyfriend from me?

Milos waited until he changed lanes to respond. "Robert Hall's body was discovered, and like you predicted, a bunch of YouTube gawkers were on the scene. They've already uploaded videos of his corpse to YouTube and other platforms."

Oh Gabe, I hope you've viewed my little message. Wasn't it clever, the way I used your boyfriend's body to deliver my warning?

As I pictured Gabe glimpsing his boyfriend's body for the first time, gazing at Rob's bloody billboard of a chest in horror, my spine tingled and my heart swelled. More than anything, I hoped Gabe was cowering in a corner somewhere, sniveling and heartbroken.

"You should be heartbroken," I murmured. "It's your fault that young Rob had to be sacrificed."

"Excuse me, Mr. del Ray? Did you need something?"

"No. Just humming. It's a beautiful day, isn't it?"

"Yes, sir."

Half an hour later, Milos pulled off the highway. He navigated the sedan through several turns and down a long, unpopulated road that dead-ended into a large parking lot. Three ugly buildings squatted in a row at the far end, all of them massive and constructed of gray metal. I looked right and then left. Not a soul in sight in any direction. Not even a broken-down car.

Milos parked in front of the middle building, and I stepped out of the car into a deep quiet. Vast expanses of empty fields stretched in all directions, insulating the area from traffic noise. Milos led the way to a solid steel door and unlocked it.

From the inside, the warehouse appeared even larger. High vaulted ceilings reached up toward the sky, giving the interior a cavernous feel, like we'd stepped inside the yawning jaw of Pinocchio's giant whale. Overhead, fluorescent lights glowed, their rectangular shapes speckled with dead moths. Far across the concrete floor sat two offices.

After inspecting the offices, which were indeed perfect for my needs, I could no longer contain the delight that bubbled up inside me like a mountain creek. I whirled, clapping my hands together. "I'm not one to heap idle praise, but this is excellent work, Milos. This space should more than adequately suit my needs."

Milos bowed his head. "I hoped it would. This warehouse used to belong to someone in trafficking. They intended to use it as storage for the mass transport of victims, but they ended up abandoning it. Their loss is our gain."

Intriguing. I cocked my head. "How do you know all of that?"

Milos shrugged, a hint of that shark's smile tugging at his sharp mouth. "I know many things."

A man who didn't want to reveal his sources. I could appreciate that. Discretion was key in my line of work. So long as Milos understood that I expected nothing less than one-hundred-percent loyalty and his secrets didn't interfere with my plans, I'd let his caginess slide.

For now.

With my hands behind my back, I strolled through the enormous space, enjoying the chill as I inspected little details. Nothing like a little history to invigorate the soul. I sniffed, imagining that over the earthy scent of dust, I could smell the lingering stench of fear left by all those lovely victims. The mottled cement floors beneath my feet appeared clean enough, but when I passed a rusty spot, my mind filled the stain with blood and tears.

Milos trailed behind me at a respectful distance. I peered into corners, opened doors to electrical closets, in search of a good spot for storing our...guests when we procured them.

Guests. I snickered at my own little joke and continued my hunt. Finally, tucked away near a side wall, I found it. A cozy little room. Perfect for housing overnight visitors.

"I need this room prepared for company." I glanced over my shoulder at Milos, who nodded.

"Yes, Mr. del Ray. When would you like me to bring Gabe to his room?"

I smiled, savoring the sweet taste of anticipation. "I've been giving the timing a great deal of consideration. Tonight, I say we find a pretty young thing and have ourselves a test run. Before we move on to the main event."

Milos cocked his head and lifted a thin eyebrow. With his sunken cheeks, bald head, and deep-set eyes, the expression reminded me of a curious skeleton.

"I know that might sound odd, but my goal isn't simply to kill Gabe. If it were, he'd be dead already."

As I warmed to my subject, I began bouncing on my heels. "Gabe has caused me a great deal of trouble. It's only right that I make him pay for every single minute that I've suffered at the hands of his betrayal. I took him in, clothed him, gave him a job, and put a roof over his head. For him to turn on me, well, it was very disappointing."

Milos nodded. "Anyone would be disappointed under those circumstances."

A bitter flavor coated my tongue, erasing the previous sweetness. My bouncing subsided. Replaced by a stillness born of vengeance. "The plan for Gabe is to wait until he's situated in his new safe house, then lure him out and grab him and bring him back here, for me to play with."

Milos's eyes narrowed, as if he too were appreciating my plan. "I understand. And the others?"

Ah yes. The others. A slow grin spread across my face. "Oh, never fear, I haven't forgotten about them. Ellie being in charge of cold cases has given me the perfect means to toy with the little bitch. Did you know what a simple thing it is to research unsolved crimes in Charleston? And I've found the perfect case to use to mess with her."

I clasped my hands together and released a theatrical sigh. "Poor Danielle Snyder, disappearing all those years ago. How could her father not contact the police when he got the call from a woman claiming to be his long-lost daughter?" I laughed. "This is already turning out to be a real hoot."

No reason to tell Milos that I'd picked Danielle's case for another reason too. That the case represented unfinished business. My smile faded. Back then, I'd ordered another employee named John Garrett to abduct two girls, not one. The imbecile! How he'd managed to accidentally kill one was beyond me. I tsked under my breath. What a waste.

Roxanne had been such a pretty little thing too. Any buyer would have been thrilled to own the pair of them, but thanks to John's screwup, my client had been greatly displeased. John's malfeasance had reflected badly on me, and such a slight I'd never forgiven, nor forgotten.

But now, providence smiled down upon me, handing me the opportunity to kill two birds with one stone. I'd send Ellie spinning in circles chasing ghosts while also finally claiming revenge on the man who'd cost me far too much in money and reputation.

Speaking of chasing ghosts... "I think it's time to make another call to Charles Snyder."

Milos rounded his bug-eyes even more and busted out laughing. Great, gaping mouth cackles that shook his angular body and deteriorated into wheezing, all of which accentuated his resemblance to a Halloween skeleton. "Charles Snyder, as in *Do You Feel Lucky?*" After naming the title, he guffawed again.

I approved of Milos's merriment. Hopefully, he wouldn't turn out to be an utter disappointment like all the others. "Yes, that Charles Snyder. I'm sure he believes the game show he hosts is suspenseful, but I'm certain we can come up with a much better game of our own, don't you agree?"

Milos nodded eagerly.

"Good. Now, why don't you get started on acquiring our

prize for this evening? Who knows how long it will take to find a promising candidate up here."

"Yes, Mr. del Ray."

As Milos walked away, I turned back toward the room. Empty for now, but not for long. I could already picture Gabe secured inside. Waiting on his chance to be a contestant in my own personal game of Do You Feel Lucky: the life or death version.

11

_____

After leaving Charles Snyder's house, Ellie eased her car to the end of the circular driveway and parked by the curb around the corner. She pulled out her phone to message Carl, who worked in IT back at Charleston PD headquarters. Hopefully, the quirky IT tech would continue his streak of being super helpful with her investigations, even now that Jillian—his longtime crush—was dating Jacob.

She typed in Elaine Morris—the new name Charles Snyder had given for his ex-wife—and requested that Carl provide her with Elaine's new address ASAP. She added the phone number of the mystery caller who claimed to be Dani Snyder at the bottom for Carl to research and hit send.

Ellie opened her GPS and entered a new location before pulling away from the curb. The black SUV fell in behind her. Hopefully, Carl stuck to his record of speedy replies, so that Ellie could head to Elaine's sooner versus later. In the meantime, there was one more spot in Goose Creek that she wanted to check out before she left.

Half a mile later, Ellie pulled up to a green field and parked. She climbed out of her Explorer and followed a winding concrete walkway. Chase trailed her by a yard or two, and Ellie knew without looking that the security guard was scanning their surroundings, checking for any hint of danger. The path led them to a play area on the west side, complete with a mini-climbing wall, two circular slides, and a pretend ship. One thing was missing, though. Swings.

Ellie drew closer to the play structure and came to another startling realization. No sand. The ground around the equipment was covered in red matting. She glanced beyond the playground, her heart sinking. Even the retaining wall was gone, replaced by planters full of well-groomed bushes and mulch.

"Ugh." Ellie sank onto a bench directly opposite the biggest slide. If she hadn't known any better, she would have suspected this was an entirely different park. A quick glance at her phone reassured her that, no. This was the right spot. This was the park where, years ago, Roxanne Freeling had drawn her very last breath. And where Dani Snyder had vanished, never to be seen again.

"Everything okay?"

The security guard's gruff inquiry came from behind her. "No, not really. Not unless your definition of okay includes a teenage girl vanishing without a trace from this spot years ago."

No reply from Chase this time. Not that Ellie expected one. She'd given instructions to the firm to keep interruptions from their employees minimal while she worked because disruptions to her train of thought could mean the difference between solving a case or not. The firm had taken her request to heart. The guards they ended up assigning her were so quiet that, half the time, Ellie forgot they were there.

She rolled her neck to ease a little of the creeping tension, then pushed to her feet. Even though nothing looked the same as in the girls' crime scene photos, she forced herself to walk the area anyway. Her hope of finding anything useful dwindled with every passing minute.

Ding!

The sound alerted her to a new message. Ellie dug her phone out of her pocket, relieved when she read Carl's reply containing Elaine's address.

Nice work, you're the best!

After sending the reply, she ducked her head and hurried back to her SUV. Stopping by the park had been a shot in the dark anyway, given the passage of time. In light of the recent remodel, the odds of discovering some missing clue were about as slim as the likelihood of Ellie piecing her old Audi back together.

She climbed behind the wheel and typed Elaine's address into her GPS. Following the robotic voice's expert navigation, she entered the westbound lanes on the 52 for two miles before merging onto 26-South. Without traffic, the trip was a pleasant thirty-minute drive. Ellie turned the volume up on a popular pop song, bopping her head to the beat as she passed back by downtown Charleston and crossed the Ashley River. After that, a short hop westbound on 700 brought her to John's Island.

The navigation led her to a nice, white wooden home on a block full of lush green trees and sizeable front yards. The former Mrs. Snyder's new home didn't come close to matching the splendor of the old one she'd shared with her ex, but the property was still plenty nice.

After parking by the curb, Ellie walked up to her second door of the day and rang the bell. A disheveled woman in her fifties greeted Ellie with curly brown hair frizzing in a halo around her head, a yellow stain on her white t-shirt, and a friendly smile that crinkled the skin around her eyes. "Hello there, what can I do for you today?"

"Elaine Morris?" Ellie already knew the answer based on

studying photos, but that was the department's standard greeting.

The woman's smile didn't waver. "Yes, that's me."

The bronze of Ellie's badge flashed in the sun. "Detective Ellie Kline, with the Charleston Police Department. Is your husband home with you?"

Ellie hated the way the woman's smile died, replaced by creeping fear. "No, he's not. Is he okay? Did something happen to him?" Elaine pushed onto her toes and peered around Ellie's head, as if searching for her husband on the street beyond her.

Ellie instantly realized her mistake. She could have kicked herself. "As far as I know, your husband is fine. I promise this isn't about him. I'm here on an old matter, nothing for you to fret about."

Even as she made the statement, the words rang hollow to Ellie's ears. Nothing to fret about? When someone had called and claimed to be Elaine's missing daughter?

Ellie dug her nails into her palms. She didn't know if it was this particular case or Gabe's blown cover or the knowledge that Kingsley was watching somewhere that was throwing her off her game, and she didn't care. Her people skills needed to be better than this.

Elaine studied Ellie's expression as though trying to read the truth. Apparently satisfied at least that her new husband wasn't in any imminent danger, she sagged against the doorframe. "Excuse my theatrics. I'm convinced I may have a little bit of PTSD from back when…you know."

The older woman cleared her throat, and the smile that followed this time looked more like a grimace. Ellie found herself missing the woman's natural smile. This part of the job sucked. "I'm very sorry to do this, but 'back when' is what I'm here to talk about. I work cold cases, and I need to ask you a few questions about your daughter, Danielle."

"Danielle?" Elaine repeated the name in a whisper. "But that happened so long ago. I don't understand. Is this just for record keeping?"

Ellie dug her fingers into the notepad, steeling herself. "Yes, and no. I was called out because your ex-husband received a phone call earlier this week from a woman claiming to be Danielle."

The woman's hand flew to her mouth as she gasped.

Ellie held up her left palm to stall the inevitable flood of questions. "Now, there's no reason at this point to believe that's true. After this many years pass in a child disappearance case, it's more likely than not that anyone coming forward is a criminal or someone with ulterior motives. But we can't rule anything out without an investigation, which is why I'm here."

The woman's mouth flapped open and closed several times without eliciting a single sound. Her body shuddered, followed by her bursting into tears.

In light of Elaine's sorrow, Ellie's own eyes burned. She stepped forward and wrapped an arm around the other woman's waist. "Is there a place inside we can sit?"

Still sobbing, the woman nodded, and together, the two of them shuffled their way to a navy-blue loveseat only a few steps inside the front door. Elaine sank onto one cushion, Ellie the other. Ellie rubbed the other woman's shoulder and made soothing noises as Elaine buried her face in her hands.

At least a minute passed before the woman's body stopped shaking. Her sobs died out, replaced instead by hiccupping. When Elaine finally lifted her head, the whites of her eyes had turned pink. "Excuse me for a second."

Ellie sat on the edge of the loveseat, waiting patiently for the woman to collect herself. A faucet splattered somewhere around the corner, then stopped. Elaine returned shortly afterward, carrying two tall glasses of ice water. A box of Kleenex was tucked under one arm.

She offered Ellie the water, setting her own glass on a wooden coffee table with spindly, curved legs. "Sorry about that. Guess I must have been storing up tears for a while now without even knowing it."

Ellie softened her tone. "No need to apologize. If anything, I'm the one who should beg for your forgiveness. I can imagine this all comes as a big shock."

Elaine swiped her nose with a tissue she plucked from the box. "Charles is the one who should apologize. I can't believe he didn't call me the second he hung up!" She bunched the tissue in her lap and started shredding, not seeming to notice when little pieces began dotting the beige carpet. Her upper body heaved. "Except, I can believe it. We didn't end things on a good note."

Ellie made an encouraging sound in her throat. Experience dictated that people talked more freely when there was a silence that needed filling.

Elaine sighed. "He blames me. I was the one who allowed Dani to go to the party that night." Her pale blue eyes glistened with fresh tears. "Can you imagine what that was like? My own husband, blaming me for our daughter's disappearance?"

"That must have been incredibly hard."

Elaine nodded emphatically. Her hands went still. "It was. Partly because I blame myself. I went back over the hours leading up to that party so many times. Hundreds. Maybe thousands. What if I'd said no? Or taken us all on a weekend getaway instead? Anything but let her go to that stupid party. If only I could rewind time and have a do-over."

"Mrs. Morris, I—"

The woman shook her head. "Please, call me Elaine."

"And I'm Ellie. Anyway, Elaine, I know it's easier said than done, but please, don't blame yourself. You had no way of knowing what would happen that night. Every weekend all over the country, teens go to parties and ninety-nine-point-nine percent of them return home, safe and sound. The only one to blame for Dani's disappearance is the monster who took her."

As Elaine worked to compose herself, Ellie considered the hypocrisy of her words. Oh, she believed what she said about Elaine not blaming herself for allowing Dani to attend that party. But when it came to forgiving herself over the party she'd attended as a teen, resulting in her own kidnapping? Ellie still had some work to do.

"Do you...do you think Dani blames me, though? And that's why she called Charles instead of me?"

The tremor in Elaine's voice squeezed at Ellie's heart. This poor woman. Her poor family. How terrible must it be, living with that kind of guilt for all these years?

"I promise you, if that really was Dani on the phone, the reason she called her father is because he lives in the same house she grew up in. If that was really Dani, she couldn't have possibly known your married name or your new number."

Hope sparked in Elaine's pink eyes. "You're right. I didn't have this cell number back then." She gave a little gasp, her hand flying to her mouth. "Do you think it could really be...?"

Ellie lifted her hands. "I can't promise you that. At this point, we have no way of knowing, but I'd caution you against getting too optimistic. Like I told Mr. Snyder, what I can promise you is that I will do everything in my power to get to the bottom of this. No lead is too small. If this person calls back as we expect them to do, we'll be ready this time, and you'll be the first person to know. Okay?"

Elaine hiccupped. "Okay. Thank you."

Ellie flipped through her notepad to remind herself of her questions. "Do you recall if anything seemed off about Dani during the weeks leading up to the party? Any new friends? Enemies? Kids who might hold a grudge against Dani or Roxanne?" She glanced up. "I know this is difficult, so take your time answering."

Elaine's forehead wrinkled before she shook her head. "No, nothing. No new friends as far as I knew, no enemies. From what I remember, Dani was her normal self before-hand. Grumpy one day, sweet as punch the next. You know, your typical teen girl."

"Okay. What about any other friends in her life? Friends who might know something about what happened after the party?"

"Roxanne was it. Dani never did anything with anyone else, but she didn't need to. Those two were inseparable. If she did have any other friends, well," Elaine's shoulders rose and fell, "I didn't know about it. Either that or I can't remember after all these years."

Disappointing, but not unexpected. Ellie knew going into this interview that uncovering new information was a long shot at best. "That's understandable. Don't get discouraged. You're doing great so far."

The woman twisted her hands in her lap. "It's been so long now that, if I go too many days without looking at her picture, her face starts to fade."

One part of Ellie wondered what that must feel like, to lose the memory of your child's face? A different part consid-ered the possibility that maybe it was for the best. Time's way of healing wounds.

She clenched her teeth. Except now, some asshole had decided to dredge up this family's pain. Slash at wounds that had barely managed to scab over, making them bleed all over again. That was why she especially hated asking the next question. "Do you have any of Dani's belongings from back then that I could look at?"

"Yes, up in the attic. I can show you, if you think it might help."

Thinking it might help was a stretch, but Ellie's conscience wouldn't rest until she covered all possible bases. She nodded, so Elaine stood and led her into a narrow hallway. Toward the end of the hall, a large square cut into the ceiling. Elaine tugged at the short rope that dangled above her head, and the door creaked open, revealing a collapsible set of stairs squished together like an accordion. After extending them into place, she began climbing, with the flimsy structure groaning and swaying with each step. Ellie waited until Elaine disappeared inside the opening before following behind her.

The attic was smaller than Ellie had expected, and mustier, with a ceiling that sloped down on each side. As she crouched her way after Elaine, a low beam grabbed at her French braid. She reached up to unsnag her hair, jerking when her fingers encountered a sticky, web-like structure. Spiders, great. Hopefully, none of them had decided to take up residence in her hair.

She wiped her hand on her pants before patting down her head. Once she convinced herself that no eight-legged trespassers had climbed aboard the Ellie Express, she continued creeping her way forward. A mishmash of discarded furniture filled one corner. The other held boxes in a variety of sizes.

Elaine stopped in front of the boxes. "This is it. Was there anything in particular you wanted to see?"

"A journal, if she had one? Or old photos from school?"

After pulling a box down, Elaine blew a layer of dust off the top and popped it open. "No journals. Dani stopped keeping those in elementary school."

She dug through the contents, extracting a pink unicorn pillow and a poofy red dress with a big bow before pulling a blue photo album out.

"You can try this, but it's almost all pictures of Dani and Roxanne. They weren't allowed to take photos at school, and she hadn't dated that boy for long before…" An emotion very close to hate flashed across the woman's features as she pushed the album toward Ellie. "That's why I keep this album in the attic. I couldn't bear to look at pictures of him, but I also couldn't stand to throw any photos of Dani away." Her lips curled downward, and she wrapped her arms around her waist, shuddering. "I know it's not fair to blame him, but sometimes, I do."

Ellie understood. How many times must Elaine have tortured herself over how things would have ended differently if only Dani's boyfriend hadn't been kissing another girl that night? Lowering herself to the floor, Ellie opened the first page of the album.

Thirty minutes later, Ellie stood up, rolling her aching neck. She'd gone through the entire photo album, along with the contents of the boxes. Not a single thing had jumped out at her. She was starting to feel like a hamster on a wheel, running in circles but never getting anywhere. All this time spent today, and she was nowhere closer to cracking this case.

She helped Elaine repack the boxes, and once they finished, followed her back down the ladder.

At the front door, the older woman surprised her by throwing her arms around Ellie and squeezing her in a tight hug, enveloping Ellie in a lily scent. "Thank you. Thank you so much for trying to help my Dani. I know you'll do your best."

Okay. Now, Ellie was going to be lucky if she didn't start bawling too. She returned Elaine's hug before stepping back.

She lifted her chin as, once again, determination filled her chest, pushing away her doubts. "That's one promise I can gladly make. I'm going to focus all my energy into solving the mystery of your daughter's disappearance. You have my word."

A quick round of goodbyes followed before Ellie retraced her earlier path back to her Explorer.

As she settled into the driver's seat, she clenched her hands tightly around the wheel. Dani's parents deserved an end to their torture. When it came to solving cases, Ellie prayed, for everyone's sake, that Dani's wouldn't be the one to bust her winning streak.

12

"And then Mr. Thompson pulled the lizard out of his box and let us take turns touching his back, and he didn't even care! His name is Larry. Larry the Lizard, isn't that silly?" Bethany giggled. "Don't you think that's silly, Mama?"

Mama.

Katarina's heart melted at the sound of that word uttered in her daughter's sweet, bubbly voice. She took her eyes off the road to drink in Bethany's animated expression as the eight-year-old launched into another story.

"And then Matt stuck two pencils up his nose and said he was a walrus, and Mr. Thompson didn't even get mad! And then..."

Katarina smiled as her daughter bounced in the passenger seat, jumping from one story to the next without any apparent rhyme or reason. The same way she did every day after school.

If only one of them could thrive in their new life in Wyoming, Katarina was glad that person was Bethany. Katarina didn't know how, but her daughter seemed unaffected by spending most of her short life being juggled between foster families. The girl's brown eyes sparkled, untouched by ghosts or guile.

At the stop sign, Katarina flipped on her turn signal. Her throat tightened as the steady tick blended with Bethany's babble. She wondered, not for the first time, what Bethany had been like as a baby. A toddler. A kindergartener. All those precious memories stolen. Her foot pounded the pedal a little too hard, and the car accelerated into the turn with a squeal of tires.

Bethany threw her hands in the air and shrieked, like she was riding a roller coaster. "Whee!"

Katarina snorted, even as she eased her foot off the gas. Maybe her daughter had a wild streak after all.

"Are we almost to Dakota's house?"

"In a few more minutes."

"Yay! I've never seen *Mulan* before, have you?" Bethany didn't break long enough for Katarina to respond. "It's Dakota's favorite movie. Also, Dakota made chocolate chip cookies last night, and she has a dog! I love dogs, especially little ones. Hers is a big one, but that's okay."

The girl chattered away while Katarina drove, passing ranch-style homes on sprawling green lots with the Grand Tetons looming in the distance. Her left leg kept jiggling. Nerves. Katarina's first instinct to the playdate invite had been to say "hell no" and whisk her daughter straight back home where she could protect her. But the pleading expression in Bethany's eyes had overruled everything else. She wanted Bethany to have as normal of a life as possible. Normal meant playdates with classmates.

Her hands tightened on the wheel before relaxing. With effort. Hard to let go when she'd just gotten her baby back. The last thing Katarina remembered about Bethany's birth was going into labor. Even at sixteen, she was no stranger to pain, but the intensity of the contractions had still caught her off guard. She remembered the feeling. Like a vice clamping down on her pelvis and wrenching her bones apart.

She'd gone into labor with Bethany camped out in her uterus and woken afterward to a flatter stomach, swollen genitals, and no baby. No cuddling the tiny infant, no stroking the soft baby fuzz on her head. Katarina hadn't even gotten to name her daughter before Kingsley snatched her away.

Katarina was so lost in memories, she passed the house the first time around. After a quick U-turn in a neighbor's driveway, she guided the car back to Dakota's address. Bethany waited for Katarina to open her door before bounding out of the car and skipping a few steps ahead. She stopped, glanced over her shoulder, and waved. "Hurry up, slowpoke!"

Katarina smiled and shook her head. Patience was a trait they'd need to work on.

The girl waited for Katarina to catch up, and once she did, slipped her little hand into Katarina's. The simple gesture flooded Katarina's heart once again, swelling her chest with emotions so strong they almost hurt. Together, they walked up the stone path to a front door painted a cheerful yellow. A handmade winter wreath filled with greenery, pinecones, and red berries hung at eye-level.

Katarina eyed the decoration. If cleaning didn't work out, maybe she'd give crafting a shot. Become one of those DIY Pinterest people and set up her own Etsy shop.

Before the visual of glue guns and beads strewn all over her bedroom floor could depress Katarina too much, the yellow door flew open.

"Come on! Mom made me wait to eat a cookie until you got here." A girl with a long, dark braid grabbed Bethany's hand and pulled her inside. Giggles trailed the pair as they disappeared into the house without so much as a goodbye.

Katarina snorted while a tall, dark-haired woman appeared in the doorway, smiling.

"Hi, I'm Kelly, Dakota's mom. You must be Bethany's mom."

"Katrina. Nice to meet you."

Of course, Katarina already knew Dakota's mom's name. Along with her dad's name, where he worked, their previous known addresses, and everything else she found with a little online research. Even their criminal history, which was limited to the dad's DUI from fifteen years ago. If she'd found a hint of anything worse, Bethany wouldn't be there at all.

After exchanging a few meaningless pleasantries that left Katarina itching to leave, the other woman finally waved her off. "See you at six."

Katarina drove away with the next several hours wide-open and no way to fill them. She could go home, but then what? More tidying things that had already been organized one time too many? Without her daughter there, the place was just lonely. Without Bethany, her mind went in too many directions. Dangerous directions.

She waited for a woman and a little boy on bikes to cross the street, drumming her fingers on the wheel. There had to be a less mind-numbing method to pass the time than cleaning. Some way to entertain herself in this quiet little pissant town.

Twenty minutes of roaming the streets didn't lead her any closer to finding entertainment, though. So far, the only place where she didn't feel like she might die a slow, painful death from boredom was the bar from yesterday. Bob's.

She drummed her fingers on the wheel again, then shrugged. Why not? A few turns later, she pulled into the same parking space. She recognized two of the cars parked nearby from yesterday. Not that Katarina was looking.

Doesn't matter if he's here or not. I'm only here to kill time.

That was what she told herself, anyway. Right up until she wrenched open the door.

A drum solo blasted her as soon as she stepped inside, but her gaze raced by the live band in search of a familiar face. She spotted him sitting at the same table as before, and a tingle shot up her spine.

Pretending not to notice the way he tracked her as she approached the bar, Katarina headed straight for the same stool she'd occupied yesterday. Unlike last time, five of the other eight seats behind the bar were taken, and most of the tables were full. The band on the little stage near the front finished their number to scattered applause and a few hoots.

With a high-pitched wail, the electric guitarist kicked off their next song. It was a classic rock number that sounded vaguely familiar to Katarina. The lead singer jumped in with his raspy voice a few beats later, and she watched him strut around the stage, his oversized mustache wobbling with each step.

Near the end of the first song, Katarina sensed a presence hovering over her left shoulder. She knew without looking who stood there, and another tingle raced across her back. Their gazes met, and the man smiled. A slow, lazy grin that landed somewhere south of Katarina's belly button.

When the song ended and applause broke out, Clayne leaned in. "You never called."

Katarina shrugged. "Didn't have a reason to yet."

He grinned and once again straddled the empty barstool next to her without waiting for an invitation. "That 'yet' sounds real promising." He winked. "So, what do you do for a living?"

Beat up brooms and fantasize about stabbing dog walkers.

"Nothing right now. I'm between jobs."

Katarina knew better than to offer up unnecessary information. And she couldn't produce a single reason why Clayne needed to know about Bethany. Or WITSEC. "What about you? I read your card, Miller Distributing. Like the beer company, or are you more into drugs?"

Same as yesterday, Clayne didn't so much as flinch at her forwardness. "Drugs, mostly. Plus a few other ventures that maybe I'll tell you about one day…if you stick around long enough."

Katarina blinked. Clayne's response surprised her, and she wasn't used to men being surprising. Not the part where he was involved in drugs, because that came as no shock at all.

No, the shock stemmed from his openness about his illegal activities. She crossed her arms and tilted her head. Clayne Miller was either more arrogant, more powerful, or more stupid than she'd originally suspected, or some combination of all three. In spite of herself, Katarina was dying to find out which one.

Using her right hand, she reached out and smoothed his flannel shirt down his chest. "Now, why would you up and tell me a thing like that?"

Clayne captured her stray hand with his own, and locking his gaze onto hers, slowly lifted it to his mouth. He kissed her fingertips, one after the next. The touch of his mouth to her skin sent fire racing up Katarina's arm, and she had to fight off a shiver.

When Clayne finished, he replaced her hand on his chest. "When you run the show long enough, you stop sweating the little stuff. I get to decide whether to tell someone or not, and darlin', I knew the moment you first walked into the bar and cased the joint that you were a woman who shared my wavelength."

Katarina playfully stuck out her lower lip. "And here I thought I was being so discrete."

He reached over and smoothed a stray strand of hair behind her ear. "I'm sure you were discrete to everyone else in this bar. Just not me. Now, how about you let me buy you that drink today?"

She considered him for a moment. Was she ready to do this? Really do this?

Although she'd spent a number of years seducing men, her encounters rarely got to the point where sex was involved. In fact, Katarina couldn't remember the last time she'd slept with a man. Most had repulsed her, and she'd hated the feeling of being used.

She didn't feel that way now.

She licked her lips. "Sure. I'll take a shot. Tequila."

Clayne slapped his hand on the bar. "Now that's what I'm talking about." He waved the bartender down. "Hey, Roy, two tequilas shots. Make them top-shelf."

"You got it."

Roy pulled a blue bottle down from the highest shelf and poured two generous shots of clear liquid. He topped the short glasses off with a lime.

Clayne raised his shot to Katarina, so she lifted hers too. "Here's to new friends. Cheers."

After the glasses clinked together, Clayne tossed his tequila back. Katarina did the same. The spirit filled her mouth with salt before burning a path down her throat. She finished the shot off with a squirt of lime.

When she licked the last of the salt from her lips, Clayne followed the motion with heavy-lidded eyes. "What d'ya say we take off and head to my place?"

"Okay."

The word slipped out without her permission, leaving Katarina stunned. Really? Go home with him? She might be new to this mother stuff, but even she felt pretty certain that hooking up with strangers in bars wasn't what typical moms did while their kids watched *Mulan* at a playdate. But the fire heating her belly didn't care.

She slid off her barstool and lifted an eyebrow. "I'm ready when you are."

As Clayne threw a twenty on the bar and led her out of the area, Katarina silently scoffed. *Screw typical moms.* Katarina had never been a typical anything, and she couldn't come up with a good reason to start now.

13

The pungent odor of sweat mixed with fear greeted me when I strolled into the small room, compliments of the man seated in the middle. Jonah. Not that his name mattered, of course.

Black rope circled around Jonah's wrists and feet, binding him to the chair while a sack covered his head and face. His body slumped against the chair back, suggesting that our guest was asleep. How disappointing.

I switched my attention to the large monitor on the desk that ran along the back wall. The screen was divided into four equal quarters, with a different video view in each. Gabe's new safe house, from multiple angles. Perfect. I smiled before turning back to the man, who sat very calm and still.

That wouldn't do at all.

Whack!

I kicked out, and my work boot slammed into the closest chair leg, jostling Jonah awake. He shrieked and bolted upright before thrashing around and tugging against the expertly knotted ropes. "Who's there? Please, help me! Get me out of here!"

I plucked the sack off his head. When his wild gaze focused on me, I lifted a finger to my mouth. "Shh, there's no reason to shout. No one else is around for miles, so I suggest you save your breath."

I stepped forward, examining his features. Pretty, with his high cheekbones and dark hair, but not Gabe pretty. A pity, but he'd do.

The stranger's gray eyes widened when he processed my words. "What?" He glanced over his shoulder and spotted Milos, who waved. Jonah trembled before turning back to me. Perspiration glistened above his upper lip. "I don't know what's happening, but you have the wrong person, I swear! I didn't do anything! Please, let me go. I won't say a word."

"Oh, don't fret. We know you didn't do anything wrong." I waited until hope filled the man's gray eyes. "We needed a volunteer, and you were in the right place at the wrong time. Although, in your mind, I guess this is more of a wrong place-wrong time scenario. Funny how that works, isn't it?"

Dark circles formed on the underarms of his gray t-shirt. "No. No, no, no."

He shook his head back and forth, and I sighed. Silly boy. As if theatrics might help. His moans continued to fill the room as I turned to Milos. "Has the package been delivered?"

Milos tapped the phone in his hand and nodded. "Yes, sir. It's done."

"Wonderful." The completed delivery meant Gabe had received and activated the smartphone we'd sent, right to the front porch of his new safe house. I paused, tapping my chin. Although, on second thought, the fact that we'd managed to locate and send Gabe packages meant that the house wasn't so safe after all.

I enjoyed my own little joke. Delivering the device had been a risk, but one that had paid off. If that marshal who babysat Gabe had been home to intercept our shipment, we would have had a problem. Milos had assured me that, once Gabe was moved, the marshal presence would diminish. Yet again, Milos had come through for me.

Across the room, I caught Milos watching me with his gleaming, predatory eyes, and my chest filled with warmth. I enjoyed the man's quiet, dependable presence. My smile slipped away, concern taking over. As long as he didn't end up disappointing me like all the others. I'd hate to add yet another name to my revenge list.

A whimper interrupted my rumination, yanking my attention back to the man in the chair. He didn't know it yet, but he would play a pivotal role in my plan to get even with Gabe. Pulling the burner phone I'd had Milos purchase from my pocket, I strolled over to the tripod positioned a few feet away from our guest. Time to get started.

A thrill shivered across my skin as I snapped the phone into the tripod and tapped the buttons to pull up the video chat. Another tap and the app started pinging Gabe's smartphone. I scooted out of the camera's frame, stroking my sculpted cheek with a growing smile. My new face was a work of art, and as such, deserved a special unveiling. Gabe would have to wait a little longer to sneak a glimpse of Dr. Sandoval's brilliance.

Chime!

My hands itched with excitement when the burner phone signaled that someone on the other end had accepted the video call. From my hiding spot, I peered at the screen, almost gasping when his face popped into view.

Gabe was even more beautiful than I'd remembered every night when I fantasized about different ways to end his traitorous, deceptive life. Breathtaking, with those full lips and chiseled cheekbones. Every bit topped off to perfection by a head of dark curls that, even now, I longed to stroke.

My face grew hot. How dare he look so good after the agony his betrayal had spawned? I studied him a little longer through the rectangular screen, and the rage subsided a notch. Upon closer inspection, the purple smudges under his brown eyes assured me that he'd suffered more than one sleepless night recently, and his fluttering hands testified to his increased stress level.

Perfect. Now, we could begin.

"Are you alone? Be honest. You know I already know the answer."

Gabe flinched at the sound of my voice. He wet his lips with the tip of his tongue. "Y-yes."

"Good, because I want us to play a little game. But before we do, it's only fair that I let you know that we're monitoring your every movement. If you attempt to alert anyone, we'll know, and that will result in some very serious consequences for you. We don't want that to happen, do we?"

On the screen, Gabe's chin quivered, his eyes brimming with tears. "No."

His image began to blur, and I realized it was because his hand was trembling so badly. "Please put the phone down on a steady surface, then back far enough away that I can see you better."

It took him a few moments to get the lens just right, and it was worth the extra time when he dropped into a chair a few feet from wherever he'd propped his phone.

Better. So much better.

I nodded, pleased with his agreeableness so far. "Clever boy. Oh, and another important item." I tapped a button on the screen, changing the camera's view from the door behind us to the man strapped to the chair. "If you hang up before I say the game is over, yet another person will die because of you."

Gabe released a choked gasp while I walked to the mask

awaiting me on the desk. After pulling the fabric over my head, I slid my hands into a pair of gloves and my arms through the sleeves of an oversized coat to better disguise my shape. Once I was ready, I nodded to Milos, who returned my nod and hit record on the iPad he'd set up earlier.

Planning ahead for this momentous occasion freed me up now to multi-task. I could terrorize Gabe, and at the same time, create a separate video to sell on the dark web. No sense in wasting a perfectly good opportunity to make some quick cash. Or bitcoin, to be precise. My idea of the perfect win-win.

Whistling a jaunty tune, I selected a razor-sharp knife from several options Milos had splayed out for me and approached the man in the chair. "I'm sure you have an inkling of which game we're going to play by now, dear Gabe, so I'll go ahead and start us off." I tapped a gloved hand to my masked chin. "Where to begin, though, when there are so many delightful options?" I turned to face Gabe more fully. "I'm feeling rather generous today, so I'll let you choose."

Gabe wavered in his chair, and I thought he might be on the verge of passing out. He managed to stay upright but didn't say a word.

I smiled, though he couldn't see my expression behind the mask. "Tough decision, I know, dear Gabe. Maybe multiple choice will prove easier?" I ran the very tip of the blade lightly down my captive's ear. "Gabe, should I start here or maybe a finger?"

Jonah responded before Gabe could. "Are you crazy? Neither, man. Tell him neither. Call the police. Call for help."

Irritated with the interruption, I stuffed the sack that had previously been on the man's head into his mouth. From where he leaned against the wall, Milos chuckled.

Turning my attention back to Gabe, I asked him the question again. "Ear or finger, my pretty?"

My former assistant's entire body was shaking as he stared in wide-eyed disbelief. When he said nothing, I raised the knife to the ear.

"Finger," Gabe screamed.

Elation washed through my every cell. I loved when they participated. The joy was indescribable.

"As you wish, my dearest Gabe."

The man's gray eyes fell on the gleaming blade as I grabbed his closest hand. The middle finger, I decided, and extended the digit until I had a clear target. A glint of silver flashed as metal caught the fluorescent lights overhead. I kept my movements slow, catering to the audience witnessing this live and to those who would witness it later. Suspense tripled their enjoyment.

Jonah shrieked, thrashing against his restraints. The cloth fell from his mouth, allowing his words to reach the world. "No! Stop, please stop! You can't do this, you can't—"

His scream ricocheted off concrete walls when the blade sank deep into his flesh.

Satisfaction coiled in my loins, making me shiver in delight. The first cut was always so exquisite. A sensation to be savored, like slicing into the most tender piece of filet mignon. The secret was in the knife. High quality and perfectly sharpened only. Otherwise, a man could waste countless time and tax his wrist, sawing away as if a body part were a grisly, overcooked cut of sirloin.

With the man's screams providing the soundtrack, I continued my work while blood splattered on the concrete floor. Each slice gave me a fresh thrill. There was a beauty to this work, an artistry that few were brave enough to comprehend. I paused, giving myself a chance to truly appreciate the scene before me.

On the fourth cut, his bone gave way. A couple of swipes later, and the man's finger separated from his hand.

While Jonah sobbed, I wiggled the bloody appendage in front of the camera. "Guess he won't be flipping anyone off anymore, at least not with that hand."

To my utter delight, Gabe's skin turned ashen, and he trembled like a child. "You're sick in the head."

I yawned. "Boring. And also, not the response I need to end the game. I guess that means you'd like to play another round."

"What?" For a moment, I again thought the young man might pass out. "No, I don't, I never said that! What do I need to say to end the game? Tell me, and I'll do it." Gabe started sobbing too.

"Three simple words. That's all you need to say to end this game and to have me cease this poor man's misery. Surely, you don't want him to suffer for your reticence? Three words, then I promise, I'll end his pain." I paused before sharing my favorite phrase. "*Die, bitch. Die.*"

Gabe reared back like I'd reached through the screen and punched him. "I don't...what? No! I can't...you can't expect me to..."

He shuddered and didn't finish. Okay by me, because that meant we'd move on to round two.

"Your choice." Ignoring Gabe's protests, I turned back toward Jonah, who'd finally traded in his screams for a high-pitched keening noise instead. I circled him, tapping my chin as I walked. "Decisions, decisions. What should I try next? Ooh, I know." After situating myself behind the man's head, my hand snaked out and latched on to the fleshy part of his left ear. He yelped, thrashing his head from side to side.

I clicked my tongue at his commendable but rather vain effort to escape the inevitable. "Now, now, I'd sit still if I were you. Otherwise, I might miss your ear and send the blade straight into your brain instead."

The man went still. The keening started up again.

"Wise choice." I met Gabe's eyes on the screen. "Anything you'd like to tell me?"

"Yes! I mean, no! Please, for the love of God, please…" He broke off with a moan, his gaze fixated on the knife.

I tsked my disappointment as I focused back on our sobbing guest. "What does it say about your beliefs if your God allows horrors like this to go unchecked? Silly boy. There is no God. Only power."

Without warning, I raised the knife and swung. The man's left ear dangled like a trophy from my hand before he knew what was happening. "See, that wasn't so bad, was it?" I lifted my prize and his screams restarted. Blood spurted from the gaping hole I'd left behind, staining his shoulder and the floor a deep red.

The poetry. The artistry. The musical accompaniments.

I grew hard as I absorbed it all.

Eager for more, I wiped my blade clean on his cheek. First one side. Then the other. A rancid odor wafted up, making me wrinkle my nose. "I believe our guest has released his bowels." I shook my head sadly. "Such abysmal manners these days, wouldn't you agree?"

Without waiting for a reply, I stroked the metal across the man's throat. "In a matter of seconds, we could end all of your pain and suffering. Don't you want that?"

The man's lips parted, but only a sob escaped.

Shrugging, I turned back to Gabe. "He seems a little ill-disposed at the moment, poor soul. What about you, dear boy? Don't you want to end his suffering? Or is there a cruel streak in you after all?"

Gabe blanched. He shook his head as he mouthed a single

word, over and over. *No.* He rose from his chair and stumbled back. First one step, followed by another.

I wagged my finger at the screen. "Ah ah ah. Remember what I said. If you try to escape my punishment, the consequences will be severe. You don't want that to happen, do you, Gabe? Not after what already happened to your little friend? Such a pity."

At the mention of his friend, Gabe stopped in his tracks. His chin dropped to his chest, and defeat bowed his posture as he shuffled back toward the camera.

His old man's walk fed my revenge-starved soul. *Oh, Gabe. Did you really think I'd let you off the hook that easily?*

"No, please, no more. Let me go! I won't tell. I swear I won't tell. Please."

I winced. Jonah's incessant blubbering grated on my nerves. That and the stench wafting from his pants. "That's not how this game works, didn't you listen? And stop making that terrible racket before I cut out your tongue."

Brightening, I clapped my hands together.

"Your tongue! Yes, I agree. That's the logical next step. At least then I can carry on with my work in silence." I twirled the knife, reinvigorated by my brilliant idea. "It's always a bit more difficult. There's the business of clamping off the nose to make a subject open their mouth and then busting out the teeth." I ran the tip of the blade over the man's lips. "But the payoff is worth the effort."

So entranced by my plan, I didn't notice Gabe yelling until I gripped the man's chin in one hand and squeezed his nostrils shut with the other.

"Stop! Please. I'll say it! I'll say the words!"

Disappointment flooded me as I gazed into Jonah's pain-glazed eyes, but I shook the feeling off. Fair was fair.

"Fine, but you have three seconds, after which our friend here will be rendered speechless by my brilliance. Literally."

Beneath my mask, I snickered at my pun before launching into a countdown. "One, one thousand. Two, one thousand."

"Die, bitch! Die!"

Like so many of my contestants, Gabe shouted the words. No matter how many times I heard them, they never grew old.

Die, bitch! Die!

So perfect. So sweet. My limbs filled with a languid warmth born of deep contentment. There was nothing quite like the satisfaction of provoking such a soft-spoken, gentle boy far beyond the boundaries of his moral convictions.

"A pity. I was quite looking forward to removing his tongue. Oh well, a deal is a deal."

I expelled an exaggerated sigh, released Jonah's nose, and stepped to the side, twisting his head toward his right shoulder and exposing his quivering throat to the camera. After all, where was the fun if Gabe didn't have a clear view of our game's climax?

"Gabe Fisher has sentenced you to death."

Jonah flinched, but I didn't give him time for more. The blade sank into his skin, severing his carotid artery with a single flick of my wrist. So simple, killing a human being this way.

Blood spurted from the severed artery in time with his dying heart. I counted down the beats as the life drained from his eyes.

One hundred beats later, the red stream had slowed to a trickle. The man's gaze turned sightless, and his head drooped to the side. He wasn't dead yet, but he was certainly beyond saving. Another game completed.

I slashed my finger across my throat, signaling Milos to stop recording. Once he tapped the screen, I sauntered closer to where the burner sat on the tripod, eager for a close-up of Gabe's suffering.

Pleasure washed over me like a warm drizzle at the sight. Tears streamed unchecked down his pretty cheeks, and he trembled all over, but his eyes, oh, his eyes! They were delicious in their agony. Twin, dark pools of fathomless horror framed by bloodshot whites.

I licked my lips as my fingers twitched in anticipation of the delights to come. "You're next, dearest Gabe. See you very soon."

The video chat ended when I pushed the button. I rolled my shoulders before tugging the mask off my head. Fresh air flooded my face and scalp, cooling my skin and filling my nose with a pungent mix of copper and feces. So rude of our guest to soil our room like that. Oh well. Milos would need to do a little extra cleaning tonight.

But first, we had another matter to address.

Grinning, I turned to face my new assistant.

"Milos, it's time to make that second call to Charles Snyder."

14

_____

From the spot where she'd taken up residence in the basement, Ellie glared at the evidence and photos strewn across the table, willing them to reveal any secrets to Danielle Snyder's case that she'd somehow missed. Nothing happened. Unsurprising, given that Ellie had already attempted this technique multiple times before without success.

"Are you doing that thing again, where you try to browbeat the case into solving itself?"

Jillian's blonde head stayed buried nose-deep in Ellie's notes when she asked the question, leaving Ellie to shake her own head in wonder. Her friend's ability to read her was downright creepy sometimes.

"So what if I am? It's not like anything else has worked so far." After one last glare for good measure, Ellie began tidying her space. "Find anything I might have missed yet?"

Jillian held a finger up while she finished reading the last page. When she got to the end, she straightened and pursed her red lips. "Not a darn thing."

Ellie had figured as much. Jillian didn't possess much of a

filter, so if her friend had found a lead, she would have blurted out the idea. Immediately.

"There has to be something I'm missing." But what? Ellie had been through this file too many times to count. Her gaze swept the entirety of Dani's investigation so far, and her shoulders drooped at the scant offering. Even the interviews with Dani's parents hadn't produced any new leads. The avenues she'd ventured down so far had all resulted in dead ends.

She cupped her chin in her palm, brooding. There wasn't much in this world more frustrating than a stalled case. Constantly reviewing evidence and facts that went nowhere felt a lot like banging her head against the wall and produced the same results: a killer headache. The light at the end of the tunnel was the knowledge that if she pushed through, Ellie could give families the relief of knowing what happened to their loved ones.

Ellie lived for that rush of solving a case, which was why she threw her shoulders back, shifted her hips into a more comfortable sitting position, and slid Dani's file closer so that she could start again. From the beginning.

Before she flipped open the first page, music blared from Ellie's phone. She tapped the screen to accept the call, her attention still fixed on the case. "Detective Ellie Kline."

"Detective Kline, it's Charles Snyder. Do you remember?"

As if she could possibly forget. Ellie opened her mouth to tell him as much, but Charles Snyder jumped back in before she could even gather her breath.

"I'm Dani Snyder's dad. You came to my house the other day and asked me a bunch of questions about my missing daughter? I'm sorry to bother you so soon, but something's happened, and I don't know what to do. This is all so much. Please, I need your help. I can't..."

He broke off his frantic babble with an audible gasp, so

Ellie seized the opportunity to reassure him. "Shhh, it's okay. Please don't apologize. Of course I remember you. Now, can you tell me what's going on?" She sprang to her feet as her muscles flooded with sudden energy.

"She called! Dani called again, or someone did, and this time she gave me an address of where she is! What do I do now?"

"Okay, Mr. Snyder, here's what I need you to do." When Ellie uttered the name, Jillian gasped. Ellie turned away. She needed to focus. "I appreciate that this is all very confusing and exciting, but the first thing I need you to do is take a couple of deep breaths and slow down." The way the older man was working himself up, Ellie wouldn't be surprised if he triggered a heart attack.

"Okay, I'll try." The hiss of his inhalations followed. Five slow breaths in total. "Okay, I feel a little better now."

"Good, that's good. Now, to answer your question, you already completed the task you needed to do. You called me. The next step is for you to tell me exactly what the caller said."

"Right. Okay." While Mr. Snyder paused, Ellie pulled out her notepad and flipped to an empty page. "She said that she was okay but trapped. A man is holding her hostage. She was able to grab his phone when he wasn't looking, but she can't escape, and she needs someone to come right away because she's convinced he's going to kill her tonight."

His voice trembled at the end, so Ellie reminded him to breathe. She asked him to repeat the message while she finished taking notes. "Okay, I've got it. Now, what address did she give?"

She jotted down the address that Mr. Snyder recited. "Perfect. Here comes the hard part. What I need you to do now is sit tight. I'll round up my team, and we'll head out to that address right away. In order to do our jobs safely, though, I need your word that you'll stay in your house and wait for me to call. Can you do that?"

A pause. "Yes. Yes, I can do that. But please, hurry. In case—"

"Don't worry, Mr. Snyder. I promise that I'll be assembling my team the second I hang up this line."

"Thank you, Detective."

Ellie hung up with Mr. Snyder and then called Jacob.

He answered on the second ring. "Everything okay?"

"Just got a call from Charles Snyder. The person claiming to be Dani called again, with an address this time. Can you and Duke be ready to go in five?"

"Meet you in the lobby."

With that call complete, Ellie dialed her boss next.

"This better be good, Kline. I'm buried up to my nose hairs in paperwork here."

Without mincing words, Ellie repeated the information about the call with Mr. Snyder. "Jacob and Duke are meeting me downstairs in five. Can you commandeer a few more bodies for me?" If this call turned out to be a trap, Ellie might need more officers on hand to deal with the threat.

"You realize that caller has more holes in her story than Swiss cheese?"

"I'm aware."

Fortis grunted. "All right. Whoever I can rustle up will be down there. I'll run a search on that address too and text you the details."

"Thanks."

Ellie lowered her phone to the table, her mind reeling. What were the odds that the caller was Dani? Low, but not zero. Never zero. She turned to Jillian and caught her friend bouncing behind her desk like a blonde pogo stick.

"So, this is it? This address could lead you right to Dani?"

Ellie plugged the address into her maps app. "Or straight

into a trap. I've got to hustle upstairs. Jacob and Duke are probably already waiting."

She moved toward the door, surprised when Jillian darted in front of her. "Hey. Promise to be careful, okay? You and Jacob both." Her eyes began to water. "And Duke."

Ellie's skin prickled at the interruption, but her impatience subsided when she noted her roommate's haunted expression. She reached out and grasped Jillian's hands, stilling their restless motion. "I promise we'll be careful."

After a last reassuring squeeze, Ellie released her friend and headed for the hallway. She took the stairs two at a time, bursting into the lobby to find three officers waiting in a loose huddle, with Jacob and Duke standing off to the side. Picking up on his partner's cues, the shepherd's entire body quivered as he shifted his weight from paw to paw.

She nodded at her crew. Todd and Lou, she recognized from her stint as a beat cop, and the unfamiliar face introduced himself as Colby. "Thanks for helping me out here. I'm sure Fortis already filled you in on the basics, but let me know if you have any questions? Time might be a factor, so the quicker we get on the road, the better."

Colby cleared his throat. "We got a name to go with this address?"

Ellie's phone dinged. "Hang on. Hopefully, this is Fortis with that information now." She checked her phone and nodded. "The name associated with that address is John Garrett. Any other questions?" No one answered so she motioned to the front door. "Good, let's roll."

Energy radiated off the beat cops in waves as she led the four men and a dog to her Ford Explorer. Not that Ellie faulted them. Heading to an unknown location to potentially rescue a decade-old kidnapping victim wasn't a call-out most cops ever experienced. "Jacob, you ride with me. The rest of you follow behind."

Doors opened and slammed. Once she was sure everyone was ready, Ellie threw the SUV into reverse and headed out to the road. Two black and whites fell in behind her.

Duke whined as she followed the GPS directions onto the highway, conveying the jitters they all felt. "You and me both, boy."

The coordinates led Ellie north of downtown, into a run-down section of Charleston, where houses turned into shacks, and in some areas, shacks into trailers. Rusted cars on blocks decorated more than one dirt yard. They passed a dilapidated house where laundry flapped in the breeze from a clothesline, then a yard where a brawny pit bull snapped and snarled at them from the end of a thick chain staked into the earth.

The deeper into the area they drove, the more Ellie's gut shrieked a red alert. "Am I the only one getting a bad feeling about this?"

Jacob shook his head, his mouth a grim line. "Definitely not just you."

A few seconds later, the GPS announced the grim news. "You have arrived at your destination."

Ellie parked and killed the engine. Jacob hopped out, with Duke bounding after him. He peered at their destination and whistled. "Damn."

Ellie climbed out of the driver's side, her stomach clenching like a steel trap. Damn was an understatement at the sight that greeted them.

Trash piles splattered a square lot where, despite South Carolina's heavy annual rains, the majority of the grass was brown and dry. A single-wide trailer dripping with rust and neglect squatted in the middle. The structure's yellow siding peeled away in spots, like even the trailer wanted to escape this place. A *No Trespassing* sign hung on a chain-link fence.

Ellie sucked in a breath. "Do you see that?" She pointed at a pipe that jutted out of the trailer's roof.

Jacob's voice sounded as strained as Ellie felt. "Yeah. Unfortunately. Meth."

Her gaze took in the black plastic tarps duct taped to the windows, blocking any prying eyes, and she gritted her teeth. "Sure looks that way." Mr. Snyder's caller had led them straight to a meth house. The muttering coming from the other officers told her they'd noticed too.

"What's the play here?" Jacob's calm manner acted like a balm on the rest of the cops. They quieted down to await Ellie's decision.

Ellie blew out an uneasy breath. They could wait on hazmat, but that ran the risk of Garrett bolting first. "Ideally, we go check this out and get probable cause to enter. Consent or plain view are our best bets, understand?"

Everyone nodded. "When we do get probable cause, no one, I repeat, no one, is to enter that trailer until we get appropriate PPE. Are we clear on that point?" More nods. "Good. Now, when we approach the dwelling, I want two of you to circle around the back and secure it in case we have a runner. Jacob, you and Duke go right at my hand signal. Lou, you take left." Her gaze drifted back to the pipe. "Oh, and in case any of you were deciding this was a good time to whip out your vape, don't."

Her joke drew a few snickers to help relieve their jitters, easing some of the tension. Good. A wrong move in this situation, and *boom*! They'd all go up in flames. Meth labs placed first responders in grave danger, both in terms of chemical inhalants causing lung burns and explosions.

She zipped her jacket all the way to her throat and motioned for the others to follow. As they approached the house, big brown patches of dead grass crunched beneath her feet. A pile of yellowing granules to their left only furthered her suspicions. She pointed, and Jacob nodded. Contaminated kitty litter was yet another common by-product of meth producers. The clincher was the expensive-looking cameras positioned around the trailer, one of which was easily worth more than the rest of the lot's contents combined.

The wind shifted directions, wafting a hint of a noxious odor their way. Ellie sniffed a combination of rotten eggs and cat urine before the smell disappeared.

"Jesus, that's nasty."

Ellie threw her hand up to silence whichever cop had whispered before motioning her team to follow her. Nothing stirred in the lot beyond the flap-flap of the window tarps moving with the wind and the flutter of leaves on a neighboring tree. She edged her way toward the trailer, stopping thirty feet away. The closer she got, the higher her pulse climbed.

She inhaled through her nose, focusing on the pathway the air traveled through her body. First, her nasal passages. Then her trachea. Finally, her lungs. She held the breath until she felt her heart rate subside. Until she sensed her body's connection to the earth, and a sense of calm banished the fuzziness in her head.

By the time she released the air in a low whoosh, Ellie was ready. Thank god for her years of yoga and martial arts training. Their mindfulness practices had come in handy during multiple tense situations.

She caught Jacob's eye and motioned her hand to the right. Jacob nodded. He tightened up on Duke's lead, and the pair took off at a swift clip.

Ellie repeated the gesture with her other hand to Todd, who set off to circle around the left. She crept toward the sagging awning that covered an ancient *Welcome* mat. The two remaining officers fell in behind her, one on either side.

When she reached the front door, she paused. Listening. Not a peep from inside, so she lifted her hand and knocked. After three loud bangs with her knuckles, she shouted. "John Garrett, this is Detective Kline of the Charleston Police Department. I need to speak to you."

Seconds ticked by. Ellie waited, then lifted her hand to knock again. Before her skin touched the door, a rapid-fire bark shattered the silence, followed by a man's yell.

"Stop! Police!"

Duke. *Jacob.*

"Around back!" Ellie didn't wait for a response from her two flanking officers. She sprinted in the same direction Jacob and Duke had traveled only moments before. Her heart pounded so forcefully that every last bit of her body pulsed with the accelerated beat.

If anything happened to Jacob on her watch...

No. Nothing would happen. Ellie kicked her pace up even more.

She rounded the corner to find Duke crouched low with his ears pinned to his head, growling over a man who laid cowering in dead grass and dirt. His dark muzzle curled up to reveal massive white teeth, only inches away from the man's exposed throat.

"Please, call him off! He's trying to kill me!"

Jacob stood by Duke's side. "If he was trying to kill you, he would have already. Roll onto your stomach so I can cuff you. Slowly, so you don't accidentally convince Duke here that you're fair game."

After a wild-eyed glance at the growling shepherd, the man eased onto his stomach.

Jacob pulled his handcuffs off his belt and knelt beside the man. Metal clinked as he snapped the cuffs around the man's wrists, then tightened them. "All right, we're good. Time to stand up."

With Jacob's assistance, the man staggered to his feet. Jacob maneuvered him until he faced Ellie and the rest of the team. Ellie grimaced. The meth ravaged face was recognizable from the photo Fortis had texted, but barely so. Scabs from clawing at imaginary bugs littered his face, and his lips oozed with more than one open sore.

"Christ Almighty," muttered one of the cops from behind her.

"I'm going to search your pockets." Jacob clearly didn't relish the idea. "Is there anything on your person that will stick me, harm me in anyway."

Their prisoner shook his head. "No, man."

With gloved fingers, Jacob dug a wallet out of the man's back pocket and flashed them a South Carolina driver's license. "It's him. John Garrett."

Ellie nodded. "Mr. Garrett, we need to question you about the whereabouts of Danielle Snyder, also known as Dani. Is Dani Snyder in the trailer?"

Now that Duke wasn't an instant away from tearing out his throat, John Garrett decided he could afford to cop an attitude. He spit in the dirt and sneered at Ellie, revealing a missing front tooth and several others brown from decay. "Go fuck yourself."

Ellie ignored his helpful suggestion. "Mr. Garrett, I'm Detective Kline of the Charleston PD, and this will go much easier if you cooperate."

Garrett stuck out his tongue and wiggled it. Ellie gritted her teeth.

"Hey, Kline, check this out. I can see empty cough medicine boxes and other meth shit from here." Todd stood on a step behind the screen door Garrett had fled through and peered into the trailer through the mesh.

Bingo.

Ellie turned back to Garrett and smiled. "Looks like we

won't be needing your cooperation after all. Based on our observations here today, we have probable cause to search your trailer for meth or items used in the production and distribution of meth."

The man's eyes rounded. "What? The fuck you do! Stay the hell out of my trailer, you crazy bitch! I know my rights!" Saliva flew from his mouth as he jerked his body this way and that, trying to thrash free of Jacob's hold. Duke lunged and barked, but Garrett kept struggling this time. Lou and Todd rushed over to assist.

"We've got him. You go check the trailer!" Jacob shouted to be heard over the still screaming Garrett. "Be careful!"

Ellie turned to face the screen door, grimacing. Now for the fun part. One experience that had never ranked high on her detective bucket list was raiding a meth lab. Oh well.

Safety guidelines recommended that all first responders don proper protective gear before entering a suspected meth lab. Not an N95 filter like Ellie had, but a full-blown gas mask to minimize any contact with hazardous fumes.

Only, Ellie didn't have a gas mask, and Dani couldn't wait.

Hurrying away, she grabbed a mask from her car and arranged it over her face. Jacob would freak when he figured out her intention, so she needed to be quick.

The trailer squeaked when she bounded up the steps. "Dani? Hello? This is Charleston PD, coming inside. Anyone in this trailer needs to put their hands in the air where I can see them."

Right on cue, Jacob shouted at her. "Ellie, don't you dare—"

Too late. Ellie sucked in a lungful of oxygen, unholstered her gun, and darted inside.

Even holding her breath, the chemical odor smacked her in the face. Overpowering, like nail polisher remover laced with a sickly sweet scent. She froze before pushing forward.

The less time she spent in here without proper gear, the better.

"Dani! You here?"

She crept past a trash can overflowing onto the dingy carpet with empty boxes of pseudoephedrine, yellow-stained latex gloves, used pH strips, and a single coffee filter stained a deep red. The living area was empty, save for a stained table and an even dirtier couch. A flat-screened TV perched on the kitchen counter, surrounded by a mess of items Ellie recognized as meth-making supplies: a two-liter soda bottle with a tube poking out of the top. A stained scale. A plastic jug of Drano and a can marked *Butane*. She noted too many jars and containers to count, some filled with white crystals, others with a red substance.

She gave the kitchen a wide berth, clamping down on her need to inhale until after she passed. She rounded the corner and peered into a room containing a dirty mattress on the floor and piles of clothes. All men's.

"Dani?"

No one replied.

She cleared the tiny closet and a bathroom. Clear. No Dani anywhere. Time to get the hell out.

On her way back past a computer sitting on an ancient desk, Ellie swung her left arm wide and nudged the mouse.

Oops. My bad.

As she'd hoped, the tap caused the monitor to blink to life. Images filled the screen, and acid scorched her throat.

Not only was John Garrett a meth dealer, but according to the awful photos on his computer, he also had a penchant for child porn.

The one thing the trailer didn't contain so far was any trace of Dani Snyder.

"Ellie! Get out here before I come in after you!"

Wincing at Jacob's threat, Ellie raced for the door. She hit the steps and almost collided with Jacob. She waited until she was several feet away before pulling the N95 off her head. "I'm fine, see? Dani's not in there."

Her former partner groaned. "You know Jillian's going to kill me, right?"

"You'll survive. Did you call hazmat?"

"On their way. CSI is on alert, and I told them to get some extra PPE ready." He frowned at her. "Although it's a little like closing the barn door after the horse escapes."

"Yeah, yeah." She headed back to her car and stripped down to her t-shirt and the leggings she'd thankfully pulled on that morning. She stuffed her contaminated clothes in a bag before squirting sanitizing gel in her hands. She wanted to scrub it over every inch of her but that would have to wait for later.

After pulling on the spare clothes she kept in the trunk, she allowed herself to breathe a little. She still needed to shower, but the worst of it was off her now.

Feeling better, she headed over to where Lou and Todd stood guarding Garrett. Her mind flashed to the images on his computer, and her jaw tightened. She read him his rights in a curt voice. Yet another predator. Where the hell did all these sickos keep coming from?

Once he was Mirandized, Ellie assigned Lou and Todd the task of driving Garrett to the station and booking him. Lou stuffed Garrett into the back seat before the patrol car peeled off down the road. She directed Jacob and Colby to set up a perimeter while she rang Fortis.

"Well? Did you find anything?"

Ellie gazed at the trailer. "You could say that." After she explained the situation, Fortis agreed to track down a judge and procure them a search warrant that granted legal permission for them to search every inch of the trailer for signs of Dani, to be on the safe side.

An hour passed before the hazmat team's van pulled up. The first thing they did was check the wind direction to make sure they were parked upwind of the trailer. Once that was settled, the members donned their puffy suits and gas masks and waddled their way toward the trailer. While Ellie waited for them to secure the area, the crime scene tech van bounced up the pockmarked street and parked near her Explorer.

A petite brunette woman who Ellie only knew as Paula bounded out of the van. "They almost done?"

Ellie shrugged. "Hopefully."

"Whelp, let's find out for sure." She cupped her hands to her mouth. "Hey, Dave, you knuckleheads almost finished? Some of us have lives to get back to, you know!"

One of the puffy suited figures raised their right hand. Even with a glove, the obscene gesture was obvious. "Yeah, right, what exciting plans you got going on tonight, Paula? Remember, Netflix and chill by yourself doesn't count."

"You touch your mama with that hand?" Paula smiled, making Ellie guess that the pair of them enjoyed giving each other shit. "And bless your heart! Look at you, finally jumping into this century and learning how to use Urban Dictionary. I bet the kids are proud."

"Man, don't remind me. I've got another one getting ready to go to college, and we're still paying for the first one." Dave pulled off his protective mask and groaned. "I expect they'll give you the go-ahead any time now. The air quality didn't register as shit as I expected."

Ellie winced and sent a mental apology to her lungs.

"Cool. Thank you, and say hi to Jen for me."

Two members of the hazmat team exited the trailer, carrying containers. Once they settled them on a plastic sheet that had been arranged a good fifty feet from the structure, they approached Ellie and the crime scene crew. "When you're suited up, you're good to go inside. We removed the riskiest compounds and will collect samples for you. Everything else should be okay, but I wouldn't recommend kicking off any sparks."

"Understood."

Ellie, Paula, and the rest of the crew began suiting up. As they pulled on the cumbersome gear, Ellie addressed them.

"Get what you need for the meth, but what I'm really looking for here is evidence that Garrett had a teen girl here. Well, woman now. Looks like we might be dealing with a human trafficker, so please keep that in mind as you collect samples."

Paula nodded and turned to her coworkers. "You hear that? Let's comb the shit out of this sicko's lair, see what we can find. Chuck, you take the lead. Remember, most or even all of this evidence could very well end up marked as contaminated and destroyed, so make sure you don't miss anything."

Another puffy-suited man wielding a video camera nodded and headed for the trailer. The rest of them trudged behind them, like a line-up of spacemen.

Thanks to the respirator, the smell didn't threaten to knock Ellie out this time. She hung back while Chuck did his job, methodically preserving the scene on camera. Once he cleared a room, Paula took over. She swept a UV blacklight along the living surfaces, checking for blood. Ellie opened a tiny closet and began shuffling through the items. An old towel, a worn straw cowboy hat. Boots.

She frowned, pulling the boots out to inspect them. "Hey, Paula. Can we get an imprint and size on these when you're done?"

"Sure thing."

A tech appeared from the back room, holding a large white shoe box with an Adidas logo on the side. "Might have found something here. It's full of women's stuff. Rings, nail polish, wallets."

Ellie perked up and waved her in the direction of the stained table. "Set it down here."

The tech placed the open box in front of Ellie. "I'll hold on to the lid, still need to print it."

The tech carried the lid away as Ellie leaned over the box. Three bottles of nail polish sat in one corner, all in differently shaped containers. One red, one sheer pink, one glittery blue. A tangle of necklaces glinted beside them. With a gloved finger, Ellie poked them aside, revealing a silver ring that wrapped around like a snake and a gold ring with pink stones. A trio of black and gold bangle-style bracelets rattled when she shifted the jewelry to expose any more hidden items.

Two small passport photos of the same blonde woman peered up from the bottom. After studying the picture and deciding the face didn't belong to Dani, Ellie moved on to a jumble of wallets. She removed them one by one and carefully arranged them in a row on the table. An icy finger slid across her neck. "They're all women's wallets."

Remnants of an overzealous pickpocket? Possibly, but Ellie doubted it. The shoe box collection gave off a distinct *souvenir* vibe. As Ellie reached for a yellow leather wallet, she prayed her radar was misfiring.

Please, don't let us be dealing with a collector.

On first glimpse, the wallet appeared empty. Still, Ellie inspected every compartment and credit card slot. The second to last spot she checked revealed a glimpse of white. She extracted the rectangular piece of plastic, and a young brunette smiled up at her from a South Carolina driver's license.

"Shit."

The word slipped from Ellie's mouth, causing Paula to

stop what she was doing and hurry over. "Son of a bitch. He kept trophies?"

Ellie's jaw locked down so tight, she was afraid the slightest tap might make it shatter. "It's sure looking that way. Melanie Conkle from Charleston. Twenty-three. We need to run her through the system."

She snapped another photo with her phone before setting the wallet aside and picking up the next. This one showed the owner's ID as soon as Ellie looked inside. Her heart sank, settling like a stone in her gut. According to the ID card, Becky Harrison was a freshman at Clemson University. So, no older than eighteen or nineteen.

One by one, Ellie opened the wallets and snapped a photo of the IDs she found. Each time, the rock in her stomach grew larger. By the time she reached the last one, her camera roll held seven pictures of women and girls. Even so, the student ID in the last wallet made Ellie gasp. Blue eyes gazed up at her from a round face. The same face Ellie had studied at least a hundred times over the past several days.

Danielle Snyder, the ID proclaimed. Sophomore at McKinley High.

A deep sorrow settled inside Ellie's chest. She replaced the wallet on the table and bowed her head. Ever since Fortis had handed over this case, Ellie had been desperate for a lead. Any lead. Only now that she had one, her heart wept for poor Charles Snyder and his untouched piano. Elaine and her boundless hope.

Ellie touched Dani's photo with the tip of her gloved finger and made a silent vow. Garrett would tell her what happened to Danielle Snyder and the other women. She owed their traumatized families at least that much.

15

R ob tilted his disposable coffee cup all the way back, draining every drop before sighing. "I want another one. Please? You promised." He clasped his hands under his chin and batted his eyelashes.

Gabe laughed. Always such a ham, his Rob. "Okay."

He got up from their cozy little table to order another coffee, but the register was so far away. He kept walking and found himself inside a tunnel. The bright lights of the café vanished, along with the laughter and chatter. A crackling sound filled Gabe's ears. Soft at first, but growing in volume the farther he disappeared into the tunnel's depths. He whirled in a circle, desperate to go back, but nothing but darkness greeted him. The coffee shop was gone.

"Rob? Rob, where did you go?"

The yawning blackness didn't answer, but in the shadows, a murky figure writhed. The crackling grew louder.

Fear pierced Gabe's heart. "Rob, is that you?"

The darkness slithered around Gabe's ankles, grabbing at his jeans with invisible hands. His breathing quickened, and he kicked up his pace. He wondered briefly why the shadows felt hot rather than cold, but the thought turned into a rat with beady pink eyes and raced away, his spindly tail twitching behind him. A rising certainty deep in his chest fed a growing dread and made him want to howl into the void.

Gabe shook his head. The dark was messing with him. Once he found the barista and ordered Rob that second latte, everything would be okay.

In the distance, a circle of light appeared. Finally. Gabe was so relieved that he laughed out loud. The sound distorted, echoing off the walls and turning into sinister whispers. Gabe froze. No, wait. The whispers were coming from the darkness behind him. Someone else was in here. Stalking him.

Shaken, Gabe turned back toward the light and broke into a sprint. The tunnel poured into a room with tall ceilings, sending Gabe tumbling headfirst into a pile of junk. The light here was bright. So glaring, after the pitch-black corridor, that Gabe couldn't open his eyes. He crawled around the objects blind, on all fours like a dog.

"Rob? Rob?"

The heat grew in intensity, and Gabe started to sweat. Where was the damn barista? This was absurd. A loud crunch came from behind him.

"Rob?" He wanted to look, but his eyes refused to open, so he patted his way along the path of scattered objects, trying to move his hands and legs even faster. Behind him, he sensed the presence growing closer.

His fingers closed around a rectangular shape in his path, preparing to fight the monster stalking him. The familiar shape stopped him short. A book. He was holding a book.

Like magic, the realization restored his vision. He opened his eyes to find himself surrounded by books: on shelves, in heaps on the floor. He laughed out loud in relief.

"Rob, you dork. Why didn't you tell me we were in the library?"

He rose to his feet and turned, expecting to find his boyfriend standing there, flashing that naughty little grin that Gabe adored.

Rob was there, but he wasn't smiling. His beautiful face was frozen into a mask of horror.

"Oh my god, Rob! I'm coming!"

Gabe pumped his legs, straining to cover the distance, but the floor seemed to have dissolved into quicksand. He had to get to Rob. He had to help. He had to fix this.

Just as he broke free, Rob lifted his head, and Gabe gasped. The side of his boyfriend's head, where his ears should be, were bloody, gaping holes. All Gabe could do was watch in horror as Rob reached up and dug his hands inside. When he pulled them out again, his fingers were gone. They dangled out of the sides of Rob's head, wiggling like lost worms.

"Stop! Please, stop! I'll say it! I'll say the words!" Gabe screamed as his boyfriend's blue eyes locked on him and filled with red hate.

"This is all your fault."

"No, please! No!"

A faceless man stepped out of nowhere, lofting a giant blade. With one swing, he cut Rob beneath his ribs and sliced all the way through. The two halves of Rob separated and tumbled to the floor, where Rob's blue eyes continued to stare up at Gabe from the top of his amputated midsection. A macabre smile twisted his lover's face as he called out to Gabe.

"Silly boy."

Both halves burst into flames, while in the distance, an invisible presence giggled.

"Your turn is coming."

Gabe jolted awake to screaming. Ice plunged through his veins, and he whipped the covers off, his gaze darting to every corner of the bedroom, seeking out threats while his muscles tensed in preparation to escape. Not until his bare feet slapped the floor did the truth sink in. The screams were coming from *him*.

He sank back onto the bed, his heart rate still rabbit high.

His t-shirt and boxers clung to him like a second skin. Wet from his nightmare-induced sweat.

The dream crashed over him again, squeezing his stomach, making the floor spin before his eyes. He lurched to his feet again and raced to the bathroom, reaching the sink as that hot, acrid taste burned a trail up his throat. He grabbed the porcelain edges and hurled.

Once his stomach was empty, Gabe twisted on the faucet and washed the vomit away. He splashed cold water on his face, rinsed out his mouth. When he lifted his head, the face that peered back at him in the mirror appeared haggard, with purple crescents underlining the eyes and skin as pale as a vampire's. His cheekbones jutted out at a sharper angle than before, a surefire tell of his recent weight loss.

His reflection showed a man a good ten years older than his true years. Funny, because Gabe felt closer to one hundred. His brown eyes held a hunted expression, which made perfect sense. Kingsley had already tracked him down successfully twice now, and Gabe knew his former employer wouldn't stop. Not until he'd had his fill of torturing Gabe by making anyone around him suffer.

Gabe's hand trembled as he tugged open the drawer to grab his toothbrush, needing to wash the lingering sick off his tongue. His gaze fell on the black razor instead. One of the reusable kinds with four blades. Sharp, because Gabe had replaced the old cartridge yesterday.

Like they were moving of their own accord, his fingers wrapped around the handle and raised the blade to his throat, not stopping until it reached the hollow below his ear. The same spot where Kingsley had sliced open the stranger's neck in the video.

The man's screams echoed in his skull, and Gabe gripped the razor tightly. He could finish this. He didn't have to serve as Kingsley's plaything anymore.

The metal was cold on his skin. Gabe shivered and pressed down while holding his breath. A stinging pain seared his neck. Not much worse than that of a papercut. Blood oozed to the surface and trickled toward his collarbone.

Do it! a voice whispered in his head. *Don't sit around and wait. Take back control. End this nightmare. Right here, right now. Press a little harder, and this will all be over.*

Do it.

Gabe's fingers twitched but refused to advance the blade.

Come on, what are you waiting for? You want Kingsley to carve you up like Rob?

Rob.

"No!" Gabe opened his hand, letting the razor clatter to the floor. His lungs burned, and he gasped, gulping down air in a frantic attempt to provide oxygen to his starved cells. This time, when he braved his reflection, the eyes staring back at him held fire in their depths. Determination. A desire to live.

"Never again. Giving up now means Kingsley wins, and that bastard can't win. Rob would want you to fight."

With a shaky but firm nod, he turned and headed back to his bed. The realization at how close he'd come to dying settled into his legs. They wobbled before buckling beneath him, sending him collapsing onto his mattress. He closed his eyes and let his mind drift.

He weaved his way through the crowded sidewalks, his feet so light, he wondered if he could walk on air. A languid, liquid warmth filled his limbs, his very favorite part of the high. A kaleidoscope of colors exploded on the street before him, making him laugh in sheer joy. He lifted his fingers to touch one of the shapes, but the colors danced beyond his reach.

A couple approaching him from the opposite direction grabbed their toddler's hand and veered to the side, giving him a wide berth.

"*Crack head.*"

Gabe giggled, unbothered by the man's scorn. Poor guy had no idea what he was missing. If he did, he'd know that Gabe wasn't high on crack. Why would he settle for that when heroin was so much better? So good that Gabe's parents had chosen to keep chasing the highs over caring for their own son.

Another gloomy thought invaded his euphoric bubble.

Heroin cost money, and Gabe was almost out. Wait. Didn't drugs have something to do with why he was out here? He blinked at the tourists passing by, trying to focus. Everything clicked when his gaze landed on a couple on the sidewalk ahead, paused to study a map.

The man's shirt was one of those expensive silk Hawaiian prints, and gold flashed on his wrist. A Rolex. The woman's purse was patterned with the telltale L and V, and diamonds glittered at her ears, throat, and wrist.

A mark! That was why he'd ventured near this stretch of beach, a tourist trap that most locals avoided like the plague. Rich marks provided Gabe with his most reliable income since he'd finished high school. Lucky for him, the pair ahead were perfect. He'd float right up, snag the woman's wallet, and vanish into the crowd before either of them noticed.

Only fleece the rich marks. That was his rule. He wasn't a bad person. He never touched poor people, or the elderly, or the disabled. He just needed to eat and a little extra to feed his habit. These two probably tipped their cab drivers more than Gabe would even take.

He drifted toward them, hands in his pockets. Before he could reach them, though, a new man snagged his attention. Tall, maybe twenty, twenty-five years older than Gabe. The kind of person who exuded wealth from head to toe. Gabe never intended to switch targets but somehow found himself gliding in the tall man's direction anyway, like the man's designer linen shirt contained a lure and Gabe was a hungry fish.

Gabe closed the gap between them, waiting for his chance.

When the rowdy group of college-aged kids coming their way passed them was when he'd strike. Same routine every time. He pretended to stumble right as a noisy group showed up, accidentally bumping the mark. After a quick apology, Gabe would disappear into the crowd. By the time the mark noticed their wallet had vanished with the stranger, Gabe was long gone.

The three boys in the front started to sing a loud ditty about girls and beer. Sweet. The more commotion, the better. Gabe edged closer to the man as the students shouted their approach from the opposite direction.

Wait, wait, wait...now!

Gabe darted forward at the same time the larger group parted to allow his target through. He was an arm's length away from nabbing the wallet when the man spun in his tracks.

Caught off guard, Gabe stumbled. For real this time. As one knee hit the ground, he glanced up. The man towered over him with his arms crossed over his chest and a stern expression etched onto his shrewd face.

"Why are you watching me?"

Think fast.

Only heroin dulled his brain to the point where even thinking at all was a challenge.

"I..." With the way the sun streamed over the man, his skin appeared to be glowing. Almost like one of the golden angels in the church he'd walked by earlier, where the man in the wheelchair sat begging. Perfect. "I was coming over to ask if you could spare some change."

The man didn't say anything as Gabe climbed to his feet, only studied Gabe with those weird eyes of his. Almost like he could peel open Gabe's skull and pluck the thoughts right out of his brain. Gabe shifted his weight onto the balls of his feet, preparing to run as certainty pierced his haze. He'd made a mistake, a big one. This man wasn't a mark. He was a hunter.

"How would you like a job instead?"

Gabe tapped his hand against his ear. The heroin must be messing with his hearing. "I'm sorry?"

"I said, instead of begging, would you be interested in a job?"

"A job?"

When the man nodded, Gabe's mouth split into a wide grin. "Yes, please. More than interested."

In his altered state, there was a moment when Gabe convinced himself that the man's weird eyes lingered a bit too long on his mouth. But to be fair, Gabe noticed many things that weren't really there when he was high. Besides, the idea that a street hustler like himself held any appeal for a successful man like this? Ridiculous.

That chance encounter changed Gabe's life. Dr. Kingsley, as the man introduced himself, was a psychiatrist who recognized Gabe's addiction from the very start. The first thing his rescuer did was send him to rehab. Once Gabe was clean, Kingsley trained him to be his assistant. Life had continued along just fine until the day Gabe found the video on his boss's computer, revealing the man had a dark side too disturbing to ignore.

When Gabe came back to the present, he still sat on the edge of his bed in the new safe house in McMinnville, Oregon. Rob was still dead. Murdered by Kingsley, along with the stranger last night on the video. Gabe's brain hurt, trying to reconcile the man who lifted him up off the streets and turned his life around with the monster he knew today.

"Why didn't I pick the blue pill?" Gabe had tortured himself with that question many times. If he'd had a choice like Neo in *The Matrix*, would he pick the red pill? Or would he stick to the cozy world he'd known. In the blue world pill, Gabe never would have learned about Kingsley's sadistic practices. He could have lived out his days in blissful ignorance.

Some days, Gabe even wished that he'd done exactly as Kingsley had requested and played along. Would that really have been so bad? Do what Kingsley said and not worry about the rest? Surely anything was better than watching the people around him die while Kingsley hunted him like an animal.

His phone chimed, yanking him from his trance. A message alert. The hairs on the back of his neck prickled as Gabe clicked to open the message. An image popped up, and Gabe stopped breathing. The picture showed a naked woman's body, except her head was missing. Blood dripped from her stump of a neck, but that wasn't even the most horrible part.

Ha-ha.

At first, Gabe mistook the sloppy red writing on her belly for paint. His vision focused, and he realized his error with a gasp. Not paint at all. Blood. No wonder the letters appeared so haphazard.

Kingsley had carved the word into her flesh so that the wounds would fill with blood to spell out a message. Like the woman was nothing more than a human version of a Jack-o-lantern.

Gabe's stomach lurched again. His gaze fell on the caption at the bottom—*your time is up*—and his hands turned boneless. The phone fell to the floor for the second time that morning, but Gabe barely noticed. He pushed to his feet, and on heavy legs, shuffled his way to the dining room table, feeling older than he'd ever felt in his life.

He sat in the chair, grabbed the notepad and pen, and started to write.

16

Katarina arched her back on the silky black sheets and stretched her arms overhead, relishing the buzz flowing through her naked body. The air was heavy with a musky-sweet scent, sex and sweat mixed with laundry detergent, and Clayne's even breathing was the only sound. For the first time in months, Katarina felt truly alive.

Amazing, what a little midday sex could do for morale. Not that she bothered deluding herself. Sex alone wasn't enough to jumpstart Katarina like this. No, she needed an extra element to really get her blood humming.

Danger.

She rolled onto her side, studying the naked man sprawled beside her. With his lashes fanned against his cheeks, he appeared softer. Sweet, even. But Katarina knew better.

She'd spent her life around dangerous men, and Clayne Miller triggered every warning signal. Goose bumps shivered along her bare skin. Clayne might be dangerous, but he had no idea that Katarina was too. Perhaps even more dangerous than him. That was a secret she would keep tucked away, to take out and savor whenever the urge arose. Watching Clayne underestimate her might be exactly the entertainment her life here in Wyoming was missing so far.

Her phone dinged on the nightstand. Katarina stretched one last time before turning over to check the screen. Damn. Time to pick Bethany up from her movie night already. If nothing else, rolling around in the sheets with Clayne had sure helped to pass the hours. So much better than cleaning.

Katarina pushed to a sit, laughing when strong hands latched around her waist and yanked her back to bed. Her skin pressed against Clayne's bare chest, and she sighed, her body tingling with renewed interest. Another round sounded like fun.

She sighed. Except, Bethany.

With regret, Katarina untangled her legs from his. "Wish I could stay, but I have commitments." She leaned over and planted one last kiss on his lips before bounding out of bed.

Clayne's eyes followed her every move as she gathered her discarded clothes. A flash of self-consciousness over the sight of her recently changed body—curvy and soft in places where muscles once rippled—made Katarina want to turn away. She curled her lip, shaking the inhibition off like a wet dog after a bath. Fretting over someone else's expectations was a way of giving up power, and Katarina had fought too long and hard for survival to relinquish hers so easily.

Much better to take that power and grow it even more.

With that in mind, Katarina discarded her momentary self-consciousness and instead flaunted her new assets. She eased into each item of clothing, like a reverse striptease. She knew the rule. *Always leave them wanting more.* His groan told her that she'd been successful in that endeavor, and she hid a grin. Toying with them was half the fun.

"Sure you can't stay a little longer? I'll make it worth your while."

Katarina finished slipping her feet into her shoes and straightened. "I'm sure you would, but I can't. Next time, maybe." She tossed a careless wink over her shoulder before heading out of the bedroom.

The front door was only a foot away when footsteps pounded the floor behind her. Clayne lunged ahead, blocking her exit. Katarina studied the large form towering over her. Intimidating, even in his nakedness. No fear flickered to life inside her, though. Only curiosity.

"To hell with maybe. I want to see you again."

Katarina bit her lip in a sensual way designed to drive him mad. Debating. A mental coin toss urged her to take the risk. "If I agree, will you tell me about your business? I'm dying to know more."

His eyebrows shot up. "Really? Why? You ever deal before?"

At his incredulous expression, her laughter bubbled out. She trailed a single finger down his naked chest. "Trust me, I've done more things than you could possibly imagine."

He leaned back against the door and cocked his head. "I'm all ears. Why don't you hang back a while and fill me in?"

"I wish I could, but I really do have to go." Katarina didn't say why. Bethany was her business.

His features sharpened. That was her only warning before he lunged, slamming Katarina's back against the door. She gasped as the unexpected contact rattled her spine.

"Are you a cop?" His big hand circled her throat.

Heat surged beneath Katarina's skin, flushing her arms, her chest. Between her thighs. "No, not a cop." Her voice sounded odd. Breathless. Not powerful at all. "But I do have some valuable skills that I'd like to put to use again."

The hand around her neck squeezed, intensifying the growing ache inside her, even as the oxygen flow decreased to her lungs. His face was so close that his warm breath fanned her nose. She smiled into his eyes, enjoying the way they turned from blue to black as his pupils dilated.

He squeezed harder, making the corners of her vision blur and the throbbing between her legs intensify. With her right hand, she reached out and found the bulge in his pants. Her lungs burned from scant air as she stroked him through the fabric, her desire spiraling higher the more he grew from her attention.

The sensations that rolled through her were almost too much to bear, a type of exquisite agony. Not pleasure, not pain, but a magical combination of both. As black spots drifted before her eyes and her brain turned fuzzy, a fleeting question materialized in Katarina's mind.

Why do I feel the most alive only when I'm so close to death?

After one last squeeze, Clayne loosened the grip on her neck, only to pry up her chin. Katarina's legs trembled as he growled and mashed his mouth to hers. His sharp teeth dug into her lower lip, biting down hard until warm salt laced their kiss and new sensations burst to life inside her, igniting her like a match to a forest. Hot. Rough. Delicious.

Violent.

He ground his pelvis against hers, and she arched up against him, pressing equally hard, shoving his force right back at him. After a long, satisfying kiss, she wrenched away, panting. "I really have to go now."

His fingers dug into her upper arms when he yanked her back to his chest. "You'd better not be lying to me. In my book, the only good cop is a dead cop."

His full lips took on a cruel twist, but Katarina wasn't worried. No one would ever mistake her for a cop for long. "Guess I'm safe then."

"We'll see. I have a test for you. I'll let you know when I'm ready."

She patted his cheek. "You do that. Now, I'm out of here."

He studied her face for another few moments before stepping aside. Katarina opened the door and sauntered down the walkway to her car, her smile widening with every step. Her hand flew to her throat, her fingers stroking the still-tingling skin.

That was the way to beat boredom in this rural Wyoming snore of a town. So long as Katarina was careful, she could have the best of both worlds: a life with her daughter and a life full of manageable risks with Clayne.

She slid behind the wheel and turned over the ignition. Her mind raced. Calculated risks were the key. A little danger here and there would help Katarina be a better mother. Like letting off steam to prevent the entire engine from exploding. Because one thing Katarina had learned over the past few months was that she wasn't built for a quiet, dull life. Her brain simply wasn't wired that way.

As she drove the darkening road toward Bethany, she tapped out a rhythm on the steering wheel, her brain bright and clear for once. If she approached her actions from the perspective of harm reduction, they made perfect sense. Wild sex with Clayne while dipping her toes into his business and creating a lucrative little business for herself. Those choices were infinitely smarter than caving to her inner darkness and murdering dog walkers who strolled by her house.

This way, Katarina could feed the monster Kingsley had created in a way that wouldn't threaten her life with Bethany.

Clayne Miller was the solution to all her problems. He just didn't know it yet.

17

E llie sipped from her bottled water before replacing the lid and turning her attention back to the surly man slouching in the chair opposite her. They'd been facing off in the stark, chilly interrogation room for over an hour now.

So far, John Garrett refused to cooperate, but the night was young. Since he'd also failed to ask for his lawyer, even after signing his Miranda rights form, questioning would continue.

She folded her hands on the table and started again. "What can you tell me about Dani Snyder?"

Garrett shrugged. About the most reaction she'd elicited so far.

"You remember Danielle Snyder, right? The pink wallet in your shoebox? Here, let me jog your memory." Ellie slid a photo of Dani across the table, along with a photocopy of her school ID.

The prisoner's gaze flickered to the photo before darting away.

"Look, I can work with the D.A. to cut you a deal if you help us find her. Where are you hiding Dani, John?"

No response, even though his gaze drifted back to the photo.

Ellie gritted her teeth and sifted through her notes. Time for a new line of questioning. "How about you tell me why you called Dani's father earlier today, pretending to be her?"

Garrett's head jerked up at the question. Ellie searched the meth-scabbed face and read genuine confusion in his creased brow. Now that was interesting. Either Garrett possessed superb acting skills, or the man was clueless about the call to Charles Snyder.

As she studied the sallow skin, the lips erupting in open sores, and the involuntary muscle twitches, Ellie started to wonder. Did a pathetic meth addict like Garrett have the chops to mastermind a scam like this? Maybe once upon a time, but now? Highly unlikely.

She hid a frown by pretending to read the file. At the very least, someone else was involved. Ellie would bet on it. And since they had zero leads on that front, she needed Garrett to talk.

Time to twist the screws.

After flipping through the file, Ellie spotted the information she wanted. She slid the report free and waved the paper at him. "The lab matched your shoe size to the prints at the scene of Dani's disappearance. Another girl, Dani's friend, died that day. Roxanne."

Garrett shifted in his chair while Ellie dug through the evidence file for a photo of Roxanne. She held up the picture. "You remember Roxanne, right? Pretty blonde girl, at the playground that night with Dani?"

When Garrett refused to lift his head, fire pulsed in Ellie's cells. She slammed her fist on the table. The bang echoed off the bare walls and made Garrett jump. "Look at her picture. Look at it."

Garrett glanced up from the floor and gulped air when he

focused on the likeness of Roxanne. Sweat beaded on his forehead.

Progress. Finally. Ellie leaned forward, ready to play her ace. "You know what I think?" She softened her voice to a tone closer to sympathetic. "I believe you were there that night, at the park, and you intended to take both girls, but something happened. Roxanne struggled, and she fell and hit her head. It wasn't murder, right, John? Just a terrible accident."

Ellie had his full attention now, so she paused to sip her water. Drawing the tension out before delivering the death blow. She shrugged and expelled a sad sigh. "Unfortunately, the D.A. has you pegged for her murder. He's going to throw the book at you, John. Unless…"

She shook her head, sighed again, and slid Roxanne's photo back into the file.

"Unless what?"

Elation surged through her limbs. She had him hooked. Now, to reel him in.

Firming her lips to hide her smile, Ellie met his gaze. "Unless you cooperate and help us find Danielle Snyder or tell us anything that might lead us to her whereabouts. If you do that, the D.A. might be persuaded to go easier on you. Otherwise…"

Ellie lifted her palms. Garrett closed his eyes and clenched his fists, appearing to wage an internal battle.

When he opened them again, he inhaled a ragged breath. "Okay. I know stuff."

He cut off, his head twitching violently.

"I'm afraid I'm going to need you to tell me a little more than that." Ellie waited with her hands balled into her lap. *Come on. Don't chicken out now.*

"Fine. I know stuff about a trafficking ring. But that's all

I'm gonna say until I get some promises about my charges. No deal, no information."

Ellie bit her lip to temper her excitement. "Okay. I'll go talk to the D.A. now and see what we can do."

She gathered up her files and headed out of the room. Once the door clanked shut, she pumped her fist in the air and released a lungful of air.

"Nice work, Kline." Fortis clapped her on the back. "Now hurry your ass to the D.A. before our scumbag changes his mind."

Ellie did as she was told. Thirty minutes later, she had the terms of the D.A.'s deal. She called to let Fortis know as she strode down the hallway. They reached the interrogation room at the same time.

"You ready for round two? This is it. You either get this guy talking now or risk him zipping his lips for good." Fortis loomed over her, his mouth taut with the same tension lacing Ellie's entire body.

She released a slow breath. "Gee, no pressure or anything, right?"

Fortis snorted. "This job is all pressure, all the time. You know that as well as anyone."

She did. Good thing Ellie performed best under tense circumstances. "I've got this." She headed back into the cramped room, determination tightening her jaw. Finding Dani depended on getting Garrett to talk. Failure wasn't an option.

Garrett glanced up when Ellie settled back into the chair, which she took as a hopeful sign. "Okay, we have a deal. No murder charges on Roxanne, on the condition that you provide us with information we can use."

The man nodded. Twitched a few times. Then started speaking. "It was like you said. When I saw the two girls in the park, I was gonna take both of them. That was my job that night. Two girls, not one."

Questions reared in Ellie's head, but she held her tongue and jotted down a note for later.

"The blonde one…uh…" He picked at a scab on his chin.

"Roxanne," Ellie provided gently, even though she wanted to scream the name at him, make it ring in his mind forever.

"Yeah, Roxanne. She tried to run. When I grabbed her, she tripped and hit her head on that concrete wall. I went over and checked, thinking maybe I could salvage, uh, save her, but she was already dead."

When he didn't go on, Ellie folded her hands on the table. "You said your job was two girls, not one. What did you mean?"

"An order came in for two girls, so that's what I went out to do. That was my job. Grabbing the girls so that the order could be fulfilled."

An order…for girls. Like they were a side of fries on a fast-food menu.

This time, Ellie gulped her water, hoping to wash away the filthy taste lingering in her mouth. "What order? Can you tell me how that worked?"

Garrett shrugged. "It was part of a trafficking ring. The leader took the orders and then sent people like me out to help fulfill them. Like, maybe one client asks for a blonde woman in her twenties. Or someone wants two dark-skinned girls, no older than eighteen. Fat girls, skinny girls, rich bitches, you name it. One of the clients probably requested it at some point."

The way Garrett offered up the information so matter-of-factly made Ellie's skin crawl. "But that night, you only came back with one."

Garrett scowled. "Yeah, and the head guy was pissed as hell at me too. Like it was my fault she hit her head and croaked. If getting girls was so easy, why didn't he get off his rich ass and do it himself?"

His nostrils flared before his anger subsided, leaving a pinched expression behind that Ellie struggled to comprehend. "The boss was so mad, I had to go into hiding because of that night. He was gonna kill me if I stayed. I could hear it in his voice."

He shivered, and Ellie finally understood. Fear. Even now, this hardened man was still scared of his old boss. What kind of man provoked such an extreme reaction? All these years later?

A premonition flitted over Ellie's skin like a frigid breeze. She swallowed hard. "Who is he, John? The ringleader?"

Garrett shivered again and then shrugged. "Dunno. Never saw his face. Only thing I know is that he used to go by a nickname. Dr. X."

All the oxygen was sucked from the universe, and Ellie struggled to breathe. She splayed her fingers on the table, attempting to find some sense of balance in a world that had begun to spin.

Dr. X. Or as Ellie knew him…Dr. Kingsley. The moment Garrett spilled the name, Ellie knew he was telling the truth. The pieces fit so perfectly.

She dropped her pen to the floor to buy time to pull herself together. When she sat back up, her face was composed.

"Okay, so you brought back Dani and then disappeared. What happened to her?"

"The buyer wanted the girls for films."

He shrugged again, making Ellie want to slam her hands down on his shoulders and squeeze until he started caring about the lives of the girls he'd condemned to such horrific fates. *Films.* Sure. Her stomach hurt at the thought of telling

Charles and Elaine that their baby had been sold into a porn ring.

"I recognized Dani later in a snuff film I bought on the web. They found some other chick to star with her." He snorted. "There's always another girl."

Ellie regulated her breathing in a vain attempt to curb the intense emotions exploding inside her. A porn ring had been awful enough, but a snuff film? Sick beyond compare.

Garrett rattled on, oblivious to Ellie's inner distress. "It was one of those fight-to-the-death setups, you know? Sorta like *Hunger Games*. One girl wins, one girl dies. The girl I grabbed won the fight."

He paused to preen a little, like he was proud of this fact. Ellie clenched her fists and imagined the satisfying crunch his nose would make if she punched him.

"But then they went ahead and killed her too."

Ellie forced the question from her lips. "How?" She didn't want to know, but she had to.

"Slow. The executioner took his time, made a whole show of it. He started by dipping her hands into bowls of acid, then her feet. He kept working his way up until he finally shoved her into a barrel of acid, right up to her chin." His expression softened as he reminisced, a smile curving his festering lips. "The guy was a master. Didn't let her screaming get him all worked up, just kept working her over, nice and slow."

Forget punching. Ellie's muscles tensed with an urge to lunge across the table and end him. The sick bastard was enjoying his memory of Dani being tortured to death. He deserved to pay.

Ellie found her center, breathing her rage out through her nose. He deserved to pay, but that wasn't her job. Her job was to serve and protect the community. Not revenge. No matter how tempting the desire might be.

"Can you show us how to find this video?"

"I can do better than that. I've got my own copy."

Ellie's lip curled into a snarl. A red film coated the room, and the sound that spilled from her mouth was pure rage.

"Ellie!"

A gentle hand wrapped around her upper arm and the contact snapped her free. She blinked, shocked to note that she was on her feet and leaning over the table. Garrett cowered in his chair, his eyes wide and frightened.

"A word, please?"

Clay gave a gentle tug on her arm. She dropped her gaze to her hands, noticed they were clenched into fists. With a shaky breath, she released them, and without another glance at Garrett, she allowed Clay to guide her from the room. The second the door clanked shut, Ellie collapsed against the cool metal.

"You okay?" Clay hovered, his brown eyes worried beneath the brim of his cowboy hat.

"No, clearly not. God, that poor girl." Ellie buried her face in her hands.

Patient as always, Clay waited her out. When she felt more in control, she lifted her head. "I'm okay now. Spill."

Clay examined her expression before nodding. They both knew Ellie was lying about being okay, but Clay understood. What Ellie meant was that she was ready to get back to work.

"Jillian and I were able to link some of the girls from those wallets with Kingsley's trafficking ring. Several of them have already turned up dead."

The news crashed over Ellie, pushing her back into the door. Her eyes stung. Kingsley. Always Kingsley.

She swayed on her feet. "What are the chances that this entire case was a Kingsley setup to hurt me?"

Clay grimaced. "Jillian and I were thinking more along the lines of a distraction technique."

Great. That was so much better. Ellie frowned. "A distraction? From what?"

Before he could say anything, the answer slammed her over the head. She gasped. "Gabe. What if Kingsley sent me after Dani to distract me from whatever he's planning with Gabe?" Ellie started pacing the hall, barely noticing his grim nod as she ran through the facts. "That has to be it. The timeline fits too perfectly. Gabe got the letter on the same day that first call came in." She whirled toward Clay, her heart racing. "Which means Kingsley could be planning his next attack today! That call came in this morning. Can you contact Gabe's marshal and make sure he's okay?"

"Yup, hang tight."

Clay disappeared down the hall, his boots clicking with his hurried pace. Ellie waited for what felt like hours but was only minutes before he returned.

"Spoke with Frank, he says everything is fine. He's on high alert now. He'll let us know if he spots anything out of the ordinary."

Relief washed over Ellie. "Okay. Thank you." At least Gabe was safe.

Now came the hard part. Ellie had to find the right words to tell Dani's parents what happened to their daughter. Only no such words existed. Ellie would explain, and once they recovered from their shock, her parents would ask why. Victim's families always asked why, pleading to the police to offer an explanation that made sense.

How could Ellie explain, though? A tragedy she couldn't make sense of herself? What rationale possibly existed that could make Dani's grieving parents comprehend why a man slowly submerged their only child in acid until she died?

None. Not a single reason in the universe worked.

Ellie pictured their horror when she told them the news.

Then her brain conjured up an image of Dani, screaming as acid ate away at her skin. Her stomach revolted.

With the images lingering behind her eyes, Ellie raced to the nearest bathroom and made it to the toilet just in time.

When she was finished, she splashed water onto her face and rinsed her mouth. While the cool water ran over her wrists, she looked into the mirror. Cold revenge hardened her features.

"I'll find him."

It was a promise to Dani and all the victims Kingsley ever hurt.

It was a promise to herself.

18

At the dinner table that night, Clay Lockwood groaned and rubbed the back of his neck. Man, what a day. Those last few hours spent listening in on Ellie's interrogation of Garrett had been intense, and the fact that all roads led back to Kingsley? That knowledge set Clay's nerves on edge.

Jillian laughed, capturing his attention before he shifted his gaze to the table's other two occupants, studying them as they scooped Caesar salad onto their plates. Kingsley's involvement in this case signaled danger to everyone in this room, but Ellie most of all.

Clay accepted the bowl that Ellie passed him and forked some greens onto his plate before unwrapping his hot turkey, bacon, and Swiss sub. The sweet aroma made his mouth water. He picked up a foil-wrapped half and prepared to dig in when a hot, stinky odor intruded on his meal.

Clay wrinkled his nose and peered over his shoulder. Two furry heads faced him: one brown, one black. Both dogs eyed his sandwich hopefully with their pink tongues dangling. "You guys are too much. Can you at least wait to beg until after I try the damn thing?"

"Hey, Sam, no begging at the table!" The lab mix acted like she didn't hear Jillian's scolding, only licked her lips and whined.

Jacob snickered. "I think you can mark dog trainer off your list of alternative career possibilities."

Jillian swatted her boyfriend on the arm. "Oh, hush you." She gestured at Duke. "Like yours is behaving any better. Sorry, Clay, do you want me to put her away?"

Clay almost said yes, but a peek at the twin sets of limpid brown eyes suckered him into reversing his decision. "No, they're fine. As long as they don't try to swipe my sandwich right out of my hand." He shot the two beggars a warning look. "You hear that? You steal food, you're going to pay the price." He deepened his voice to show them that he meant business. Sam's bushy tail thumped the floor harder in response.

"I can tell that Sam is very concerned."

After she made the teasing comment, Ellie laughed, a musical sound that eased some of the residual tension in Clay's neck. Ever since they'd left the station, she'd acted a little deflated. Pensive and quiet, which wasn't like her.

He smiled in return. "Well, I tried." He bit into the sub and sighed as the delicious flavors melded on his tongue. "At least now I can understand why they're so keen. This sandwich is delicious."

"It's my favorite sub shop in Charleston."

Clay frowned at Ellie's plate. Could have fooled him. She kept stabbing the salad greens, only to shake them off the fork and start the process all over again. She had yet to try a single bite of it or the sandwich sitting neglected on the plate.

Clay chewed more of his sub. This time, worry dimmed

some of his pleasure. "How are you holding up, given what all happened today?"

Ellie dropped her fork, sparing the piece of Romaine speared on the plastic tines from further torture. "Not great, to be honest. Calling up Dani's parents and telling them how their daughter died is an experience I hope to never repeat again." She pushed her plate away before slumping into her seat.

Jillian made a soft, sympathetic noise. "Sorry, Ellie. That had to be incredibly tough."

"Yeah. It was hard enough telling them their daughter was dead, but after all this time, at least they were both expecting that news. But the way she died? What's a good way to tell someone, 'I'm sorry, sir, but as it turns out, your daughter's last hours on earth were spent screaming in agony while a man slowly submerged her in acid, all to entertain a bunch of monsters on the dark web?'" Ellie wrapped her arms around her waist and rolled her head on her neck, grimacing as if the movement caused her pain.

Clay's heart ached for Dani's parents as well as for Ellie. He couldn't even begin to comprehend how traumatized he'd be if an officer showed up at his door and explained that Caraleigh had suffered horrific torture before having her young life snuffed out. The possibility alone turned his blood to ice.

He reached out and covered Ellie's warm hand with his, desperate to ease her guilt. "There's no good way to tell someone that kind of news. What's important in these situations is that the family sees that you care, and I know you made sure that came across."

Ellie's hand twitched beneath his as she inhaled a shaky breath. "Thank you. I do care, so hopefully, you're right." She sighed. "They said they want to attend Garrett's trial."

Jacob set down his beer and wiped a hand over his mouth. "Do we know what the charges are yet?"

Ellie lifted her shoulders, using the motion to pull her hand away from Clay's. "Not yet. Attempted kidnapping and possibly involuntary manslaughter at most for Roxanne's death because of the deal. Kidnapping and who knows what else for Dani. Then we have the other women, and that will take weeks or months to figure out. Right now, the D.A.'s waiting to see if Garrett will give them more information on the trafficking ring before they formalize anything."

Jillian's jaw dropped. "That's it? Kidnapping and maybe involuntary manslaughter? For the role he played in destroying Dani and Roxanne's lives?"

"Right? It's bullshit!" In her anger, Ellie waved her hands and struck her beer bottle. Clay steadied the container before the amber liquid spilled everywhere. "Our justice system sucks sometimes. First Katarina gets off scot-free in WITSEC, now Garrett."

Jillian stabbed a bite of food with her fork. "It's not fair."

Clay admired the fire shining in her green eyes as Ellie warmed to her topic. "Do you know how many cases actually go to trial these days?" She only waited a second before jumping in with the answer. "Three percent. That's it. The rest of the cases are pled out. Can you believe it? That's not how our system was intended to work."

After he finished chewing, Clay nodded. "No argument here. In my opinion, the fact that plea bargaining has become the rule rather than the exception is one of our biggest judicial fails."

"Right? And all to save money." Ellie's upper lip curled in disgust. "Apparently, trials cost too much, so what do we do instead? Plea deal."

"Money plus plea deals make legislators look good. We have

mandatory minimum sentencing laws from back in the seventies to thank for that." At the sight of Jillian's wrinkled brow, Clay leaned forward. "Back then, drug users faced long sentences for minor crimes. So instead of going to trial, which with mandatory minimums meant running the risk of serving out decades in jail, defendants started pleading guilty to a lesser charge. On the surface, it doesn't sound too terrible, right?"

Jillian shook her head. "No, it doesn't. What's the catch?"

"The catch is, innocent people end up taking plea bargains out of fear. You plead guilty, you almost always get a lighter sentence than if you're found guilty by a jury. Some estimates say as many as fifteen percent of the people who plead out are innocent."

Jillian choked on a crouton. "Hold up, fifteen percent? Wow. I had no idea. That's terrible."

"On one end of the spectrum, we have fifteen percent of people who end up in jail when they shouldn't be there, and on the other end, we have our John Garretts of the world. Bastards who traffic in human lives and end up with a slap on the wrist. The whole system is maddening." Ellie smacked her plate to emphasize her point, rattling the table and sending a tomato squirting out of her sandwich.

Clay unleashed his own frustration by wadding his empty foil wrapper into a tight ball. Ellie put her heart and soul into her work and genuinely cared about doing the right thing. In his experience, there was nothing more demoralizing to a good cop than when the system failed to work properly.

A loud ring made Clay grimace. He tossed the foil ball onto his plate and stood up. "Sorry."

Jacob waved his apology off. "Please. With three LEOs at the table, it's a miracle when one of our phones doesn't ring during dinner."

Clay was still smiling over Jacob's sad but true comment when he answered the call. "This is Special Agent Lockwood." Cradling the phone to his ear, he crossed into the kitchen.

"Agent Lockwood? We have a problem, a big one. Gabe's gone MIA."

Like he'd flipped a switch, Clay's amusement snapped off. He leaned his hands on the counter, bracing himself. "Okay, Frank, tell me everything you know."

Everything Frank knew didn't turn out to be very much. Within minutes, Clay hung up and muttered a curse. *Gabe, what the hell were you thinking?*

"What's going on? Did something happen?" Ellie was twisted in her chair, alarm pinching her pretty face.

Clay stalked back over to the table, wishing he had better news for her. "That was Frank. Gabe left the safe house."

Ellie's eyebrows knitted together. "Left as in, he went on a coffee run without telling Frank?"

"I wish." Clay's jaw tightened. "Left as in he wrote Frank a note saying Kingsley found him again and that he didn't feel safe. He's in the wind."

"Oh my god." Ellie reared back like she'd been struck.

"What was he thinking?" Jacob echoed Clay's earlier sentiment.

"I don't know, but hopefully we can find him and ask." Clay wished Ellie would say something else, but she only sat there staring at him, her green eyes wide with a fear he didn't like to witness.

"How did Kingsley find him again?"

Jillian asked the question that haunted them all, and Clay's jaw clenched even tighter at the possible explanations. None of them were good. Kingsley locating Gabe not once but twice sure seemed to indicate they had a leak in the WITSEC program, and if that were the case?

The hair on Clay's forearms lifted. A breach in the federal witness protection program meant they were in a shit load of trouble. Clay was still reeling when Ellie's phone chimed.

She tilted her screen so he could read the display —*unidentified caller*.

Clay sat up straighter. Could be nothing. Only one way to know for sure.

"Hey, quiet down." He tossed the command down the table before motioning Ellie to answer. Jacob and Jillian quit their hushed conversation, watching as Ellie placed her phone on the table and accepted the call in speaker mode.

"Hello, Detective Kline speaking. May I ask who's calling?"

A high-pitched wheeze, like the sound a person made when they struggled to draw air into their lungs, was the only response.

Ellie lowered her voice. "Gabe? Is that you?"

A pause. "Y-yes."

The stuttered reply cracked the tension in the room like an ice pick. Gabe was still alive.

For now.

Ellie wiped her palms on her pants before replying. "Are you okay? Where are you? What were you thinking?"

Sobs erupted into the dining room. "I'm s-sorry," Gabe gasped, "I d-didn't know what else to d-do."

Clay bit back an angry retort, reminding himself to let Ellie talk first. Watching her chest rise and fall in an obvious sign of distress wasn't doing much to keep his temper in check, though.

"Shh, it's okay. I'm the one who's sorry for snapping like that. I'm just worried about you. Can you take a few breaths and let me know what happened?" Ellie's voice was soft and soothing.

Gabe hiccupped. "Y-yeah."

Clay squeezed the wooden back of his chair, preparing

for Gabe's explanation. Whatever had spooked the man into running probably wasn't pretty.

Duke's whine from his dog bed broke the silence first. After giving up on begging, the shepherd had curled into a ball to nap, but the tension radiating from the dinner table must have roused him. While Jacob shushed him, Gabe sniffled and cleared his throat.

"Kingsley found me again. I don't know how. When Frank was away, he had a smartphone delivered to the new safe house, and later that same day, I got an alert prompting me to accept a video call. It was him. Kingsley. He wore a mask, but I'd recognize his voice anywhere."

Clay exchanged a grim look with Ellie. This was bad. Real bad.

On the other end, Gabe drew in a shaky breath, as if he needed extra strength to get the next part out. "He...he wasn't alone. There was a man tied to a chair. Kingsley, he... he tortured him in front of me. Said I had to play his game." Another sniffle. "Kingsley cut off the man's finger, then his ear. That poor man, he was screaming so loud...I had to say the words. I couldn't let him suffer like that. I—"

While Gabe broke off and struggled to compose himself, Clay performed a sweep of the table. Jillian's face had turned pale. Jacob was glowering at his plate. Ellie was still, her green eyes glazed. Like she was trapped in an internal nightmare.

"Then he sent me a photo of a woman. He, oh god, he chopped her head off and carved *ha ha* into her belly." Gabe was speaking so softly now, Clay had to strain to hear. "The caption was, *your time is up*. After that, I wasn't about to stick around until he made good on that promise, so I bolted."

Clay's concern for Ellie grew when Gabe's announcement appeared to have no effect on her. She didn't react. Didn't move. She stared at that same spot on the table while a fine layer of perspiration glistened on her cheeks.

Clay tapped her shoulder to get her attention, breaking the spell.

"Bolted. Right." Ellie blinked a few times, and he could practically see her giving herself a mental shake. "Where are you headed? Do you have anywhere to go?"

"Portland, for now. My plan is to find somewhere to lay low and then leave the state."

Ellie lifted her chin, and Clay's locked muscles eased a little. For a moment there, he'd been worried that Gabe's story was triggering her own Kingsley PTSD and causing her brain to shut down. He should have known better. The woman sitting by his side was one of the strongest people he'd ever met. "Okay, when you get to Portland, sit tight. I'm booking myself on a flight out to Portland first thing tomorrow morning." Ellie tugged at a stray curl. "For now, though, you should head to the nearest police station."

"No. No police station. I won't chance it. Not when we don't know how Kingsley keeps finding my safe houses."

Ellie bit her lip before glancing up at Clay for his reaction. He nodded, unable to fault the other man's logic. With two safe houses blown, chances were that someone in law enforcement was leaking information on Gabe's whereabouts. She sighed, still fidgeting with that same curl. "Understandable. Do you have cab fare to get to Portland?"

"Not that much, no."

Clay's shoulders tensed again. Wandering the streets without money upped Gabe's risk even more.

"Okay, what if I wired you some money?" Ellie asked.

Gabe hesitated. "I'd be too afraid that someone might trace it."

"Okay." Ellie clasped her hands on the table and exhaled. "You know you can trust me, right?"

"I do know that. Right now, you're the only person I do trust, Ellie. But for all we know, Kingsley could be spying on you as we speak too."

Jillian's hand flew to her mouth, covering up a tiny gasp while Ellie flinched. Clay balled his hands into fists, wishing he could reach through the phone and slap a piece of duct tape over Gabe's mouth. The other man wasn't telling them anything new, but still. Ellie didn't need the reminder right now.

The skin over Ellie's knuckles blanched as she clasped her hands even tighter. "How about a burner phone? Do you have enough money to buy a new one?"

"M-maybe? I think so. I'm going to dump this one as soon as we're done talking, but I'll contact you if I get a new one."

"And if you can't get a new one? What area of the city can we find you in?"

"I'll figure out a way to contact you somehow." A prolonged noise blared in the background. A truck driver, Clay guessed, laying on his horn. Gabe waited until the racket stopped before finishing. "I've gotta go now. I'll be in touch."

Gabe cut out, and red letters flashed across the screen. *Call ended.* Ellie glared at the phone before tossing the device aside and turning to Clay. "We need to book flights to Portland, first thing in the morning."

Jacob shook his head. "I'm not sure—"

"I wasn't talking to you." Ellie crossed her arms over her chest and glowered at Clay, like she expected him to disagree too.

Clay lifted his hands. "Hey, no argument from me. Let me call Frank back, and then you can call Fortis and let him know what's going on."

When she realized he wasn't going to fight her on this, the belligerence eased from Ellie's expression, softening the lines of her face. "Okay." She pressed her fingertips to her temples. "Thanks."

"I've got your back. We'll find him."

Clay vowed right then and there to turn his reassurance into reality. He called Frank back and quickly filled the marshal in on their plan. "Yeah, you too. Talk soon." When he finished, he nodded at Ellie. "You're up."

Ellie entered Fortis's number on her screen and then waited. The phone rang four times before the head detective answered.

"You again?" Fortis groaned. "You're off the clock now, you know that, right? More important, I'm off the clock. I was just settling in with a Corona and an episode of *The Great British Bakeoff*, so make it quick."

Across the table, Jillian snorted and clapped a hand to her mouth to smother a giggle. Even Jacob snickered. Clay couldn't blame them. Not to stereotype, but he was also struggling to picture the gruff detective cheering on contestants as they sifted flour and assembled baked goods.

"Does that mean there are some homemade cookies in my future? If so, I like chocolate chip."

At Ellie's quip, Clay bit his cheek to hold in a laugh. If she was back to giving Fortis the business, then he knew she'd snapped out of her funk. For now.

"*Kline...*"

Ellie smirked before growing serious. "Right. So, we had a little development this evening. Gabe called. Apparently, Kingsley tracked him down again, so Gabe left the safe house on his own. He doesn't trust anyone except me, and I can't say I blame him."

"Jesus. Okay, start from the beginning and don't leave out a single detail."

As Ellie walked Fortis through the last hour, Clay planned ahead. He'd need to let the local FBI office know his itinerary, then give the Portland office a heads-up that they'd be in the area. Then, they needed to come up with a course of action for when they touched down in Oregon. Especially if Gabe wasn't able to contact them again.

Of course, all of this was dependent on Fortis giving Ellie the okay to go.

If only he'd gotten all the pieces of the task force put in place sooner...

Clay tuned back in, right when she got to the big ask. "I want to fly out to Portland with Clay. We can't strand Gabe there, with no money and nowhere to go." The pink flush to her cheeks and stubborn tilt to her chin testified that she was prepared to fight, if necessary.

"You have my blessing to go to Portland, on one condition. Make sure that you attend any and all relevant press conferences and when you do, let everyone know you work for Charleston PD. Can you do that?"

Ellie rolled her eyes at the phone. "Yes, I can do that."

"Good. Send me your flight details once you've booked it. Now, if that's all, I'm hanging up. No offense, but the only voices I want to hear right now have British accents."

When the call ended, Jillian burst out laughing. Duke padded over to the table to investigate what all the commotion was about. "I'm sorry, but I would never have guessed in a million years that Fortis was a GBBO super fan." She turned to study Jacob through narrowed eyes. "You know, I wouldn't mind if you decided to take up baking as a hobby, just saying."

Duke barked at that precise moment, making all of them laugh. Especially Jillian. "See, even Duke agrees, don't you, boy?" She scratched behind the shepherd's triangular ears, and his tongue lolled out of his mouth.

Ellie rose from the table and disappeared into her

bedroom. She returned with her laptop, plunking it down on the table. "Aisle or window?"

Clay shrugged. "Either. As long as we're sitting together."

The dining room filled with the steady tap-tap of her fingers as they flew along the keys. The sound plucked at Clay's nerves, like a crow pecking at a power line. Sure, Clay worried about Gabe's safety. Mostly, though, he was uneasy about a trip that might once again lure Ellie closer to Kingsley's web.

"All set! We fly out at 8:03 a.m."

When Ellie finished with her laptop, her green eyes blazed, like she was ready to take on the entire world if that was what saving Gabe required.

Clay made a new vow, right then and there. For the duration of the Portland trip, he wasn't going to let Ellie out of his sight.

19

Headlights cut the evening sky as Gabe hurried down the darkened sidewalk, training his eyes on the ground ahead. Despite the plummeting temperature, a handful of pedestrians still scurried back and forth on either side of the street in the Portland suburb, huddled into sweatshirts and jackets.

He tugged his own hood lower over his forehead, the gesture as much to protect him from the cold air and icy northwestern wind nipping at his cheeks and nose as it was to hide his identity from any onlookers. Gabe had hoped that leaving the safe house would soothe his jangling nerves, but he'd been deluding himself. At least in the safe house, he'd had walls to protect him. Out here, alone on the street, he felt too exposed.

A clatter rang out from behind him, and he nearly jumped out of his skin. A thump followed. Gabe froze, straining to hear. *Footsteps?*

As he glanced over his shoulder, his quads tightened, preparing to run. The soft glow of a diner's interior lights revealed an orange tabby, racing away from a tipped trash can. Still, Gabe hurried his pace, pulling his hood even tighter to his face. After waiting for a red pickup truck to whoosh past, he darted out into the street, rejecting the crosswalk at an intersection that was only a half a block ahead. Once he hopped onto the opposite sidewalk, Gabe risked another peek behind him.

The path remained clear. None of the other walkers paid him any attention. So far, anyway.

Gabe reached the intersection, crossing when the light turned green. About a half-block up, he ducked into a drug store. After the anonymity of the gathering darkness outside, the fluorescent lights made him twitch. He grabbed a red basket, idled his way through the aisles, and once satisfied that Kingsley wasn't going to pop out at any second, selected a sharp-looking knife from a shelf.

Gabe wanted to stay at a motel for the night, but he'd fled the house with little cash. An encampment might be his best bet anyway in Portland. He could disappear into the crowd of other homeless souls, like a scrap of hay in a haystack. Didn't matter where he ended up crashing because, either way, he'd feel more comfortable with a weapon tucked beneath his head.

Even the sight of the knife in his basket inflated Gabe's courage. He took his time meandering the rest of the store, pausing in the refrigerated section. He added a bottle of water to the basket and headed for the cashier. Two teen girls giggled as they approached him going the opposite way, so Gabe ducked his head and kept walking.

His basket bounced off a solid object, stopping Gabe in his tracks.

"Oof. Sorry."

Gabe muttered the apology to the man he'd bumped into, catching a glimpse of a shiny, balding head and bushy eyebrows before hurrying past. This had been a mistake. The store's lights glared down on him like he was on a stage, leaving him far too exposed. The sooner he disappeared back into the night, the better.

Luckily, no one waited in line at the register. Gabe scooted his two items onto the counter, jiggling his leg while the bored mid-twenties man with a goatee rang him up at glacial speed. Despite the cold air, Gabe's armpits were damp with sweat by the time he grabbed his bag. He scurried from the store at a pace a few clicks shy of a run.

The night swallowed him up again, and Gabe's anxiety ebbed. To be sure, he found a hidden spot near a purified water fill-up station, where he crouched on his heels and waited. Several minutes ticked by, without anyone else exiting the store. Gabe swiped his forehead on his hoody sleeve and finally allowed his muscles to relax. His imagination was working overtime. No one was following him.

Your time is up.

Gabe shivered and readjusted his hood as Kingsley's caption rolled around in his head. A perfect reminder that even if he was acting paranoid, he had a damned good reason. Three innocent people. By his count, that was the number of people Kingsley had already murdered to get back at Gabe. At least. So, when he'd threatened Gabe with that message, claiming he was next, Gabe tended to believe him.

On the street ahead, brake lights flashed red. A horn beeped. Gabe shivered again and resumed walking. An aroma of sweet cheese wafted from a pizza place down the road, but Gabe's gut churned too much to consider eating. His mind replayed scenes from Kingsley's video call, souring his stomach even more.

That poor man. If Gabe wasn't such a wimp, he would have said the three magic words sooner. Instead, he'd frozen, letting the man suffer for his cowardice. Those brutal images, along with the shrill pain in the man's screams, would haunt Gabe until his dying day. All those deaths piled high on his conscience. The man. The headless woman.

Rob.

His heart twisted at the reminder of what he'd lost. Gabe quickened his pace, as if moving his legs faster could help him outrun the past. One block passed in no time. On a side street, he spotted a flickering motel sign.

His breath puffed little clouds in front of him. He hesitated. The homeless encampment in Portland was probably his safest bet, but a hot bath sounded divine right now. Maybe he could sweet-talk the owner into giving him a late-night discount. Rob always told him that his grin could charm the pants off anyone.

Another sharp pain in his chest. God, he'd do anything to bring Rob back, but that was a child's dream. All Gabe could do was keep moving. His gaze drifted up to the motel sign. But first, he'd try to haggle his way into a tub and soft bed.

Decision made, Gabe tucked his hands into his pockets and rounded the next corner, only to pull up short when a figure blocked his path.

"Excuse me," Gabe muttered while staring at the ground. He veered to the left.

The figure veered left too.

Gabe's pulse shot up. He forced himself to breathe. Probably an accident. "Sorry, looks like we're dancing. I'll go right this time."

He lifted his head to offer the stranger a smile and stumbled. His legs shook, and he blinked in rapid succession. The streetlights spun as Gabe tried and failed to deny reality. The balding head and bushy eyebrows belonged to the customer at the convenience store. The man Gabe had bumped into on his way to the register.

Run. Now.

Adrenaline flooded his veins, urging his body into fight

or flight mode. Gabe pivoted to flee, but two strong arms locked around his chest from behind.

Frantic now, Gabe wiggled and thrashed, only to have his captor squeeze so hard Gabe worried his ribs might crack. The bald man from the convenience store was skinny but strong and seemed to have no trouble turning Gabe toward a van idling by the curb. The side panel door slid open.

Gabe drew air deep into his lungs. His captor's hand clamped over Gabe's mouth, smothering his scream with a fleshy palm that reeked of garlic. The man shoved him toward the van while Gabe's head jerked left and right, seeking a bystander. A witness. Someone to call 911.

As he was propelled toward the open door, Gabe spotted two pedestrians. Hope flared in his chest. *Please. Help me.* They lifted their phones to film his kidnapping, and the flame died as the truth seeped in. No one cared about him beyond their next social media story. His kidnapping would be documented, but by the time the police found him, Gabe would be long gone.

Gabe fought harder the last two steps, kicking and squirming for everything he was worth. His captor overpowered him, shoving him into the van with an ease that was embarrassing. Instead of bird-watching these past few months, he should have been lifting weights and taking self-defense classes.

Even as he renewed his struggle, Gabe tripped and hit the floor. Dazed, he laid there unmoving for a few moments, inhaling a pungent mix of garlic and sweaty feet. The door slammed shut behind him, and tires squealed as the van accelerated into the street.

"Hello, Gabriel."

Gabe rolled over at the greeting from a voice that sounded all too familiar. The man from the convenience store was gone, and a new stranger leered down at him, holding an object in his hand. A syringe. Gabe scooted away, but the man grabbed his leg and yanked him back.

The man's bright smile was the last thing Gabe saw before the sting of a needle pierced his neck. The drug burned on the way into his bloodstream. As the van swerved around a corner and Gabe's world blurred at the edges, the man sat down on the van floor beside him, pulling Gabe's head into his lap.

"Sweet dreams."

The world went dark to the sensation of the strange man stroking Gabe's hair.

20

B ethany climbed out of the car and adjusted the straps of her pink backpack before turning back to Katarina to wave. "Bye, Mama!" With her rosy cheeks and twin braids peeping out from beneath her purple knit pom-pom hat, she resembled one of those dolls Katarina had always wanted as a kid but never gotten.

"Bye, baby. Have a good day."

"You too!"

The girl slammed the door closed and skipped away. Katarina waited until Bethany disappeared into a crowd of kids in rainbow-colored jackets before pulling away from the curb. She took a circuitous route on the way back to the little house, driving up one street and down another. Another long day full of TV, brooms, and boredom loomed before her. There was no reason to hurry home.

After a while, though, the sprawling neighborhoods all started to look the same. Katarina grew tired of ranch-style homes and Subarus. Even the majestic Tetons that towered over the town like sentinels were losing their appeal. Katarina stabbed the button to roll her window down and screamed.

"Ahhh!"

For an instant, the release softened the edges of her angst. But then the breeze ripped her cry away, letting the frustration rush back in. Katarina exhaled and accepted defeat. Soap operas and vacuums, coming right up.

Resigned to her fate, Katarina navigated to her own address, but as soon as she turned into the safe house driveway, her cell phone dinged. After shutting off the engine, she checked the message.

Meet me at the Statehouse restaurant at noon. Dress nice.

Katarina stared at the text until the meaning sank in, and her mood pivoted in a complete one-eighty. A new restaurant and a chance to meet up with Clayne? Yes, please.

Smiling now, she bounced her way inside. After a long soak in a bubble bath, she toweled off and sifted through the contents of her closet. What to wear, what to wear. She inspected a shin-length, cream-colored knit dress before discarding the idea. Pretty, but the material clung too much to hide the knife Katarina planned on carrying.

She ended up choosing a gray wool turtleneck dress that skimmed her curves and ended above her knee, pairing the look with black suede over-the-knee boots. Sexy but sophisticated, and more importantly, the skirt hid her thigh sheath. A gun she'd managed to buy from a Craigslist ad fit perfectly in her purse. After styling her dark hair into soft waves and adding a pair of small gold hoop earrings and a matching wrist bangle, Katarina was ready to go.

When she pushed open the carved wooden door and entered the restaurant, she paused in the marble entryway to admire the elegant interior design. Chandeliers glittered down upon sleek dark tables surrounded by chairs upholstered in rich burgundy and gold. A well-dressed group chatted over plates of game fowl and perfectly charred steaks, and the sweet aromas reached Katarina's nose, making her stomach rumble. A gold bucket in the middle of the table held a bottle of champagne on ice. Not bad, Wyoming.

"Can I help you?"

Katarina inspected the blonde hostess smiling from her little station. Good haircut, chic black dress, and the diamonds sparkling in her ears were real. "I'm here to meet Clayne Miller."

"Yes, of course. If you'll follow me, please."

To Katarina's surprise, the hostess led her to the far back corner of the dining room, where a door opened to reveal a private conference room.

"Here you go, enjoy your meal."

The hostess exited the room and closed the door behind her, leaving Katarina to scope the place out. She did a double take when she spotted Clayne decked out in a charcoal suit that made the most of his strong body. Wow. She never would have pegged Clayne as part of the men-who-brunch set.

As she approached, Clayne shook the hand of another well-dressed, dark-haired man wearing a beautiful navy suit, the cut of which pinged Katarina's internal radar. Sure, Clayne cleaned up nice, but she'd bet money that the newcomer's suit was custom-tailored. If Katarina had to guess, she'd peg the price tag at five thousand. Easy.

Katarina licked her lips. Things were about to get interesting.

Tossing her hair, Katarina sauntered over to the well-dressed duo, adding a little extra swing to her hips. Clayne caught sight of her, and his face broke into a wide grin. Before she guessed his intention, his arm whipped out and wrapped around her waist. She didn't need an explanation.

She knew a man who was staking his claim when she saw one.

"Well, don't you look good enough to eat?" Clayne's blue gaze raked over her from head to toe before he turned to the other man. "Katrina, I'd like you to meet Lance Martinez. Lance, this is my girl, Katrina Cook."

His girl.

Katarina shook Lance's hand without so much as blinking at Clayne's unexpected introduction. "Nice to meet you."

"Likewise." Lance's gaze lingered on Katarina's thighs a beat too long before he released her hand and stepped away. He looked down his long nose at her and gestured to the table. "Shall we sit?"

Katarina didn't mind the peep show. On the contrary, Lance's distraction equaled power. She eased into the chair that Clayne held out for her and studied the menu. As soon as she noted that neither man bothered, she snapped the embossed   leather   binder   shut   again.   "Any recommendations?"

"Everything here is good, but the steaks are out of this world."

When the waitress came to take their order, Katarina made sure to order a steak. The filet, medium-rare. Clayne and Lance both ordered the rib-eye. Clayne asked for his to be cooked medium-rare while Lance glowered at the server.

"Rare as in I expect the damn thing to be this close to mooing." Lance held his thumb and pointer finger a fraction of an inch apart to demonstrate.

"Yes, sir."

Lance flicked his hand in dismissal, and the waitress scurried over to fill their crystal goblets from a wine bottle near the fresh floral centerpiece. As soon as she gathered their menus and left them alone, Clayne jumped right down to business. "Good news. Lance here is looking to expand his

Denver business and wants me to work under him. That means more revenue for both of us. Isn't that great?"

Katarina sipped the white wine that Lance had ordered without her input and remembered how much she despised taking commands from other people. Men like Kingsley, for example. And Lance.

Always so arrogant, with the way they sneered down their noses in their expensive suits. She laid her hand on Clayne's forearm. "Great, baby, but I can't help but think this organizational chart is all wrong. You should be in charge of the business, and Lance here can work under *you*."

Katarina hid a smile when Lance choked on his wine. "Excuse me?" The dark-skinned man patted his mouth with a linen napkin and pinned his bored smile back in place. His brown eyes burned into Katarina, though. "Clayne, you should educate your friend about the vast scale of my empire, so we can avoid embarrassing misunderstandings like this in the future."

"Of course." Clayne turned to Katarina and proceeded to do as requested. His closest hand slipped under the table, though, stroking her thigh as he rattled on. Appreciation, she guessed, for her vote of confidence. "Although, it might not be a bad idea to give me a little bigger chunk of the business to run. I have the contacts out here to make sure we're successful."

After a little back and forth, Lance stroked his chin and agreed. "Okay. We'll give it a try. Better make sure you can deliver." Mild tone or not, his warning was clear.

"Not a problem." Clayne squeezed her thigh as he replied, making Katarina's skin tingle.

The men were ironing out the details when the waitress reappeared, placing their meals in front of them. Katarina inhaled the delicious mixture of beef and garlic-mashed potatoes wafting off her plate. She sank her teeth into the first bite and almost moaned when the juices washed over her tongue.

"What'd I tell you? Good, right?"

Katarina finished chewing the tender bite. "Delicious." After sampling her potatoes and finding them equally divine, she set down her fork. "I don't mean to overstep, but I'd be happy to offer up a few ideas on how to grow your business if you're interested."

Lance's hands stilled in the process of cutting off another bite of steak that appeared bloody enough to satisfy a vampire. He flicked her another condescending look before leaning back in his chair and yawning. "Sure, why not?"

When he checked his Rolex, Katarina's eyes narrowed, but she kept her cool. She spoke for ten minutes, and his entire demeanor transformed. Maybe Kingsley had served a good purpose in her life after all. He certainly had taught her how to run a profitable business.

By the end, Lance hung on her every word, his bloody meat forgotten on his plate. He surveyed her with an appreciative gleam in his eyes. An expression Katarina much preferred to his snooty one.

"Aren't you full of surprises?" Lance mused out loud. Katarina sank back into the plush burgundy and gold chair with both her belly and pride satisfied while he and Clayne shook on the deal.

After they finished eating, they headed outside, where a beefy man with sunglasses and close-cropped hair waited to usher Lance into an SUV with tinted windows. A driver with an identical brawny build sat behind the wheel.

Katarina studied the men, her internal radar pinging once again. These men were way too fit to be chauffeurs, not to mention the telltale gun-shaped bulge beneath the closest one's jacket. Security detail, in Wyoming? Unexpected, to say the least. Her eyes narrowed. Maybe Lance Martinez hadn't been inflating the magnitude of his operation, after all.

The bodyguard opened the back door of the SUV wide. Before Lance stepped inside, he turned to address them both. Katarina noted with satisfaction that he didn't talk over her anymore. "You'll be hearing from me soon." His gaze lingered on Katarina for another few seconds, and then he ducked into the back seat.

Clayne tracked the SUV as the vehicle accelerated out of the parking lot, then picked Katarina up by the waist, planted a big kiss on her lips, and spun her around in a circle. "Woot! That went great, and I owe part of it to you!"

Even as she whirled through the air, her mood buoyed by Clayne's obvious excitement, Katarina's skin bristled over his short-sightedness. She waited until her feet touched the ground to ask the question burning her tongue. "Why didn't you tell me that I'd be attending a meeting when you texted me?" One thing that Katarina despised more than anything was feeling unprepared.

Her irritation must have shown because Clayne flashed her his little boy grin. "Uh oh, is someone miffed at me? Sorry, darlin', but I needed to watch how you'd handle yourself in a business situation without advance warning. That was the first part of the test, which you passed with flying colors. Now all that's left is the second part."

Clayne's car pulled up before Katarina could respond. Probably for the best. Her mind was whirling with ideas over what the second part of the test held in store. Excitement crackled through her body, zapping any lingering remnants of irritation and boredom, and instead, it fired her muscles with pure energy. She spent the fifteen-minute ride feeling on edge in the most delightful way.

Focused. Alive. Full of purpose.

The car stopped in an industrial lot. Katarina climbed

out, and Clayne guided her to a massive white warehouse. Using a keypad, he unlocked the outer door and led her inside. The first thing Katarina noticed were the men with semi-automatic weapons. By her count, no less than fifteen patrolled the building.

Her attention shifted from the men to the objects filling the long rows of shelves, which was when Katarina noticed the second thing. She stifled a gasp. Cocaine. Tons and tons of cocaine. More packets of the white powder in one place than she'd ever seen in her life.

She didn't have time to take in much beyond those two details because Clayne kept walking, winding his way past the shelves. He led her toward an enclosed room in the middle of the warehouse and paused with one hand on the doorknob.

"I want to show you how we treat traitors in my operation."

He opened the door with a flourish. Two men sat inside a bare room that reeked of cigarettes and urine, both of them tied to chairs.

Katarina's heart drummed harder in her chest as she entered the room, only she wasn't quite sure what was triggering her body's reaction. Fear over what Clayne had planned for the men? Maybe a little, even though she'd taken part in plenty of similar scenarios in her life. Or stress over how her involvement in this could affect Bethany? Possibly. But as Katarina eased into an empty chair and watched Clayne remove his jacket and shirt in preparation, the electricity sizzling through her veins intensified, and she knew.

Katarina was broken. Undeniably. Permanently.

What else could explain the fact that sweeping and dusting made her feel like a withered, hollowed out old tree, whereas crime and pain lit a spark inside her soul?

She gritted her teeth, rejecting the idea. That was the old

Katarina. Not Katrina Cook. Katrina had Bethany, and the two of them were a family. But the humming in her veins told a different story.

"If this gets too bloody for you, baby, holler." Clayne tossed that comment over his shoulder as he approached the first man.

Katarina's breathing quickened. She leaned forward in her chair as Clayne prowled around the cowering man and lectured him in his easy drawl.

"You really thought you'd get away with it, Luis? Steal from me?" Clayne cracked his knuckles, one by one. A sharp, ominous sound in the quiet little room. "Come on, buddy. How could you be that dumb? You should know me better by now. I'm a greedy man, and no one takes what's mine without paying the price."

His fists flew without warning, striking the man in the face and gut. When blood spurted from Luis's nose, Clayne turned to the other man, who'd squeezed his eyes shut after the first punch. "And you, Shawn. You think so little of me that you'd steal from the business that puts clothes on your back? That feeds your family?"

The man shook his head, which only aggravated Clayne. He struck Shawn several times, until the man's face began to swell and blood dribbled off his chin. By the time Clayne quit swinging and retreated, his knuckles resembled raw meat.

He turned to Katarina and squatted down. "See, baby? That's how it's done. You doing okay? Not too much blood for you?"

Katarina shook her head to reply. Horror held her tongue hostage.

Not horror over being a party to torture, but rather over the stark realization that struck her like a shovel to the skull. Katarina was bored again. The anticipation leading up to the first blood draw had faded away, leaving her skin itching to jump in and teach Clayne more artful methods.

Clayne rose and focused his attention back to the first man, Luis, and Katarina rationalized her next steps. To keep Bethany safe, Katarina needed to feed her inner monster. Her sharp edges kept her alive, and after weeks spent wasting her wits away, Katarina understood that the longer she was trapped in that little house, the quicker her edge would vanish.

Only the strong survived, and denial of this hard-learned lesson wouldn't change that.

Katarina owed it to her daughter to be strong.

Acceptance flowed over her like a sun-kissed breeze. Katarina rose and walked over to the armed man guarding the doorway. His sneer as he stepped aside to allow her to exit told her he'd assumed she was weak and running away. A nasty grin curved her lips. Proving arrogant men wrong never failed to fill her with joy.

She reached beneath her dress and whipped the knife from the thigh sheath, relishing the widening of the guard's eyes at the way the weapon materialized in her hand. "I came prepared, but I need you to grab me an additional knife and two sets of pliers." When the doofus only stood gaping, she feinted closer, until the blade's tip hovered less than an inch from the fleshy spot beneath his left clavicle. "*Now.*"

The guard's sneer fell away, and he backed out of the room. He returned with the requested items quickly. Katarina didn't bother to thank him as she plucked the tools from his hands and carried them back inside. Still shirtless, Clayne leaned against the wall, with his defined chest speckled red from other men's blood. He watched her approach like a jungle cat, all lazy posture and predatory eyes.

"How about a little change of pace?" Katarina extended one of the pliers toward him. He pushed away from the wall and prowled over to her. She dropped the tool into his outstretched hand. "Right or left?"

Clayne tapped the pliers against his open palm. "Left."

"That means Shawn is all yours, and I get Luis."

Katarina sidled up to the man on the right and sighed. It felt good, no longer fighting to deny her enjoyment of his delicious, wide-eyed panic. "I was raised to appreciate torture for what it should be, an art form rather than brute force. When you're strategic and use the right tools, inflicting pain doesn't require great strength or effort. Only a plan. Watch."

She inserted the last digit of the man's pinky finger between the grips of the pliers and squeezed. The man's scream pierced the air as his nail cracked beneath the metal. Once the nail was crushed, Katarina released the pressure on the pliers. Lowering her grip, Katarina applied the curved tip to dig into the exposed pink skin. Luis's screams intensified as she pried the entire nail away from his flesh.

"See? No injuries," she flashed her pristine knuckles, "and I didn't even break a sweat, and yet, by the sound of Luis's screams, this method was more effective. You want to give it a try?"

Clayne smiled. "Hell, yeah!" He lifted the pliers and repeated the process on the other prisoner. Not as effortlessly as Katarina, but she expected him to be a little clumsy at first. When it came to torture techniques, practice really did make perfect.

When Clayne finished and faced Katarina, he was grinning from ear to ear. "That was fun, now what?"

She shrugged. "Weren't there some questions you wanted answered?"

Clayne nodded. "Yeah, I want to know if anyone else was involved with these two peckerheads in the theft, among other things. I wouldn't peg either of them as the ringleader."

Twirling the knife, Katarina turned back to the men. "Look at me." She waited until she had their attention. "Now, we're going to play a game involving speed and timing. I know that sounds like a lot, but I promise it's very simple." She crouched in front of Luis so that she could look him right in the eye. "I'm going to ask a question. Afterward, I'll count to three. Are you with me so far?"

Luis choked out a, "Yes."

Katarina patted his head. "Good job." She straightened and crossed the short distance to where Shawn sat. "On the count of three, you will both answer the question at the same time. When your answers match, then you win, and we skip additional persuasive tactics for that round. But if your answers aren't identical, well…" Katarina tapped the knife against her open palm, and Shawn shuddered.

When she moved to stand between them, both men's foreheads and cheeks were drenched in sweat. "Are you ready?" Katarina ignored the men's shaking heads and whimpered *noes*. "The first question is…tell me the name of who came up with the idea to steal from your boss in the first place."

She paused a beat and then kicked off the countdown. "One." Katarina watched the men squirm. "Two." One more second ticked by. "Three."

Shawn blurted his answer a millisecond before Luis. "Andy!"

"Me!"

Katarina clucked her tongue. "Uh oh. That answer does not appear to match, sorry." Without warning, Katarina lunged forward and plunged the knife deep into Luis's thigh. He was still shrieking when she feinted to the right and stabbed Shawn in the exact same spot. As she danced away, a sharp, ammonia-like odor stung her nose. She smiled. Loss of bladder control was a sign of success. Katarina returned to

Clayne's side and gave his bicep a quick squeeze. "Be a dear and pull those out for me, won't you?"

Clayne did as she asked. Once Katarina held the knives, now streaked red with blood, she started over. "Now, let's try that again, shall we?"

This time around, both men yelled the same thing. "Andy!"

Clayne's employees turned out to be quick learners. Katarina only had to stab them once more in the opposite thigh before all their answers matched. Too bad. The session ended so fast, Katarina feared she hadn't gotten a chance to showcase her skills to the max. Oh well, there was always next time. She shrugged as she turned to Clayne. "What's your plan for them now?"

Clayne tucked a loose strand of hair behind her ear. "I was gonna off them, but maybe you have something better in mind?"

Katarina glanced over her shoulder at the two sweaty, bleeding men. "I thought we might use them to send a message."

Clayne sucked on his lower lip. "Yeah, I can get behind that." He barked at the door. "Get these peckerheads out of here, lock 'em back up for now."

Two of the armed men entered, slashed the men's restraints, and dragged them away, trailing a path of bloody track marks behind them. As soon as they disappeared, Clayne grabbed Katarina by the shoulders and slammed her up against the wall. His fingers dug into her hips while his mouth ground into hers.

The violence of the last hour acted like an aphrodisiac, shooting liquid heat through Katarina's cells and filling her with need. She raked her nails into his shoulders while she kissed him back, giving free rein to the frantic passion that arched her spine and plastered her body to his.

His teeth nipped at her throat, and she sighed as the pain-filled pleasure washed over her. She allowed her head to fall back, savoring the sensations while she still could.

She needed to commit the pleasurable feelings to memory now, because Katarina doubted she'd let Clayne live long enough to create many more.

21

A t five-thirty the next morning, Jillian whizzed down the highway toward the airport, slamming on the brakes when a silver BMW changed lanes at the last second and cut her off.

"You knucklehead!" She reached out to make sure her travel mug was still safe in the cupholder before shaking her fist at the other car. "You're lucky you didn't spill my coffee!"

"We're good too. Thanks for checking."

Jillian rolled her eyes at Ellie before focusing her attention back out the windshield. "Hey, a girl has her priorities in the morning. Coffee comes first."

"I'll drink to that."

Jillian's rearview mirror showed Clay saluting her with his cup from the back seat.

"Now that our lives are no longer flashing before our eyes, can we get back to discussing our game plan once we get to Portland? Or lack thereof, I guess I should say."

At Ellie's reminder of the trip's purpose, Jillian's humor melted away. Right. Ellie and Clay were flying to Portland to track down Gabe without a clear strategy in mind for achieving that goal. She changed lanes to get around the terrible driver in front of her, but now her mind was too preoccupied with Portland to bother with flipping him off. "Are you two sure this is a good idea? Maybe you should wait until you hear from Gabe again."

Clay leaned forward, resting his forearm on the back of Ellie's seat. "We're not sure of anything, but this is what Ellie wants to do, and I support her decision."

Jillian bit her lip. She didn't like this. Not at all. "Ellie?"

Her friend blew out a frustrated breath. "I'm not feeling much more confident than Clay is. What I do know is that, until Gabe contacts us again, our hands are tied. The one thing we do in the meantime is make sure we're already on the ground in Portland, ready to go when he calls."

If he calls, Jillian corrected, but only in her head. Ellie was stressed enough without Jillian adding to her friend's worries. She sipped her latte, hoping another injection of caffeine might calm her fears.

"Once he makes contact, we'll pick him up and let Frank know. Then we'll figure out a way to transfer him to a new safe house. Although…" Ellie released an angst-filled growl.

Out of the corner of her eye, Jillian caught Clay giving her friend's shoulder a reassuring squeeze. "Hey. I have faith that we'll figure out where the leak came from, but if for some reason we can't, then we'll hide Gabe ourselves until we do. Deal?"

Ellie sighed. "Deal."

After one more squeeze, Clay released Ellie's shoulder and dropped back into his seat.

Jillian snuck a quick peek at Ellie's grim expression and sighed. Not for the first time, she wished that her friend and Clay would quit being so darned stubborn and give in to their feelings for each other already. The fact that they were still into each other was so obvious, even Jacob had noticed.

For a big tough FBI agent, Clay wore his heart pretty openly on his sleeve. As for Ellie...

She studied her friend's tight-lipped profile before turning her attention back to the road. Ellie hid her feelings better, but every now and then, Jillian detected an intense yearning in her friend's green eyes when she watched Clay from across the room.

Jillian made an impatient noise in her throat. Maybe she should mind her own business but living with the pair of star-crossed lovers made butting out tough. Especially for her. She had Ellie to thank for the happiness she'd discovered with Jacob. Was it so wrong that Jillian wished for that same happiness to find her best friend? Clay and Ellie were perfect for each other. Nothing like that spoiled ex of hers.

She navigated the morning traffic, marveling over how much had happened over the past year. If Fortis hadn't banished Ellie to the basement to work on cold cases, she and Jillian might never have become friends. In turn, Ellie wouldn't have introduced Jillian to Jacob, and the four of them wouldn't be cohabitating in a house with two dogs. Yeah, so Jillian could have passed on being kidnapped or almost getting blown up by Kingsley.

Behind her eyes, the Audi exploded into orange fire all over again, and her lungs seized with remembered fear. The deafening boom, the flying chunks of metal shrapnel. Jillian had been steps away from going up in flames herself.

Red lights flashed in front of her, so she tapped her brakes and tossed her head. If skipping the bad parts meant having no Ellie, Jacob, or Clay in her life? Forget it. The trade-off was worth every terror-filled moment.

Her spine chose that moment to twinge, and Jillian grimaced. Okay, the back pain, she could really do without.

"Hey, isn't that the airport exit?"

Ellie's question jerked Jillian from her memories. She

glanced at the sign and flipped on her turn signal. "Hold on." She gassed the SUV and swerved across two lanes of traffic at the last possible second, accelerating into the exit lane without a moment to spare. The driver behind her slammed on their brakes and blasted the horn. Yeesh. She totally deserved that one.

Jillian glanced in the rearview mirror to wave an apology but dropped her hand when she spotted the silver BMW from earlier. "Ha! Karma's a bitch, jerkface."

Clay whistled. "This is a side of Jillian I've never seen before."

"Oh yeah, I carry a mean grudge. You best remember that, Clay Lockwood." Jillian ruined her warning by snickering.

Her levity faded by the time she pulled up to the curb outside their gate and threw the SUV into park. Clay grabbed their duffle bags from the back while Jillian rounded the front of the SUV and threw her arms around Ellie. "You be careful out there, you hear me? Otherwise, I'm going to let Sam roll around on that white suit you love so much."

"Don't you dare!" Ellie squeezed her back before stepping away. "And okay already. I'll be careful, I promise."

Clay walked up with the bags, so Jillian pointed her finger at him.

"You too, Clay. Be safe." Before the FBI agent could protest, Jillian gave him a quick hug too. Over his shoulder, she noticed a nearby airport security guy giving her the stink eye. "All right, I've gotta go before they throw me in airport jail for exceeding my curb time allotment. Text me when you get there."

Jillian hurried back to the driver's seat, waving off approaching security. "I'm leaving, okay? Chill!" Flicking on her turn signal, she took one last look at her friends, catching sight of Clay's cowboy hat and Ellie's red braid before they disappeared between the sliding doors that led to the gates.

Once they were gone, an odd sensation slithered across her skin at the sudden emptiness of the SUV. She rubbed the back of her neck and scowled. What was she, five years old again, and afraid to be alone? She told herself to quit acting like a fool.

A driver waiting for her spot blasted his horn, prodding Jillian to finally put her middle finger to use while she hit the gas. She followed the airport signs to the 26-East and merged into the slow-moving rush hour traffic. Every so often, Jillian found herself checking the rearview mirror for signs that someone was tailing her. Her heartbeat stuttered for ten minutes straight when she noticed the same white Honda Accord on her butt. She signaled and cruised into the slow lane. The car whizzed on by.

"Idiot. Of course he was following you. You're on the freeway. That's what cars on the freeway do."

Despite her muttered joke, the uneasiness persisted. Served her right for brushing off Ellie's security detail this morning. At the time, she'd dismissed the offer as silly, figuring why waste their time by forcing them to follow her to the police station? She regretted that choice, but too late for a do-over now.

Jillian checked the rearview mirror again. Her lungs seized at the white car behind her. She slammed her foot on the brake, and the car swerved into the next lane. Only then did she spot the blue, black, and white emblem on the hood. A BMW. Not a Honda.

At this rate, Jillian would end up in an accident long before she ever made it to work.

Annoyed by her jumpiness, she clicked on the radio, turning to a morning news program in hopes that would soothe the cold, oily sensation that stretched across her neck, her shoulders, down her spine. The DJs' chatter as they traded jabs sounded like gibberish, though.

Jillian turned the volume up and attempted to concentrate, but her attention diverted back to her life over the past few months. As much as she loved that her proximity to Ellie and Clay allowed her access to cases and secret information that no one else knew, Jillian had to admit that the downside was pretty terrible. Because of his sick obsession with Ellie, Kingsley had targeted her. Multiple times. Now, the sociopathic doctor was going after Gabe.

People around Ellie ended up hurt.

Jillian eased off the gas to let a car in the next lane merge, her shoulders hunching at the traitorous thought. No fair. Ellie couldn't help that a madman was obsessed with her. She flipped the buttons until hard rock blasted from the speakers, turning up the volume until the noise drowned out the static in her mind.

When she parked in Ellie's usual spot in front of the Charleston PD, Jillian clicked off the radio, but she didn't get out right away. Instead, she gripped the wheel and stared straight ahead. The truth was, Jillian was right to be on high alert. They all were.

Gabe had only thwarted Kingsley to save Jillian's life, and look what was happening to him. Guilt twisted her gut. If anything, whatever Kingsley did to Gabe as a result fell on her head, not Ellie's.

But guilt alone wasn't responsible for the invisible bugs crawling along her skin. Jillian had experienced fear enough times to recognize the sharp, coppery taste. Because Kingsley would stop at nothing to get back at his former assistant, and once he did? He'd move on to the next person on his list. The man got off on torture, and his appetite for pain would never be quenched.

Jillian trembled. One of those names on that list that Kingsley had yet to scratch off was Ellie's. Jillian was deluding herself if she didn't believe her name showed up on the list too.

She dragged her hand down her face before shutting off the engine and climbing out. Speculating this way got her nowhere, unless she wanted an ulcer and a heart attack by forty-five.

Pessimism was a trap. A mental state that sucked away all hope, the way a black hole did light. Jillian smoothed her hair and reapplied her red lipstick. She was an optimist. Time to start acting like one.

Jillian flung back her shoulders as she marched toward the station's entrance. There was nothing wrong with being extra cautious, or keeping her senses switched into high alert. Caving to panic and allowing fear to infiltrate every aspect of her life was the problem.

As she entered the building, a reedy Christmas tree towered in the far left corner, snagging her attention with its joyful, twinkling lights. Her hand flew to her chest. Wow. With all the craziness lately, Jillian had pretty much spaced on the holidays. She bet Ellie had too.

While she gazed at the festive tree, a wonderful idea struck her. She clasped her hands together. Yes, a little holiday spirit would go a long way toward elevating all their moods right now. As she bounded down the stairs that led to her basement office, Jillian's anxiety all but vanished.

Jillian might be useless to change the outcome of Clay and Ellie's rescue mission in Portland, but one thing she could do was ensure their homecoming was full of hope and light.

22

G abe drifted through the darkness, almost like he was floating underwater. In the distance, a noise blared, low and throaty. Familiar, yet wrong. The sound penetrated his weightless world, bobbing along with him as he tried to place the intrusion. It was on the tip of his tongue but vanished into the ether before Gabe could solidify the idea to words.

The noise blared again. Louder this time. Gabe's eyelids twitched as he floated in that direction. He pushed, but they were too heavy to lift.

Buzz. Buzz.

Tiny feet danced across his cheek. Gabe flinched and attempted to bat away the tickle, but his arms remained boneless. Too heavy to move.

Buzz.

A new tickle on his nose. Gabe wanted to scratch, but he still couldn't move. He frowned. Something was wrong.

A whirlpool materialized in his tranquil lake. The current tugged at his legs and accelerated his pulse. Now he remembered. His pool wasn't safe. Monsters lurked below the surface, circling until they decided to pull him under.

He had to get out. Now.

His eyelids still felt weighted, like someone had taped rocks to the skin, but his growing sense of dread made him push harder against the restriction. After a huge effort, he managed to blink. Only the world resisted sharpening into focus. Awareness returned to his limbs, one cell at a time. A chair. He was sitting in a chair.

Gabe frowned again, somehow disturbed by that realization. Why a chair? Had he fallen asleep? That same noise blared again, and recognition clicked. A foghorn! But wait. Didn't a foghorn imply that a boat was nearby?

As the drugs continued to wear out of his system, Gabe blinked his eyes again. He managed to keep them open in a squint. Everything was still blurry, but through his altered vision, he could make out the shape of a man sitting a few feet away.

Gabe tried to lift his hands to rub his eyes, but he hit resistance. Same thing happened when he attempted to move his feet. Not weightless at all. Restraints. Around his wrists and ankles. He was tied down.

Adrenaline surged, pulsing the last of the fuzziness away. As he regained consciousness, disjointed memories flashed behind Gabe's eyes. Packing up his few belongings and sneaking out of the safe house. The bright lights of a convenience store. A bald man with bushy eyebrows. Flickering letters that spelled out M-O-T-E-L. Strong arms grabbing him from behind and shoving him into a van. The smell of garlic.

One of the last things he remembered was a needle piercing his neck, and a soft hand stroking his hair. The rest was a blank until he woke up...here. Wherever *here* was.

He'd traded the imaginary monster from his drug-induced haze for a real one.

Gabe drew in a shuddering breath, cautioning himself not to panic. Not that his pep talk helped. He was in a strange place, tied to a chair, waiting for Kingsley to torture him until he screamed for mercy. His focus sharpened, allowing him to make out the features of the man sitting opposite him. Except, that made no sense.

Gabe blinked, but the image before him stayed the same. The man examining him from a few feet away appeared to be no older than forty, with brown skin, thick hair, and sharp cheekbones. Not Kingsley. A stranger.

But that didn't make any sense. "Where am I?"

The stranger's impassive expression didn't change, nor did he respond to Gabe's question.

Desperate, Gabe fought his restraints, yanking with all his might. He tired far too quickly. An aftereffect, he suspected, of whatever poison had been in that syringe.

Gabe relaxed, giving his wobbly limbs time to regather their strength. Not too much time, though, because he had to get out of here. Before Kingsley came back.

As he waited, Gabe appealed to the stranger again. "Please, help me! Cut me free. The Feds will be coming any minute now, but if you hurry up and cut me free, they won't have to know about your role in this, whatever that may be. *Please.*"

Again, no reply from the stranger. The man leaned forward in his chair, though, which Gabe grasped at as a hopeful sign.

"Do you work for Dr. Kingsley? We don't have to tell him. You could say I escaped. Please."

This time, the man's lips quirked upward. Before Gabe could process that reaction, a door squealed open behind him before clinking shut again. He froze. Oh god, was he too late? Was that *Kingsley*?

With his pulse thundering in his ears, Gabe swiveled his head to the left, toward the newcomer. The constriction in his chest eased when the man's long, gaunt face and sunken cheeks registered. Another stranger. Not Kingsley.

Gabe's chin fell to his chest in silent thanks. He lifted his head again, and his gaze snagged on an object that flashed in the newcomer's hands. The gaunt man carried a tray, and on that tray gleamed a display of knives arranged in a fan. Gabe's throat turned into a desert as the invisible force resumed squeezing his rib cage, forcing the oxygen from his lungs.

The man walked the tray over to the brown-skinned stranger, who continued to study Gabe with that same odd smile. "Here they are, Mr. del Rey. Freshly sharpened and polished, as requested." The gaunt man stopped within reaching distance of the brown-skinned man he'd called Mr. del Rey. He lowered the tray so that Mr. del Rey could inspect the contents without leaving his chair.

Gabe racked his brain for clues as to why this was happening. He'd been so sure Kingsley was behind his kidnapping, but he didn't recognize these men at all. Who was this Mr. del Rey, and what did he have against Gabe? Or the gaunt man, for that matter?

A shiver slid down his arms as the brown-skinned man stroked a single finger down one of the gleaming blades. Gabe yanked his arms and legs, testing the ropes binding him in place. If anything, the knots tightened.

Mr. del Rey glanced up from the knives and clucked his tongue. "Relax, dear boy. The fun is about to start."

The words stopped Gabe cold. No, not the words, he realized. The voice.

His muscles froze in instinctual panic as the pleasant,

lilting tones sifted over him. His mouth opened on a silent gasp as he stared at the man, searching for any proof that his ears weren't failing him. But no. The brown-skinned face smiling back at him was a stranger's. The voice, though. That voice would accompany Gabe to his grave.

He shook his head, dazed. Maybe he was stuck in a nightmare, and fear was playing tricks on his brain. That made more sense than the other possibility that tugged at Gabe's consciousness.

"No. No."

Gabe didn't hear his own whimpers until the brown-skinned man shushed him. "Now, now, stop that. Pretending not to know who I am won't change a thing."

This time, the familiar voice triggered a visceral reaction. Gabe's internal organs mashed together into a single, giant lump before plunging to the soles of his feet. His head jerked backward, snapping his teeth shut in the process.

Laughter boomed out. Sinister. Familiar. A sound that had haunted his nightmares for far too long for Gabe to deny the truth any longer.

Del Rey and Kingsley were one and the same.

"So, what do you think of my new look? A nice change, don't you agree? The old one was getting a little dated."

Del Rey/Kingsley presented Gabe with his left profile first, then his right. Like they were old buddies, discussing the results of a little Botox. Gabe tasted bile and wished he could will himself back into unconsciousness. Anything to escape this living nightmare. "H-how?"

"A good plastic surgeon can do wonders these days. Not that you'd have any reason to know that, what with your exquisite bone structure and skin. A shame, really, to carve up such a beautiful face, but what can you do when the boy you pulled out of the gutter and granted a new life stabs you in the back?"

Del Rey/Kingsley began whistling as he examined each of the knives on display. Gabe wanted to close his eyes but found himself glued to every detail of the horror movie in which he starred. Del Rey selected a long, thin weapon and tested the sharpness of the blade on his index finger. A red drop welled up at the faintest touch. Red, like the blood that had spurted from that man in the video's head.

That man. The video. Oh god. The awful reality crashed over him like ice water in a snowstorm. This was the same room from the video.

The room where Gabe had condemned a stranger to death.

Gabe started shivering and couldn't stop.

"Excellent, Milos. Thank you for getting these into tip-top shape for tonight's festivities."

Kingsley bounded to his feet and approached, waving the knife like a baton. Gabe's gaze flitted between the shiny blade and the strange new face. Back and forth, like a metronome. As if his panicked brain was struggling to choose the bigger threat.

Gabe swallowed the plea climbing up his swollen throat. Gabe knew his former boss well enough to accept the truth. Sociopaths like Kingsley delighted in the suffering they inflicted. Begging would only push the sociopath's joy over the top. Gabe's eyes fixated on the knife, and he trembled. Not that Gabe was deluding himself about his pain tolerance. Sooner or later, Kingsley would break him. Probably sooner.

Like Gabe's racing mind was an open book, Kingsley cackled, and his eyes glittered. "Aren't you adorable, showing some backbone? We'll see how long that lasts as the night progresses." Those odd brown fingers reached out for Gabe's leg, causing his entire body to tense, but all he did was smooth the material of Gabe's pants. "There, that's better."

Kingsley lifted his arms up high, and for a solitary, breathtaking moment, Gabe hoped he might retreat.

"Now, let the games begin."

Metal sparkled overhead. In a blur of silver and flesh, the knife whizzed past Gabe's face and plunged into his thigh. White-hot pain seared his quad.

Drawing on an internal strength he'd never realized existed, Gabe bit back the first scream. The second scream wrenched free. By the third scream, Gabe stopped counting.

Pain swallowed him whole as Kingsley sawed tiny squares into Gabe's muscle and plucked them out one by one.

23

By the time Clay parked their SUV rental in front of the driveway of Gabe's neat little McMinnville safe house, Ellie had already chewed off all the nails on her left hand. The hour-long drive from Portland to the suburb had started out pleasant enough, but toward the end, every mile they traveled increased the anxious twist of Ellie's gut.

She grimaced at her self-manicure, glad her mother wasn't there to witness her failing. *Nice young ladies keep their fingers out of their mouths.* How many times had Ellie stuffed her hands under her thighs at the dinner table to hide the evidence, only for Helen Kline to arch one of her cool reddish brows until Ellie caved and allowed her to assess the damage? Too many to count.

Oh well. Ellie felt certain that nice young ladies also didn't inspect dead bodies, or study blood spatter patterns, or chase serial killers all over the country, either. Good thing she'd given up on fitting into that well-mannered Southern belle mold a long time ago.

Ellie checked her phone one more time, deflating when her screen showed zero new alerts. Still no word from Gabe.

She raked her teeth over her lower lip and jumped out of the SUV. The sooner Gabe contacted her, the quicker her stomach would end its internal tumbling act. She spotted Clay waiting for her on the brick path, so she broke into a jog to catch up.

As she and Clay approached, Frank unfolded his tall frame from where he sat on the front porch. "Any word yet?"

Ellie shook her head, sending a jolt of pain down the back of her neck. One of the many downsides of air travel mixed with stress. She massaged the taut muscle while Frank tossed Clay a small cardboard box. Clay plucked two latex gloves from the opening and passed the box to Ellie. After she slipped her own gloves on, Ellie covered her shoes with a pair of blue paper booties. Gratitude that Frank had covered their bases filled her. Best to preserve the scene, just in case.

Once she was ready, Frank bent down to shove the key into the front door. The lock clicked, and the marshal ushered them into a tidy, well-lit home with an open floor plan. "Divide and conquer?"

Ellie nodded. "Sounds good. Let's start in the back of the house and work our way out? I'll take the hallway bathroom."

Clay nodded. "Frank and I can split the bedrooms."

Single file, they headed down the hall. Ellie flicked on the bathroom light and settled in to search. She divided the room into four quadrants, beginning on the top left with the medicine cabinet. Only three items were inside. After popping the top off the deodorant and checking for hidden items underneath the white stick, she discarded the tube and moved on from the cabinet to the mirror and counter. She continued her search, slow and methodical, pulling out the drawers all the way to ensure nothing was taped beneath them and testing every toiletry item to check for hiding spots.

Nothing yet, so she moved over to the toilet and removed

the lid to peer into the tank. Clear. The porcelain clattered when she replaced the lid. So far, not even the tiniest of clues, at least in the bathroom. Ellie straightened and prepared to move on.

"Got something!"

At Clay's announcement, Ellie raced to the bedroom. She skidded to a stop inside the door. Over by the bed, Clay gripped a tiny plastic square between his thumb and pointer finger. "What did you find?"

Clay glowered at the object in his hand. "This was taped under his nightstand."

Ellie hurried over, baffled by Clay's reaction. When she got close enough to identify the thin square, she wanted to scream. A SIM card. *Dammit, Gabe.*

Frank's mouth drooped. "Whelp. At least now we know how he was found. What the hell was he playing at, taking a risk like that?"

Ellie wished they could question Gabe in person to find answers. She checked her phone again. Nothing. Her stomach lurched, kicking off a fresh somersaulting routine. "I'm done in the bathroom, so I'll take the closet."

She opened the door of the small walk-in. Not much inside beyond hangers and a few discarded t-shirts. A single pair of gray tennis shoes sat in the middle of the scuffed wooden floor. Ellie didn't expect to find much, but she took her time anyway, carefully inspecting each item. *Was the SIM card really the only reason Kingsley had tracked Gabe?*

After examining and discarding the shirts, Ellie sighed and picked up the first tennis shoe. She checked the laces, the tread, removed the sole, and shined her flashlight app inside while her fingers felt for any inconsistencies. Nothing there, so she replaced that shoe and moved on to the second one, repeating her process all over again.

Once again, she detected nothing in the laces or the tread.

But when she pulled up the insert and traced her fingers over the material, her breath caught. Was that a slim crack in the lining on the interior side, halfway to the toe box? She aimed her camera light at the spot and spied a narrow slit. Too perfectly straight to be a tear.

Praying that, in her desperation, her mind wasn't conjuring leads out of nothing, Ellie pried open the crevice with her remaining intact nails and turned the shoe upside down. A tiny disc fell to the floor. "Uh, guys? I don't think Gabe taking risks was the only reason Kingsley found him."

She scooped up the minuscule device, no bigger in diameter than a Cheerio and less than a tenth as wide. Clay appeared over her shoulder to investigate what she'd found, so she lifted her palm to show him. "GPS tracker in his shoe. Maybe part of Gabe being found is on him because he hung on to that SIM card, but my guess is that a big part is due to the very smart man with nearly unlimited resources who was determined to hunt him down."

"Can I see that?"

Ellie passed the tracker to Frank, whose expression turned pained. "Damn, that's on me. I should have caught this. I thought when we moved him to the new safe house…"

Clay shook his head. "Hey, don't beat yourself up. That was a reasonable assumption to make. Plus, this device is so tiny, not many of us would have known to look for it until after the fact."

The marshal's dejected posture didn't ease up, so Ellie decided to distract him. "How was Gabe acting these past few days? Did you notice anything different?"

Frank straightened. His brow wrinkled. "I'm not sure. There was this one time where his eyes looked a little red, but I figured—" A loud ringing interrupted him. Frank dug his phone out of his pocket. "Excuse me one second."

Ellie and Clay continued searching the room until Frank's

footsteps thudded down the hallway. He reappeared in the doorway, his ruddy skin ashen beneath his dark hair.

Ellie's heart stalled. *Gabe.* "What's wrong?"

"That was the home office in D.C. One of the secretaries there and her two children were killed in a car accident. I knew the family, so they called to let me know."

Ellie's initial relief over not hearing bad news about Gabe gave way to sorrow. "Oh no, that's awful. I'm so sorry. What a tragedy. Those poor kids."

Clay clapped a hand on the marshal's shoulder. "My condolences, Frank. That's rough."

Ellie's phone rang, making her miss whatever Clay murmured next. Hope raced along her veins when she checked the number. *Unknown Caller.* This could be Gabe! Finally.

In her excitement, Ellie forgot to answer her phone with her usual *Detective Kline* greeting. "Hello? Is that you, Gabe?"

"You look so pretty standing there, but are you getting enough sleep? Those circles under your eyes suggest otherwise."

Every hair on her body bristled at the familiar voice. Not Gabe.

Kingsley.

Ellie lifted her other hand to tap the speaker button.

"Ah ah, I wouldn't do that if I were you. This conversation is intended to be private."

At Kingsley's warning, she froze, with her finger a mere inch away from the button. Goose bumps erupted across her flesh. *What the...? How?*

Without alerting the others, she performed a slow scan of the room. Nothing, nothing, nothing...*there!* The teeny-tiny camera peeked out from the corner of a picture frame on Gabe's desk.

Sonofabitch!

"Why, hello there, my puppet. It appears that you've finally found me."

Ellie glared into the lens, stepping even closer as Kingsley gloated into her ear. "This hardly seems fair. You can see me, but I can't see you. I know," she snapped her fingers, "why don't we meet face-to-face?"

Kingsley's laugh made her skin crawl. "Aren't you a funny girl? I promise we'll meet soon enough, but I'm a little...tied up at the moment. Or, more to the point, your friend is."

Her hand vibrated as her phone announced an incoming text. Ellie checked the message, and what she saw ripped the oxygen from her lungs. Kingsley had sent her a photo of Gabe, tied to a chair, dripping blood from too many parts of his body to count. She stood statue-still, transfixed by the horror.

"You remember our game, don't you?"

Kingsley's question penetrated her daze. Her heart slowed, then accelerated. Please, no. *Gabe.* "Not this time. I refuse to play."

He chuckled. "Refusing to play is a choice, my puppet. Surely you remember that much?"

Acid pooled in Ellie's stomach. This couldn't happen. Not again. She whirled, stumbling in her frenzy to do something. Anything. Clay grabbed her arm to prevent her from face-planting on the floor. He ducked his head and mouthed the words. *What should I do?*

The skin-on-skin contact of his hand to her arm grounded her, transferring enough calm to tame her racing thoughts and concentrate. Who could help them right now, who? A name popped into her head.

Carl.

The Charleston Police Department's IT guy had come through for her in the past. Maybe he could trace the call. Ellie understood the idea was a long shot, but Carl was all she had for now, and anything was better than nothing. They had to at least try. They owed Gabe that much.

A scream ripped her back to the phone. To that terrible room where Gabe was strapped to a chair. His life draining away.

"Are you ready to play now?" Kingsley's lilting voice held a sharp edge this time.

"No." Ellie squeezed her eyes shut, but of course, that did nothing to block out the next round of screams. The sound was worse than a thousand nails screeching down chalkboards, scraping along Ellie's nerves until her fingers burned with the urge to cut every last neuron out.

She grabbed Frank's arm and mouthed a command. *Katarina! Find Katarina!* Kingsley's former protégé knew more about the man than anyone, but she was in WITSEC, so her whereabouts were guarded. As a marshal, Frank was the only one of the three of them in the room who might be able to track her down on short notice.

Frank's forehead creased as he stared at her lips. He shook his head. *What?*

Find. Kat-a-rin-a. Frustrated, Ellie tried exaggerating each silent syllable. Frank shook his head again and lifted his hands. Ellie dug her nails into her palm to keep from shrieking the command out loud. Too risky by far, with Kingsley listening in. The element of surprise might prove to be their sole advantage.

This time, the scream broke off halfway through, which chilled Ellie to the bone. Her hands grew clammy, and her pulse thundered in her ears.

"Gabe is begging you to play, my puppet. Can you hear him over your frantic pantomime?"

A howl of useless, bitter rage built in Ellie's throat. She pivoted to face the camera again and opened her mouth to scream. "Fuck you!"

Kingsley's amused cackle blended with Gabe's shriek this time, forming a discordant, hellish melody. "Come on now, Ellie, don't be that way. Play with me."

Gabe screamed again, but his voice petered out at the end, dropping into a hoarse, anguished moan. Ellie gripped the phone tight, bracing against a wave of helplessness. Desperation chipped away at her convictions, and tears stung her eyes as she felt herself begin to cave.

She hated to let Kingsley win his sadistic game, but she hated to let Gabe suffer even more. No one deserved this kind of agony, and Kingsley got off on it. Gabe's tormentor wouldn't stop until either he got what he wanted or he'd tortured poor Gabe to death.

She licked her dry lips. Opened her mouth. Commanded her mouth to form the words. But her vocal cords clamped down, refusing to sentence yet another person to death.

"P-please!" Gabe's sobbed plea cracked her heart in two. Ellie felt trapped, in a hell worse than most people ever imagined. Condemn a good man to die, or say nothing and listen to him suffer? Both choices were brutal and filled her mouth with ash.

"Hear that? He wants you to play too. Three little words, my puppet. That's all you have to say. Then this round can be over for good."

Ellie dug her fingers into her hair and pulled, welcoming the physical pain. Anything to relieve the emotional torture. But the burn only helped for an instant and brought her no closer to a decision. Ellie couldn't...wouldn't say the words, but she had to.

In the end, the thing that sent her over the edge was Gabe's soft whimper. Ellie licked her lips again, swallowed the lump that clogged her throat. She inhaled and lifted her chin. Determined that this time, she'd force the words out. No matter how much they hurt.

"Die—"

Before she could get past the first word, a hand flew out of nowhere and yanked the phone from Ellie's grip. She spun, lunging to reclaim her device. "Wait, stop! Please, don't hang up—"

Too late. Clay stabbed the *end call* button before she even stopped talking. Ellie gaped at the phone. Kingsley was gone.

And Gabe. Gabe was gone too.

24

"...**B**ut with a twitch of her black tail, the fierce warrior leopard leapt from the tree branch and landed in front of the wild dogs, her muscles bunching under sleek skin as she prepared to pounce."

Katarina glanced up from the pages of the fantasy novel to savor the joy of her own fantasy come-to-life. Curling up together with Bethany on the bed while reading her daughter a nighttime story was one of Katarina's favorite parts of the day.

Even after two months together, the sight of the little girl's face, a miniature of hers except innocent with clear eyes, round cheeks, and a splattering of freckles, still filled Katarina with that otherworldly sensation, like her heart existed outside her body and inside Bethany's. She smoothed the fine blonde hair, still damp from the bath, and inhaled the sweet fragrance of strawberry shower gel.

So perfect. The two of them, all warm and cozy. Cuddled together like a regular mom and child. No one better dare threaten to steal that from them.

A fierce protective instinct flooded her limbs, causing

Katarina to squeeze Bethany tighter. The little girl squirmed in protest, so Katarina slackened her grip and told herself to chill.

Her stupid conscience, or anxiety, or whatever the hell had been making her act jumpier than a rabbit who'd spotted a hawk ever since she'd returned home from Clayne's warehouse, could shut up now. Lots of people managed to lead double lives with no problems. Like in that Lifetime movie Katarina had watched the other day that was inspired by a true story. If some stupid man could go most of his life having two separate families tucked away in different states with no one the wiser, then an occasional outing with Clayne should be a breeze.

A warm hand patted Katarina's cheek. "Mama, you can't stop there! What happens next?" The bed rocked as the little girl wiggled around in her impatience.

"Right. Let's see…" Katarina scanned the page until she located the spot where she'd left off. "Dingo, the leader of the wild dogs," she paused, rolling her eyes at the author's utter lack of creativity when choosing the name, "planted all four paws and stood his ground, even though inside, he shivered like he had that day the strange white powder fell from the sky…"

The little girl sighed her contentment and nestled her pajama-clad body closer, melting Katarina's heart. As she continued to read, the muscles of her neck relaxed, and the last of her nervous energy seeped away.

Katarina stroked Bethany's hair again and gazed down at her with wonder. Ever since returning home from Clayne's warehouse, Katarina's body had behaved like the switch to her nervous system had remained stuck in the "on" position, an unsettling sensation that persisted all throughout homework, dinner, and Bethany's bath. She'd been unable to sit still, and every little noise rattled her. Bethany had even called her out on that first one, asking her why Mama was shaking the bed with her leg.

But now, like magic, the simple act of snuggling the little girl while reading her a bedtime story soothed Katarina's residual jitters until they were only a weak vibration. Good riddance.

Katarina couldn't say that she'd enjoyed the novel sensation, or even fully understood. She didn't regret her earlier choices. That would be silly. Katarina was pragmatic enough to recognize that her impromptu torture session had provided her with a valuable service. The satisfaction of cutting those men had acted like an air valve, easing her internal pressure to inflict pain until she no longer felt ready to burst.

Every single required parenting class she'd attended so far emphasized the importance of parents setting aside some time every week to relieve stress. It wasn't Katarina's fault that the teachers never specified whether or not torture qualified as an approved stress-relief method.

Bethany flinched beside her. Her daughter's eyelids drooped shut, popped back open, and then fluttered closed once more. Katarina lowered her voice to a more soothing tone and hid a smile. Every night, Bethany struggled to stay awake, and every night, sleep won the battle. But defeat never stopped her from picking up the gauntlet the very next evening.

Pride filled Katarina's chest. Her daughter was a fighter. Just like her.

The rise and fall of Bethany's chest slowed and grew rhythmic, and her dark lashes fanned her cheeks and stayed there. Katarina closed the book, pressed a kiss to her daughter's sweet-smelling forehead, and eased up from the bed. She tucked the green down comforter around the sleeping girl before tiptoeing from the room.

Once the door clicked shut, Katarina stifled a yawn and turned right into the hallway to head for her own bed. A soft tapping noise from the opposite direction stopped her in her tracks. She froze, not daring to breathe while she strained to hear.

Several seconds passed, with no further sounds. Katarina's shoulders began to ease. *Dumbass.* Probably another icy Wyoming wind, causing a tree branch to rattle against one of the windows. She chided herself for being a wuss, until the sound came again.

Rap-rap-rap.

Far too rhythmic to be a tree. Katarina's adrenaline spiked, prompting her heartbeat to thunder in her ears. Someone was on her porch. Knocking at her front door.

Shit. She whirled and sprinted to her bedroom. Nightmare scenarios battled in her head while she grabbed the gun off the top shelf of the closet. The weight of the semi-automatic in her hand comforted her as she crept to the foyer, but not enough to calm her rioting pulse.

Who was outside? Clayne? One of his associates from earlier? Her step faltered. Child protective services? Katarina had no way of knowing. Each night, she followed the instructions the marshals taught her to the letter. Draw all the blinds, then pull the curtains. And no way in hell was Katarina stupid enough to look out the peephole.

She ducked behind the couch for cover and snapped the safety off the gun. As quietly as she could, she dialed 9-1 on her cell, waiting with her finger hovering over the remaining digit.

Rap-rap-rap!

The third knock rang out louder than the first two times, like whoever waited on the other side of the door was losing patience. The change in volume startled Katarina. So much she nearly dropped the gun when her phone buzzed a moment later. She checked the screen and almost fainted from relief.

It's me at the door.

The message came from Tonya, the U.S. Marshal assigned to her in WITSEC.

"Christ, Tonya, you about gave me a heart attack." Once Katarina flipped the safety back on, she shoved the gun under the couch and hurried toward the entryway. New doubts slowed her pace before she reached the door.

What if Tonya knew about Clayne? Or worse, someone had ratted out how Katarina had spent her afternoon? Katarina hesitated and then reached for the lock. Drug dealers weren't likely to spill her secrets, and besides, it wasn't like she had much of a choice. Either she answered the door, or the U.S.M.S. would do it for her.

The grim expression on Tonya's ruddy face when the marshal barreled her way inside didn't do much to quell Katarina's concerns. Neither did her marshal's size. Tonya was a big woman. Over six-feet tall and built like a linebacker. Katarina was scrappy, but if the situation deteriorated into a physical fight, the marshal had a good fifty-pound advantage.

Think fast.

As her mind whirred, Katarina escorted Tonya into the living room, pasting a fake smile on her face and sealing her lips shut. One mistake Katarina knew better than to make was letting her nerves rule her vocal cords and cause her to blabber. For all she knew, the only proof Tonya had about Katarina's involvement with Clayne was when they'd sat together at the bar. Katarina had lied her way out of far worse situations. Patience was key.

"Didn't expect to see you here tonight. Can I get you something to drink?"

The marshal shook her head. "Sorry to disturb you at

night, but I'm afraid I have some bad news. We should probably take a seat."

I don't want to take a damn seat, just tell me already! Instead of screaming the words, though, Katarina followed the larger woman to the couch and perched on the edge of the cushion. She was no idiot. Alienating her marshal right now would only make things worse. She clenched her hands in her lap instead and sifted through possible excuses and lies. None of them helped prepare her for Tonya's grim statement.

"Kingsley is back in the picture."

Tonya's lips moved, but Katarina couldn't hear anything else over the loud whooshing that pulsated through her ears. Not Clayne. *Kingsley.* Her frantic gaze darted to the front door.

"Where is he? Here, in Wyoming?"

Oh god, *Bethany.* They had to leave. Now.

Katarina sprang to her feet, but a hand circled her wrist, snapping her attention back to the marshal.

"It's okay, calm down. We believe he's somewhere on the West Coast, not here. Hey, are you hearing me? I said he's not in Wyoming."

Katarina stared into Tonya's concerned face while her brain worked to process the woman's statements. When they clicked into place, she collapsed back to the couch and hyperventilated into her palms. Once her breathing calmed, Tonya spoke again.

"I'm sorry, I should have told you that from the very start. I'm here because the detective thinks you can help them."

Katarina lifted her head, wondering if her mind was playing tricks on her. "What detective?"

"Detective Kline, and Special Agent Lockwood."

A vision of the red-haired officer flitted behind Katarina's eyes and made her hands clench with instinctual loathing. Help Ellie Kline? That interfering bitch? If it weren't for her,

Katarina would have escaped with Bethany years ago, when she'd snatched the little girl from the people pretending to be her parents.

Instead, the flame-haired cop had spotted the pair, grown suspicious, and run Katarina down. Charged her, even, for the crime of kidnapping her own daughter! What a joke. The most unforgivable part was how Bethany had been tossed back to her fake parents when Katarina was right there. Desperate to be a mother to the daughter stolen from her at birth.

Now that they'd been reunited, though, the memory of the Charleston detective stung less. And Special Agent Lockwood wasn't so bad. He'd helped Katarina get into the WITSEC program with Bethany. She relaxed her hands. Still. Katarina wasn't about to sign up to bake him a fucking cake anytime soon.

"What kind of help?"

Tonya pinned Katarina with an intense stare. "Kingsley is holding one of his former employees hostage. They're hoping you can help them track down where that might be. Give them some insight into the type of place he might pick to torture his victims."

The last of Katarina's terror ebbed, leaving her body feeling drained, like she'd finished running a marathon. So much for capping off her exciting afternoon with a relaxing evening at home. Screw the detectives. All she wanted to do now was collapse on her bed and sleep twelve hours straight.

She leaned forward, ready to tell Tonya she had no clue where Kingsley might be hiding. The sooner she ushered the marshal out, the sooner she could crash.

Katarina was about to do exactly that when an atypical tug of uncertainty trapped her in place. Were there any downsides of Katarina helping them try to hunt down Kingsley? None that came to mind. On the flip side, benefits definitely existed.

For one, if her assistance did manage to lead the police to her former mentor, Katarina could free herself from future incidents of Kingsley-inspired terror. Far-fetched, but possible. And even if she failed to provide any tips that led to Kingsley's capture? She'd still come out of this looking like a model witness and generate a boatload of goodwill for herself and Bethany.

Given her recent risks with Clayne, Katarina would be foolish to turn an opportunity like this down. Especially one that cost her nothing.

"Sure, I'll try, but I can't promise anything."

Tonya's eyebrows lifted, telling Katarina she'd surprised the marshal by agreeing. "Great, they'll be very happy to hear that. I'm sure whatever you can share will be helpful."

Katarina drummed her fingers on her sweatpants while she racked her brain. If she were Kingsley, where would she be hiding with her latest victim? "He likes big, open spaces."

Tonya frowned. "Open spaces. Like empty fields or lots?"

"No, indoor spaces. Like abandoned warehouses."

"Got it. That's good." Tonya typed a note into her phone. "Anything else?"

Katarina searched her memory. "Shell companies. He likes to use them to make any big purchases, and he often puts an X in the name as a tag, because he goes by Doctor X."

Stupid, really, once she stopped to consider it. Katarina sneered. Men, always letting their egos get the best of them.

"Great. What else?"

Katarina chewed on the inside of her cheek as she concentrated. She felt a surprising pang of disappointment when she came up empty-handed. "Sorry, that's all I can come up with for now."

Tonya rose from the couch, so Katarina followed her lead

and did the same. "Thanks for your help. I'll be sure to pass this along. If you think of anything else, call me."

"I will." Once again, Katarina experienced a jolt of surprise to find that she wasn't lying.

The sturdy marshal opened the front door before turning back to spear Katarina with a hard stare. "And if you get a phone call, a package, a letter, or notice anything that seems remotely off, call me immediately. Do not wait...unless you want to end up in the same shoes as the poor bastard Kingsley is holding hostage as we speak. Understood?"

Katarina's nails dug into her palms. A desperate attempt to battle the fresh wave of unwanted fear that washed over her. She hated feeling scared like this. Fear reminded her too much of when she was a little girl and used to creep around, terrified of how the slightest mistake or noise at the wrong time could trigger one of her foster parents to punish her. Like the Davidsons.

As she'd stood by Kingsley's side and watched flames devour the Davidsons and their house, she'd made herself a promise. From that day forward, Katarina had vowed never to be that vulnerable or frightened again. And she'd succeeded. Mostly. "Understood."

Now, only two things on this earth plunged that stark, icy terror into Katarina's chest: fear that someone might hurt or steal her daughter and fear that the very man who'd rescued her all those years ago would one day punish her for daring to leave him behind. Well, that and take a chunk of his money when she left.

After studying Katarina's expression, Tonya grunted. "Good. Now, make sure to lock up behind me. I'll be in touch."

The second the door thudded shut, Katarina did as instructed and clicked the locks back into place. Wow. Not the way she'd predicted her night going at all. Katarina hurried over to the couch and knelt down to retrieve the gun before heading for her bedroom. Hard to believe that half an hour ago, she'd been close to nodding off in her daughter's bed. Now, every cell in Katarina's body pulsed with energy, like she'd guzzled down an entire pot of coffee.

She bounced on the edge of her bed, tempted to call Clayne. But no, that wasn't a smart move. Katarina couldn't afford any mistakes right now. Just because she and Clayne had slept together and shared a little emotional intimacy through their torture session didn't mean that he could be trusted. In fact, she knew better. The only person Katarina could truly rely on in her life was Katarina.

The headboard thumped the wall when she collapsed on the blue and white checked comforter. She sighed. Too bad, because having a badass like Clayne to watch her back would feel pretty damn good right about now. Katarina knew better than to indulge in fantasies, though. From her parade of foster parents to Kingsley to the random men she'd picked up along the way, no one else had ever, truly protected her.

She didn't kid herself that someone would start now.

25

The crime scene and IT techs scanned every nook and cranny of Gabe's safe house with the precision of carpenter ants scouring a picnic for crumbs while Ellie's shoes wore out the same five steps back and forth across the entryway. She hated this part. Stuck on the sidelines twiddling her thumbs, waiting on other people to finish their work and loop her back in.

Impatience pivoted her feet toward Frank. "Are you sure they knew how important it was for Katarina's marshal to call us back right away? Maybe you should try again."

A muscle twitched in Frank's jaw. "Look, I appreciate that you're impatient. I'm on pins and needles here too. But if I call the marshal's office back one more time, they're gonna bust my ass from here to Sunday."

Ellie turned to Clay, who shook his head. "He's right. You already had him check back in twice. They'll call."

They'll call. Clay made everything sound so simple. Meanwhile, each minute that ticked by was another minute that Gabe suffered at Kingsley's hands. Too many minutes, and…

Ellie shoved the rest of that thought into a mental box,

slammed the lid shut, and locked the damn thing away. She went back to pacing. From the exasperated sighs Frank kept releasing, her constant motion was getting under his skin. Too bad. Pacing beat the hell out of allowing her brain time to travel unchecked down dark paths.

A phone rang, jolting her to a stop. She whirled as Frank punched a few buttons on his screen. "Hello, Tonya?"

"Yeah." A raspy voice, deep for a woman, emitted from the phone's speaker. Ellie and Clay moved in closer, until the three of them formed a loose huddle. "I talked to her. She didn't come up with much, but she did say that Kingsley has a thing for open, abandoned warehouses and shell companies. Look for names with the letter X in them. That was all. I hope it will be enough."

Ellie hoped so too. While Frank continued probing Tonya for information, Ellie dug her own phone out and dialed. She bounced on the balls of her feet while she waited for Carl to pick up.

"Detective Kline?"

"Carl. Yeah, it's me again. Were you able to geo-locate a signal from Kingsley's burner phone yet? Sorry, I wouldn't pester you if it wasn't urgent."

"I was actually finishing up when you called. Like I told you before, burner phones are next to impossible to trace with any precision. The most I can tell you for sure is that the phone is pinging off towers in the Vancouver, Washington area."

Despite the tech's lack of precision, hope stirred in Ellie's chest. Sure, trying to locate Kingsley in Vancouver without anything else to go on was a little like searching for a needle in a haystack. But that information was a lot more than they'd had a second ago. At least now, Ellie knew where the haystack they needed to examine was located. "You're the best. Thanks, Carl. Talk soon."

She hung up right as Frank ended his call with Tonya. "That was Carl. Kingsley's burner phone shows him being in the Vancouver area."

Frank perked up. "Okay, we can start with that. It's time to rope in the Pacific Northwest Violent Offender Task Force, let them know we need immediate technical assistance in tracking Gabe and Kingsley down. They incorporate a shit ton of local agencies into that group, so they should be able to provide us with some bodies."

"Sounds good. I'll brief the Portland members of the Kingsley Task Force, then call the local field office here in Vancouver too. See if we can't recruit a few more hands on deck." Clay pulled out his phone and stepped outside.

Stuck once again with nowhere to focus the restless energy crackling through her limbs, Ellie shook out her arms and eavesdropped on Frank's call.

"Hello, this is U.S. Marshal Frank Otto. I need to be connected with Stan Lewis. Sure, I'll hold." A brief pause followed while Ellie tapped her foot. "Yeah, hey, Stan. Good to hear your voice too. Listen, I have an imminent danger situation on my hands here with a witness and could use some task force help. We have reason to believe he's being held in a warehouse in Vancouver that's either owned, rented, or leased by an individual, or more likely, a corporation with the letter X in the name. How soon can your team generate a list for me?"

Another long pause followed, which Ellie filled by gnashing her teeth.

"Yeah, okay. I'll be here. Thanks."

The moment Frank ended the call, Ellie pounced. "What did they say?"

"They'll perform the search as quick as possible and get back to us. Might be fifteen minutes, could take up to an hour."

Ellie threw up her hands. "Great. More waiting, my favorite." The front door cracked open, and she pounced on Clay as he slipped back into the house. "Well? Any luck?"

Clay leaned his shoulder against the wall. "I've got them running down the same information as Frank. Between the two, I expect we'll have that list soon. Jo McPherson from the Kingsley Task Force is on her way here from Portland. We'll keep her in the loop as information comes in."

Frank grunted. "Good. Making progress."

Ellie resumed her pacing, unable to generate much excitement. Pieces were falling into place, but the clock was running out. None of them could predict how much time remained before Kingsley delivered the killing blow.

"You keep that up, you'll be exhausted by the time we get the call." Frank shook his head.

Clay snorted. "You clearly don't know Ellie. All of that moving around acts like a battery charger for her. The more stressed she is, the more energy she produces."

Ellie ignored them both and chose to watch the IT guys sift through the room instead. She itched to join them, but these techs worked together like a finely calibrated machine. As competent as Ellie was, she was honest enough to admit that she'd only slow them down.

While she watched, one of the techs slid his gloved fingers all along the intricate scrollwork of the mirror hanging over the fireplace. The tech paused, teasing at an object beneath a curled bit of metal. Moments later, he stepped back and peered into his gloved palm. "Looks like we've got another camera."

"What the hell?" Frank stormed over to the tech to inspect whatever tiny object the man held. By the time the marshal stomped back across the living room to rejoin Ellie and Clay, red patches splotched his cheeks and neck, and he was cursing under his breath. "This is unbelievable. How could anyone know about the location of the safe house? The whole point of a safe house is that it's fucking *safe*. Christ."

"Kingsley has the means to do most anything," Ellie murmured, feeling pity for the man.

With an unexpected flash of motion, Frank punched his right fist into his open palm. "Anonymity is the backbone of the entire WITSEC system. Without it, we're basically a glorified moving company."

Clay dropped a hand on the other man's shoulder and squeezed. "Sorry. I'm sure the U.S.M.S. will get to the bottom of this." He hesitated. "Do you think it could be a staff member who got turned? Maybe the money was too good to pass up?"

Frank wrenched his shoulder out from under Clay's grip. "Jesus, Clay, whose side are you on here?" His nostrils flared.

Ellie admired the way Clay stood his ground. The man exuded utter calm in the face of Frank's storm, the picture of an easy-going cowboy in his broad-brimmed hat and sympathetic hazel eyes as he waited his friend out. Ellie marveled over his self-control. Here she was, puffing her chest out, ready to leap to Clay's defense. Meanwhile, the agent's half-lidded eyes made him appear close to dozing off.

Ellie eased back onto her heels and sighed. Quick tempers. The eternal curse of redheads everywhere.

The blaze faded from Frank's eyes, and his expression turned sheepish. "Sorry, that was a low blow. I know which side you're on. It's just…we're known for our success rates in keeping witnesses protected. The only time we tend to lose one is when the witness breaks the rules. But…" He shoved his hands into his pockets and shook his head. "I guess you never really know for sure what's happening in someone's private life that might make them turn bad."

The sight of the big, tough marshal looking so forlorn over the idea of a traitor in his midst slashed at Ellie's heart, erasing any remaining irritation. She understood the sickness that spread through you when you suspected fellow officers of foul play. Charleston PD had their fair share of dirty cops. In fact, Ellie owed her current job to one. Her predecessor, Detective Jones. If it hadn't been for the CPD veteran dropping so many cold cases, Fortis might never have realized what a knack Ellie had for solving crimes that others gave up on long ago.

Then again, if it weren't for Ellie, Jones probably would have enjoyed his retirement without anyone ever being the wiser that the detective took bribes from criminals to keep cold cases unsolved. Instead, Detective Jones had ended up in a coffin.

This time, even Frank jiggled his leg with impatience as the three of them waited. The clink of his keys accompanied Ellie's renewed pacing. Five steps up. Five steps back. She felt like she'd been walking that line for hours when the marshal's phone rang. Ellie stopped moving while Clay straightened up from the wall. Both of them hoping for some good news.

Frank murmured into the phone, then listened. No speakerphone this time. Ellie seethed with impatience, studying Frank's expression for a sign. After another brief exchange, the marshal flashed them a thumbs-up.

Ellie's fingers tingled as she barely dared to hope. Had they found a warehouse with X in the name? Already? She glanced at Clay to get his take, but the FBI agent was zeroed in on Frank.

"Right. I need you to rally the Special Operations Group ASAP, as soon as you send me that address."

Special Operations Group? As in the federal SWAT team? The tight leash holding Ellie's hope in check snapped, and the sudden change made her both light-headed and even twitchier. By the time Frank finally hung up, Ellie bounced on her heels and practically frothed at the mouth. "Well?"

Frank lifted his head, revealing a determined grin. "They found a warehouse that fits the criteria that Katarina shared, about an hour from here."

An hour. Ellie closed her eyes and uttered a silent plea. Gabe still had a chance. If they hurried.

When she opened her eyes again, Ellie no longer noticed the bustling crime techs around them. Her world had narrowed to two simple objectives.

"Let's go save Gabe and put a stop to Kingsley's twisted games once and for all."

"Count me in," Clay said.

Frank nodded, his expression equally determined. "I'll drive."

He led Ellie and Clay out the door to his SUV while a single thought pounded through Ellie in time with her heart.

Hang on, Gabe. We're coming.

26

After strapping on their Kevlar vests in the SUV, Ellie, Clay, and Frank joined the rest of the vehicles carrying the Special Operations Group at the prearranged destination, which turned out to be the side of the road about half a mile from the warehouse.

Frank led them over to the SUV in front and introduced them to the driver and leader of the tactical maneuver, Federal Agent Scott Willis. He had a wide, crooked nose that looked like it'd met one too many fists and brown hair buzzed about an inch long. His gaze performed a quick inspection of Ellie before he switched over to Clay. "Lose the cowboy hat before we get there."

Some of his FBI coworkers would have taken offense at the federal agent's barked command. Clay didn't understand the point. He tipped the cowboy hat in question at Willis and winked. "Planned on it."

Agent Willis nodded before shoving his phone beneath Frank's nose. "Here are the blueprints we pulled up. Short notice, so might not be complete, but better than pissing into the wind."

While the three of them took turns studying the layout, Willis filled them in on the plan. "Two teams. Team One will be led by me, and we'll breach the front door here." He tapped the corresponding spot on the blueprint and then craned his head to look into the back seat. "Yo Donny, wave your hand."

The tall blond man with a broad forehead sitting behind the shotgun position lifted his hand and waved.

"That's Donny. He's leading Team Two. That's your team. It'll be you three, plus two more of our guys, Johnson and Blake. Once Team One gets inside, we'll radio him, and your team will breach the back entrance here. We'll also have snipers positioned here…and here."

Clay peered over Ellie's shoulder to find the spots Willis indicated. Once they finished, Willis folded his arms across his barrel-chest and narrowed his eyes. "Remember, you are guests on this mission, so please act accordingly. Do not get in the way, and for the love of everything that is good and holy, don't get yourselves shot. The paperwork alone is a nightmare bitch that I guarantee will put me in a piss-poor mood. Clear?"

Clay could almost see the tension coming off Ellie. No surprise there. Between her stress over Gabe and her tendency to get fired up when other LEOs treated her like she didn't know one end of her gun from the other, Clay bet she was primed to explode. He bumped her shoulder with his. A reminder to let this go for now.

His tactic worked. Ellie muttered, "Clear," before stomping back over to Frank's SUV.

Frank and Clay trailed her. They fell into the line of SUVs and followed Willis the last half mile into the warehouse parking lot.

From that point on, things moved quickly. One of the

SUVs veered off to the right, while the others pulled straight up. Doors opened quietly, and agents slid out on nearly silent feet. Willis's group of five glided off in the direction of the main entrance. Donny waved them over to join two others who Ellie assumed were Johnson and Blake. The federal agents were all decked out in identical black tactical gear. "Headed around the left side to get into position. Stay low."

Donny motioned them to follow him around to the back of the warehouse. The two other Special Ops Group members fell in directly behind him, leaving Clay's group to bring up the rear. Clay trailed a few feet behind Ellie as their team crept along the darkened asphalt.

The night vision goggles always threw Clay's equilibrium off at first. The eerie green hue the NVGs cast over the world made him feel like he was in an underwater dystopia full of seaweed and Loch Ness monsters.

They stayed low as they skirted the perimeter of the building, pausing every so often to listen. Nothing stirred, not even crickets. As far as Clay could tell, the only lifeform out there was them.

The leader waved them around the rear corner of the warehouse and over to a rectangular metal door, large enough to drive a truck through. They divided up, with two of the SOG members slinking over to the far side of the rear entrance, leaving Clay, Ellie, and Frank to wait opposite them. Donny stood in the middle, facing the door while reaching for an object tucked into his belt. The green lighting messed with Clay's visual acuity, but he guessed the tool that Donny extracted was a breaching bar. With an efficiency of movement and time, the black-clad agent was ready to go.

Now, they waited for the signal from Team One.

In front of him, Ellie jiggled her legs. That same nervous energy crackled through Clay's limbs. He'd simply had more practice learning to contain his. Part of him hoped that, unlike him, Ellie never learned to hide her physical tells. Her unabashed openness was one of many qualities that had hooked Clay and reeled him in.

Another trait he found irresistible was Ellie's courage to plunge right into the battle, especially when that meant saving others.

As the silence stretched out around them, Clay fingered his gun, reassuring himself of the weapon's presence. That very same bravery also caused him endless worry because it led to Ellie placing herself in harm's way. The moon peeked out from behind a cloud, washing over Ellie. His gut clenched. Like right now, for instance. Once again, conflicting emotions tore at Clay. Fear, over the way the beautiful woman in front of him flung herself straight into the belly of the beast, and pride, over the same damn thing.

Their team leader whispered into the microphone attached to his earpiece before motioning them all to stand back. He held up both hands, splaying all his fingers. Clay had been on enough of these types of missions to understand.

Breach in ten.

Exactly ten seconds later, Donny applied the tool. The door burst open.

They were in.

Soft light spilled from the warehouse, illuminating their path inside. The breached door yawned open into the cavernous interior like a monster's mouth. Clay flipped the NVGs up and stayed close to Ellie's lithe form while Frank tailed him. With their guns extended at shoulder level, the three of them worked together, clearing their quadrant of the building one segment at a time. They covered ground quickly. Not tough, when empty cement flooring and a few dusty shelving units comprised the majority of the space.

Ellie whirled around one of the shelving units, gun ready. "Clear."

The rest of the shelves failed to reveal any hiding spots. So did the pile of decaying boxes in the far corner. Nothing there except grime accompanied by a strong whiff of earth and mildew and the faintest hint of ammonia.

Clay didn't like this.

The longer they went without running into Kingsley or Gabe or receiving confirmation that another SOG member had contained the pair, the more acid churned in his stomach. He wouldn't put it past Katarina to send them on a wild goose chase.

Ellie waved them over to a rectangular structure built into the warehouse. Clay closed in and saw what had captured her attention. A door. Probably led to an office. He feinted to the opposite side and pressed his back to the concrete wall. Ellie held three fingers in the air. Then two.

Clay tightened his grip on his gun and waited.

One.

Ellie sprang forward, grabbed the door handle, and twisted. A second later, she kicked close to the lock. The metal swung wide, slamming into an unseen object with a loud crack and creating an opening. Ellie lunged into the space, her gun swinging left to right. Clay fell in behind her, his muscles taut as he surveilled the enclosure for movement.

"Clear."

His lungs eased at Ellie's announcement. Nobody home. A sliver of shiny green beckoned from the table closest to the door. Clay frowned. Someone had been here at some point in time or another, based on that empty granola wrapper.

When? Recent enough that it hadn't gathered the same layer of dust as everything else, but he couldn't pinpoint the time any closer to that.

Clay waited for Ellie to move farther into the room so

they could perform a quick sweep. Instead, she stayed rooted to the spot, a yard or so past the door. Her head and body stood rigid as she stared straight ahead. Alarm bells clanged in his head. Clay moved to the side, to figure out what held her so transfixed. When he did, the acid burned halfway up his esophagus.

A chair sat in the middle of the space. Empty, save for the blood pooling on the plastic seat. "Shit."

Clay approached the chair and squatted, careful to avoid stepping into another red puddle on the floor. A quick dip of his finger into the red, viscous liquid told him what he needed to know. "Still warm compared to the ambient temperature in here. Whoever was here hasn't been gone long."

Clay dropped his gaze to the floor. That change in perspective showed him what he'd missed on his way in. Blood. He pointed out the thin squiggles, camouflaged by the dark, stained concrete...unless you were looking. "See those two red lines there?"

His question snapped Ellie out of her trance. She studied the spot. "Drag marks?"

"Definitely." Clay rose and followed the parallel bloody streaks until they stopped at the door. "And there, see how the lines disappear and are replaced by drops? That's good news."

Frank hovered outside the room, frowning at the floor. "What? You think someone or two someones picked him up and carried him?"

"I do."

Frank grunted his agreement while Ellie's head whipped back and forth between the drag marks and the drips. Frustrated green eyes connected with his. "Do you think Gabe's still alive?"

Clay didn't want to lie, and he didn't want to give false

hope either. "Alive when they left this room. Why bother carrying a messy, bleeding dead man when you're worried the cops are hot on your trail?"

Relief lit up her face, but only for a moment. Frustration was like a living thing crawling over her features. "I can't believe Kingsley outsmarted us again."

"Hey guys, you'd better come check this out."

Clay and Ellie hurried over to where Frank waited to usher them into another room. Clay entered first and let out a long, low whistle. "That bastard saw us coming from a mile away." He circled the room, counting ten large monitors spaced out along tables that lined up against the walls. Each monitor featured a different video feed. One of them came from a camera positioned along the road on their drive in. The remaining cameras provided images from outside the warehouse and from various points within.

Ellie scooted over to the tables for a closer look. Her harsh inhalation a moment later made Clay's head whip up.

"What is it?"

"He left me a note." Her voice trembled, and Clay thought he heard more anger than fear in the words.

Clay rushed to her side, his throat dry. *What had Kingsley done now?*

He found his answer when he spied the white piece of paper. The careful, neat way the edges lined up perpendicular to the table made the message all the more grisly.

Wait your turn, Ellie, there's a queue.

Unlike the paper alignment, the letters were vibrant red and sloppy, marred by smears and drips. Almost like Kingsley had written the thing in—

"That's Gabe's blood, isn't it?" Ellie spoke in a hush.

Clay steeled himself to be straight with her. As much as he yearned to sweep her up in his arms and protect her from any more pain, he wouldn't lie. "Probably. Yes."

Ellie stared at the red slashes dissecting the white paper for another few seconds before jerking her gaze away. Her chin jutted out. "Let's get back to Frank's vehicle. We need to hurry if we're going to catch that asshole, and we could use some help."

27

R age curled my fingers around the steering wheel, building in me like a crescendo as we raced down the dark street away from the warehouse. That was a close call. Much too close. Otherwise, I'd still be safely tucked away inside, toying with my latest puppet.

When I spotted a dimly illuminated parking lot coming up fast, I pushed down on the gas and yanked the wheel hard to the right. The tires squealed as they veered off the asphalt and bumped onto a stretch of dirt and foliage. I hit the brakes before we crashed into a towering green bush. One quick turn to the left and the car was hidden from the street by another overgrown shrub. My fury boiled over as I wrenched the gear into park.

"Damn you, Eleanor Kline! How dare you interrupt my plans like that? You will pay for this!" I pounded the steering wheel, the vibrations reverberating up my arms. Again and again, unleashing wave after wave of sheer frustration.

How? How had this happened? What a complete, unmitigated disaster. Milos and I were on the road, covered in blood, with a half-dead man trapped in the trunk. Running away with our tails tucked between our legs like frightened mongrels. To top things off, this car was no longer safe. Not with cops flooding the warehouse at this very moment and spying on us with our own video feed.

I battled to regain control as my throat grew raw from yelling and pain radiated up my forearms. Plan now, rage later. We didn't have time for this. "We need to switch cars. Go steal us one from that parking lot and then follow me up the road."

Milos nodded and slipped out of the passenger seat like a ghost. He crossed behind the bush and slinked into the parking area from the rear. Only a few cars were scattered throughout the lot. Milos chose the one closest to us, a silver four-door that also happened to be farthest from the misty glow of an overhead light.

I narrowed my eyes in an attempt to decipher the make and model of the dumpy-looking sedan. When I did, I beat the steering wheel once more for good measure. No Mercedes or BMW, but an older model Honda Civic. Of course. Why should anything about this night work out in my favor?

In less than a minute, the Civic's engine turned over. I reversed my way back over the dirt to the road. No blaze of headlights broke the darkness from either direction.

Yet.

I accelerated onto the asphalt, keeping my speed down until Milos pulled the Civic out behind me. Over the next two miles, my sense of calm returned. Ellie might have gotten close to catching us this time, but so what? As the saying went: close only counted in horseshoes and hand grenades.

When I pulled off on a deserted stretch of the road, I was humming. Evolution favored adaptability, and I was nothing if not flexible. I shut off the ignition, hit the button to pop the trunk, and walked around to the back of the car. I lifted the trunk, triggering the interior light to bathe the man stuffed inside with a soft glow.

I tsked. "I've seen you look better, that's for sure."

Blood splattered Gabe's body from head to toe. His eyelashes fluttered open at the sound of my voice. He twitched, his feeble arms trying to push him into a sit. They wobbled, then collapsed.

As I stared down into his pale, blood-splotched face, the desire I once felt for this pitiful man transitioned into disgust. "Once upon a time, you were so beautiful. A star like no other. Now, look what you've made me do to you. You're ruined."

Heat burned in my chest again, and I balled my fists in impotent rage. We'd been so good together, until Gabe had gone and ruined everything.

Him, and that bitch, Ellie.

"Mr. del Ray?"

I swiveled with a snarl, livid at the intrusion.

Milos stood like a scarecrow by the trunk, watching me with his shrewd, sunken eyes as he held out my duffle bag and a bottled water. "We need to go, sir."

I seethed with the urge to yell at him. I decided when we needed to go, not him. Pragmatism held my tongue. Milos was right. The longer we dallied here, the more likely Ellie and her little entourage would catch up to us. All my delicious plans for Gabe, destroyed. That redheaded bitch would regret ever being born.

"I suggest we get cleaned up here before heading back on the road." He lifted the contents in his hands a few inches higher. "That way, we can burn everything at once."

Burn. A thrill raced across my skin. Maybe this night wouldn't be a complete loss, after all.

I removed my ruined shirt. My pants came next. Once I'd stripped down to my boxers, I squirted the bottled water on my bare skin and used a patch of my discarded shirt to scrub Gabe's blood from my arms and neck. I emptied the entire bottle before stepping into the clean slacks and shirt I found in the duffle bag.

Removing the stained clothing did wonders for my mood. This time when I studied Gabe's mangled but somehow still exquisite face, my heart filled with an unexpected warmth, along with an intense, stabbing urge. Those beautiful, full lips. It was now or never.

I leaned over and pressed my mouth to his, sighing against his soft skin. I inhaled deeply. Beneath the coppery tang of blood and a faint sourness, I detected a hint of that delicious soap Gabe had always favored. Even if nothing else had gone as planned, at least this one fantasy had finally come true.

Our lips still touched when Gabe's eyes flew open. He jerked his head back and lurched onto his side, whimpering like an animal. Our connection severed. Even in his weakened state, Gabe was desperate to escape me. So much for my little fantasy.

Pretty boys, they were all the same. Always believing they were too good for me. A growl built in my throat, and my fingers curled into claws, eager to teach him a lesson, but I was too aware of Milos's sepulchral presence nearby to degrade myself like that.

Instead, I watched Milos shake a gas can over our pile of bloody clothes. He kept pouring until gas fumes polluted the air, creating a path from the clothes to the car. The cleansing liquid saturated the interior and baptized Gabe where he lay.

Milos worked with an efficiency of motion. Without any needless prattling on. The admiration already seeded in me for Creighton's referral sprouted into a deeper appreciation.

Here was a man who didn't require any prompting to jump into action. Milos was a regular Boy Scout. Although, the troop leaders might not approve of the way my gaunt assistant went about earning his fire badge.

I snickered as Milos upended the can to drain the last of the liquid before tossing the empty container into the back seat. He returned to me, holding a matchbook in his hand.

Thump!

The sudden noise startled me in the quiet night, drawing my attention back to the trunk. One of Gabe's hands curled around the side as he strained to pull himself up.

I clucked my tongue. Silly boy. What a wasted effort. He should know by now that no one escaped me.

Without taking my eyes off Gabe, I held out my hand to Milos. "Give me the matches."

Milos dropped the package into my open palm. I removed one and struck the red tip along the rough patch. The tiny stick sparked to life.

"Goodbye, sweet Gabe." I reached down to drag my knuckles over his soft cheek, excitement rushing through my every cell when his wide eyes reflected the tiny orange flame.

"D-don't."

With a gentle smile, I drank in one last glimpse of that lovely face before stepping back and flicking the match. The orange light landed in the clothes piled a scarce foot from the bumper. I cherished the joy that swelled within me as the nearby air whooshed and the material erupted into a wall of flames.

Gabe's screams accompanied our return to the silver Civic, the perfect soundtrack to end this act. With my heart still brimming with joy, I rolled down the window, wanting to relish my former assistant's howls of pain before the night swallowed them for good.

Milos accelerated, and the orange-red flames grew

smaller until they disappeared. No matter. Cold air roared inside the open window. Instead of rolling it up, I reached out, grinning while I splayed my hand to feel the icy rush between my fingers.

"Look out, Katarina and Ellie. I'm saving the best for last."

28

F or the first mile, no one spoke as Frank gassed the big SUV down the street, propelling the three of them away from the warehouse. Ellie peered out the windshield from the back seat, her nails dug deep into her thighs in an attempt to ward off yet another wave of urgency.

They'd found so much blood at the warehouse. Gabe's blood. Time was running out, and they still had no idea where to find Kingsley. "Can't you go any faster?"

Frank grunted. "Not if you want us all to stay in one piece."

Despite the marshal's testy reply, the SUV lurched forward. Darkened blobs that represented trees whizzed by Ellie's window at an even faster clip. "Any word from the locals yet?"

"Yeah, Vancouver PD and Clark County Sheriff's Department are working together on roadblocks as we speak." Frank swerved around a bend, cutting Clay off momentarily. He grabbed for the ceiling handle and waited for the road to straighten back out. "If luck is on our side, we'll catch them before Kingsley can disappear again."

Ellie gritted her teeth and sank her nails into the cloth seat. When it came to Kingsley, luck never seemed to be on their side. She prayed tonight would be the night that all changed.

"Hey, you see that?"

Clay pointed out the windshield, so Ellie leaned into the middle of the seats to get an unobstructed view. The hairs on the back of her neck bristled. Up ahead in the distance, off the right shoulder, an orange light glowed.

"I see it." Frank sounded about as happy as Ellie felt.

Fire.

"What are the odds that's unrelated to our guy?" Frank didn't wait for an answer before hitting the gas. The speedometer climbed higher.

"I'd guess about one in a million."

"Clay's right. There's no way that fire wasn't started by Kingsley or one of his men." Ellie double-checked her seat belt, even as she willed the SUV to go faster.

"Could be a decoy, to buy them time," Frank said.

Clay nodded. "Only one way to find out."

The tiny orange glow grew bigger and bigger. The SUV ate away at the road, bearing down on the fire quicker than Ellie expected. Frank too. Metal shrieked when he slammed on the brakes. The SUV jerked, the impact slamming Ellie's head against the headrest. She bounced forward, her sternum smacking the taut nylon of her seat belt before Frank swerved the SUV to the side and cut the engine.

"Jesus, Frank." Even the typically stoic Clay sounded shaken. "Remind me never to ride shotgun with you again."

Ellie didn't catch Frank's reply. Her focus was too intent on the scene ahead, where an object started to take shape within the dancing flames. Ice slid across her back.

Car. The thing on fire was a car.

She wrenched open the door and jumped out, into night

air polluted by the stench of gas and melting plastic. She was on her feet and sprinting toward the burning car before her companions had even unbuckled their seat belts.

"Ellie, wait! Dammit!"

Ellie ignored Clay's curse and pumped her legs harder. She refused to wait. She couldn't. Not now. Not when she was sure she'd heard a muffled scream.

The air Ellie raced into grew warm, then hot. Flames engulfed the car, crackling and licking toward the sky like a hungry god, and the acrid stench grew stronger. A second scream emitted from beyond the fiery curtain blocking Ellie's view.

Raw. Terrified.

The high-pitched cry burrowed into Ellie's ears, triggering her to run harder. A faint voice in her head whispered a warning, about gas tanks and explosions. A possibility, even if they weren't nearly as common as cop shows portrayed. But she overrode that warning now that she was certain.

Based on those screams, someone was trapped in the car.

She skidded to a halt when the temperature shifted from hot to boiling, searching the flames for a glimpse of a human shape. Squinting into the brightness, she could just make out the structure of the car. Her best guess placed her location as directly behind the trunk.

A shriek rang out. Ragged and shrill with agony. Only a couple of yards away.

"Gabe?!"

No answer. With heat singeing her cheeks and eyelashes, Ellie inched closer to the open trunk of the burning car, desperate to reach whoever was trapped inside. The heat intensified, pushing her back. Frustrated, she cupped her hands and yelled again.

"Gabe! It's Ellie!"

Nothing. Until another scream pierced the night.

Ellie's breathing slowed. Stopped. She couldn't be one-hundred-percent positive, of course, but she knew all the same. It was Gabe...being burned alive.

And there was nothing she could do to help him.

"Watch out!"

Ellie whirled, then skittered back as Clay rushed toward the fire, swinging his jacket at the flames. Frank appeared on his left, brandishing a small blanket. Sweat glistened on their faces as the two men beat at the flames, and hope unfurled in Ellie's chest.

A hope that wilted when Clay's jacket ignited.

"Dammit!" The agent cursed as he relinquished the garment to the greedy flames.

Frank's blanket wasn't faring much better. The small rectangle of fabric was no match for the fire's rage. From a logical standpoint, Ellie recognized that the odds of a successful rescue were slipping away. But her heart refused to concede. Desperation fueled her legs as she panted and spun, searching for some kind of miracle. Gabe couldn't die like this.

In her distress, Ellie tripped and crashed to the ground. Her palm scraped the dirt, burning as she tore the skin.

Her gaze fell to her hand where it still touched the earth.

Earth. *Dirt.*

In a dim recess of her mind, Ellie understood the cause was lost before she ever started clawing at the ground. Even in the summer, when the freezing temperatures didn't pack the earth into an intractable surface, she would have run out of time, trying to gather handfuls of substance to smother the flames.

But Ellie didn't care. She clawed the ground like a rabid creature. Again and again, scraping up handfuls of dirt in hopes of forming a big enough pile to quash a section of the fire.

A mound formed, but so slow. Too slow.

She had to work faster.

Adrenaline spiked, injecting her cramping fingers with new life. She lost all sense of time, crouched over the earth, digging her nails into bloody stumps.

Gabe. The young man who had risked everything to save her and Jillian. She had to save him in return.

Ellie had no concept of how long she'd been working when strong hands gripped her upper arms and pulled her up. At first, she fought like a person possessed, lashing out with her elbows and kicking with her feet. "Put me down! We have to help him! If I can just get enough dirt...the fire..."

One of her kicks landed, and Clay released her with a muffled curse. Ellie staggered back a step and whirled, wild-eyed.

He edged toward her with his hands lifted. The way one might approach an injured animal. "We tried, but the fire was too strong. I'm sorry, but he's gone."

Ellie scrambled a step back, refusing to believe the words. Refusing to believe what she could see with her own eyes.

"No. You're wrong. We have to keep trying."

But even as she uttered the words, she knew Clay was right. No further cries spilled from the trunk.

Gabe was gone.

The fire climbed higher, the whooshing of the flames the only living thing out there besides the three of them. New odors wafted to Ellie's nostrils. It took her dazed brain a few moments to place them, but when she did, her stomach lurched. Charcoal mixed with the reek of hair left on a curling iron too long.

Clay gripped her shoulders and attempted to turn her

away from the apocalyptic scene. "You don't have to torture yourself like this."

Ellie resisted the desire to take the comfort he offered. To bury her head in his chest and hide. Because torturing herself was exactly what she had to do. What she deserved. Hiding wouldn't bring Gabe back. Nothing would.

So Ellie stayed, watching the car burn while fat tears rolled down her cheeks. She waited until she was sure that no last-minute miracle option would present itself. Then, when she couldn't stand to watch any more, she allowed Clay to gather her in his arms and lead her away. "Come on, Kingsley can't be far," he said. "Let's get back to Frank's SUV and see if we can't track that son of a bitch down."

At first, a peculiar numbness engulfed Ellie, like her entire body had been injected with Novocaine. She barely noticed as Clay ushered her to the SUV with his hand curved around the small of her back, steadying her.

Too late.

They'd been too late again, and now another man was dead by Kingsley's hand. On autopilot, Ellie climbed into the back seat. Clicked on her seat belt. Stared ahead at nothing at all.

This was too hard. Too much. What was the point? Nothing she'd done so far had brought Kingsley down, and now Gabe was dead. Because of her.

She wanted to sink back into the seat, close her eyes, and pretend none of this was happening. She wanted to give up trying, because failing hurt too much. But deep inside her, that spark that had prompted her to become a cop in the first place refused to snuff out. As Frank started up the engine, that spark turned into an ember and then a flame, burning away Ellie's numbness and filling the void with red-hot determination.

Frank accelerated onto the road, and Ellie forced herself

to look out the window at the burning Civic and the site of Gabe's awful death. This time, she welcomed the pain that swept through her. The agony fed her determination.

"You okay back there?" Clay craned his head to appraise Ellie, his brow creased with worry.

"No. But I will be, once we bring Kingsley in."

Clay studied her expression. Apparently satisfied, the agent turned to Frank. "Got an ETA until we hit that first roadblock?"

"Five minutes."

"Good. I gave the order to be alerted immediately if personnel working the roadblocks find anything that makes them so much as lift an eyebrow."

Ellie chewed her lip. "What about alternate routes to escape, is anyone running those down? Bus routes, airports, trains?"

"FBI is sending out an APB with his name and description at all of the airports within a two-hundred-mile radius. Ditto with trains. I'm not sure where we're at with buses. Are there any that run this time of night near here?"

"Checking right now." Ellie searched on her phone and found the local schedule. "The closest one is about a mile away. Should we head there first?"

"Give me the address."

Frank typed the address that Ellie recited into his GPS. As he navigated them there, another idea popped into Ellie's head. She should have thought of it first, but her brain had been hijacked by the horror she'd witnessed. "What about private airfields nearby? Helicopter pads?"

"On it." Clay dialed a number and held his phone to his ear. "Special Agent Lockwood here again. We need a list of any nearby locations that house private airfields or helicopter pads. Send that to me as soon as you generate. We'll need agents checking out each and every one."

Four hours of fruitless searching later, Frank pulled the SUV in front of a hotel. "You two look like you're about to pass out on your feet, and the last thing I need right now is to drive both of your sorry asses to the hospital. It's late, so get out. Get some sleep. We'll be at this again before you know it."

Ellie wanted to argue, but Frank was right. The adrenaline keeping her going had slowly worn off over the last hour, leaving her body exhausted and her brain foggy. A few hours of sleep would do them good.

When they entered the sliding doors, the lobby was empty except for the few on-duty hotel staff. Clay walked straight up to the young dark-haired man behind the reservation desk. He slid his driver's license and credit card across the counter. "Can we get two rooms, please?"

The idea of sleeping alone in a strange room after everything that had transpired over the last twenty-four hours made Ellie shiver with dread. She tugged on Clay's sleeve. "Can we share a room? Please?"

The sharp lines of his face softened. "You bet." Relief washed over Ellie as Clay turned back to the employee. "Scratch that. We'll take one room with a king bed."

Ellie didn't even care that the young man flashed Clay a knowing smile before tapping away at his keyboard. "Certainly. That's one room with a king bed."

The panel beeped when Clay swiped his key card. He held open the door, letting Ellie enter first. The room was spacious and decorated in soothing, tasteful shades of blue and gray, but the entire thing could have been the size of a closet and the walls plastered with pictures of clowns for all Ellie cared. All she really needed at that particular moment was a hot shower, followed by a bed.

Clay caught her in the bathroom doorway, gazing longingly at the combo shower/tub. "You go first."

Ellie shot him a grateful smile. "Thank you. I'll try not to take too long."

"Don't rush. Showering for as long as we want is the least we deserve after this night. I'll be fine."

No argument from her. Especially once she stepped under the hot spray. The water soothed her tense muscles, and the lavender-scented soap lathered up with thick bubbles and washed the grunge from the day away. She stood under the spray until her skin flushed pink all over and her legs felt wobbly.

Once she dried off and pulled on her warm nightclothes, Ellie padded barefoot into the bedroom, dressed in flannel pajama pants and oversized t-shirt. "All yours."

She waited for the bathroom door to click shut before sinking onto the bed. To her horror, her eyes welled with tears and sobs barreled up her throat as the day's events hit her all over again.

She rolled onto her stomach and buried her head in the comforter as she cried. She sobbed for Gabe, for Kingsley's other victims. For herself. For the seemingly endless suffering that the master continued to inflict.

What happened if they never found Kingsley, and he haunted her forever? How many other people were yet to suffer? How many of Ellie's friends, loved ones, and colleagues could Kingsley attack and kill before she finally snapped for good?

Ellie didn't know how long she cried, only that at some point, the mattress dipped and Clay gently rolled her over and gathered her into his arms. His touch unleashed a whole new torrent inside her, and she buried her head against his chest. He rubbed her back and held her close, letting her sob until there was nothing left. When she lifted her head, the front of his gray shirt was dark with her tears.

Ellie cringed. "S-sorry about your sh-shirt."

Clay used one finger to tip her chin up. "Hey. Don't do that. This shirt has survived a lot worse than a little water. Crying is good for the soul, sometimes we need to unload so that we can keep going. I'm just glad that I was here for you. Talking helps too."

Ellie hiccupped, then sighed. She knew Clay was right. Bottling up her worries and fears only made them grow. So, she told him. About all of the terrible questions ringing in her head. The worst-case scenarios. The endless string of what-ifs. And even though Clay didn't speak, he was right. Talking loosened the painful knots inside her. The strong arms wrapped around her didn't hurt, either.

Once the floodgates opened, Ellie couldn't close them again. She kept talking. She told Clay about her childhood, going into detail about what happened the night that started all of this. How she'd lied to her parents about meeting a boy who'd ended up ditching her at a party, only for events to go from bad to worse when Kingsley kidnapped her on the walk home. Even though her skin crawled and her stomach turned, Ellie told him what Kingsley had made her do. She left nothing out.

"I can't help but think that I started all this. If I'd stayed home that night or gone to the movies like I was supposed to, none of this would be happening right now. That all of this is somehow my fault."

Clay's hand was gentle as he stroked her damp hair. "I understand that it's easy to fall into that trap, but that's exactly what it is, Ellie. A trap. Sure, if you hadn't gone that night, then Kingsley might never have targeted you, but then it would have been some other girl. Likely one who wouldn't have been able to get away. Kingsley is a serial killer. He loves to inflict pain. He needs to. He will never stop unless we make him. And it's only thanks to you that we're as close as we are now to stopping him for good."

Logically, Ellie understood all of that already, but the sentiment resonated more when coming from Clay. "Thank you. And wow, look at that. Time's up on my talking allotment for the evening." She rolled onto her side and propped herself up on her elbow so that they faced each other. "Now that you know all my deep, dark secrets, it's your turn, right? Anything you want to share, to even the scale a little?"

Ellie was mostly teasing, so she was surprised when Clay took a deep breath and closed his eyes, like he was gathering his courage. When he opened them again, they held a faraway look.

"When I was thirteen, my family went to a local fair. My parents, me, and my sister, who was eleven at the time." He paused, and his voice dropped to a reverential whisper. "Caraleigh."

The way he said his sister's name sent goose bumps skating up Ellie's arms.

"Being eleven and thirteen, the last thing we wanted to do was spend the whole time hanging out with our parents. So, after begging them for half an hour to let us go ride the rides on our own, they finally caved." A distant smile curved his mouth. "My dad never could resist Caraleigh for very long. She had big blue eyes like my mom and knew how to work them, ever since she was old enough to talk."

He lapsed into silence as he stared into space. Ellie's sense of foreboding grew, and she twisted the comforter between her fingers to ease the building tension.

"They let us go, on one condition. That I not let my sister out of my sight. And I did that. At first. We rode a few rides, right up until I saw Jana Danielson. At the time, I couldn't believe my luck. There was the girl I'd had a crush on all year, hanging out with a few of my friends. So we joined their group. We rode one of those spinning rides that makes you want to puke, then played some carnival games. Jana actually sat next to me on the roller coaster and touched my shoulder. I still remember how excited I was in that moment."

He broke off again. Ellie's chest tightened. *Please, don't let this story be going where I think it does...*

But she was pretty sure she knew the truth long before he ever finished.

"It was after the roller coaster, in line for churros and pretzels, when I realized Caraleigh was no longer with us. We looked everywhere. We retraced our steps, scoured the entire damn fairgrounds. But even then, I was really only worried about what my parents would do when they found out. I figured worst case, Caraleigh had gotten mad that I wasn't paying attention to her anymore and run back to tattle, and I'd be grounded." His throat bobbed as he swallowed. "We never saw her again."

The horror hit Ellie hard. Even though part of her had been expecting this punchline, her hand flew to her mouth. "Oh, Clay."

"They tried police, search dogs, even cadaver dogs. They never found so much as a trace. It was like she'd never been there at all. But you know what the real kicker is?" He lifted his head and his eyes glistened with so much agony that Ellie felt his pain like a physical punch. "I can still remember all the rides I went on with Jana, how she touched my shoulder on the roller coaster, that she wore a maroon sweatshirt with black jeans, and that she wanted the salt on her pretzel on the side. But to this day, I couldn't begin to tell you how long Caraleigh was missing before I noticed."

Self-loathing was etched into his twisted upper lip and rigid jawline. Ellie reached out and cupped his cheeks in her hands, tugging until their faces lined up with their noses only an inch apart.

"Hey. Look at me." She waited for him to comply. "I

understand the compulsion to blame yourself, probably better than anyone. But you were a kid, Clay. Thirteen. And that's the kind of thing that happens to thirteen-year-olds. They get caught up in crushes and friends and forget their responsibilities sometimes. Your parents knew that when they agreed to let you and Caraleigh go off on your own. I'm sure they factored that in, along with the risk of one of you actually being snatched, which, even in our line of work, we know is incredibly low."

He shuddered beneath her fingertips. "I don't—"

She pressed her fingers to his lips. "Like you told me earlier, it's not your fault. Not yours, not your parents'. Not Jana's or Caraleigh's. The only person at fault is the monster who snatched her."

Clay shuddered again before letting her pull his head to her chest. He clutched her upper arms like his life depended on it while she stroked his hair and made soothing sounds, blinking back a fresh batch of tears.

After enough time had passed, she gave a strangled laugh. "Wow, here I was thinking both of us were pretty deep, but all along, we're about as basic as can be. Doesn't take a genius to figure out why both of us ended up in law enforcement, does it?"

Clay snorted before he lifted his head. "Guess not."

Her humor faded, and the burst of warmth was replaced by thick, ugly shame. "I'm so sorry, Clay, that I didn't know this before. I should have asked you more about your family." She hung her head. "I've been selfish, too caught up in my own stuff. Forgive me? Be—"

Warm lips pressed to hers, silencing the rest of her sentence. "Hush. That's the biggest bunch of baloney I've heard in my entire life, and in my line of work I've heard a hell of a lot. You are without a doubt one of the kindest, most giving people I've ever had the good fortune of knowing.

Ellie Kline, I thank my lucky stars all the time that you were brought into my life. There's no way you could have known about Caraleigh because I never talk about her. Or didn't, until now. So, thank you."

No matter what Clay said, Ellie didn't believe for one second that she deserved his thanks. But she'd be lying if she didn't admit that her throat clogged with emotion over how he'd described her.

"I'm thankful that you're in my life too." She toyed with an errant curl. "Isn't it odd, how both of us had childhoods that centered around kidnappings and we somehow managed to find each other?"

Ellie wondered if that old, shared trauma was part of what had drawn them to each other from the start. Maybe their injured souls had recognized a kindred spirit in each other, long before they'd consciously made the connection.

"When was the last time you searched for her?"

Clay traced his thumb over his eyebrow. "It's been a couple years now. Before that, I was letting the search take over my life, almost like an obsession. Wasn't sleeping well, spent my free time hunting for clues. I stopped when the sleep deprivation started impacting me on the job. Good thing. I'm guessing I was a lot closer to some kind of nervous breakdown than I ever realized at the time."

"And now?"

He gave a helpless shrug. "Now, I compartmentalize. I have to. The victims of my cases deserve to have my undivided attention, which I can't give them if there's always a corner of my mind dedicated to catching a glimpse or a sign of Caraleigh." He rubbed the back of his neck. "Besides, it's been twenty years. There's a good chance I wouldn't recognize my sister if she walked right up to me and said hello."

The hollow note to his words told Ellie just how much

that thought haunted him. She squeezed his hand, unsure of how to ease his pain.

He yawned and stretched before pulling Ellie back into his arms. "Enough with sharing hour for one night, let's try to get some sleep. Tomorrow's going to be a long day."

His yawn triggered Ellie to do the same, and the mere mention of sleep prompted her eyelids to droop shut. She snuggled up against him, stealing comfort from the warm, hard length of his body spooned around hers.

As the steady rise and fall of his chest lulled Ellie into drifting off, she made a silent vow.

The moment Ellie returned to her desk at the Charleston PD, she was adding a new cold case to her list.

Caraleigh Lockwood, I will find you. One way or another.

29

My glee over dispatching Gabe to his fiery death only lasted as far as Grand Mound, Washington, a gas stop that was virtually indistinguishable from any other town in the state in that both greenery and Subarus were plentiful. By the time Milos guided the Civic off the Northbound 5 and into the outskirts of Seattle, my joy had vanished completely, replaced by a seething dissatisfaction that made my body itch in unreachable places.

Now, Milos was out finding us dinner, while here I was. Trapped in this cesspit of a motel room. The hideous orange comforter might as well have been constructed from wool scouring pads, the way the fabric scratched at my arms and bare feet. As for the mattress, well. I scooted over and winced when a loose spring dug into my shoulder blade. This old relic was better suited for one of my torture sessions than some of my hand-picked tools.

Depressing. That was the word for this hovel. My lip curled as I surveyed the dingy space. To temper my growing rage, I visualized lighting one of Milos's spare matches and flicking it into the middle of the grim little room in an attempt to summon a bit of the joy I'd feel if I watched this entire rat trap structure burst into flames. The owner deserved no less for taking such liberties with the name. Seattle's Best Motel? What a joke.

This place was a pit that hadn't been remodeled since the seventies, and that was being generous. I looked up at the ceiling, grimacing at a large, yellow stain that resembled the state of Florida. Nothing would convince me that these rooms had even been deep cleaned over the past five decades.

This was not how today should have turned out. Today was meant to be spent separating my former assistant from a variety of his body parts and savoring the steady drip-drip-drip of his life's blood hitting the concrete floor. After the hours of distress he'd inflicted on me, I deserved to enjoy the melody of his scream, over and over again.

Once I'd bored of my torture sessions, Milos and I had planned to jet off from the private airstrip to a first-class resort of my choosing, where we'd enjoy all of the creature comforts we deserved while I planned the next step of my revenge with meticulous care.

But thanks to the Feds turning up the heat, the man providing our private jet got cold feet and backed out. Which led to our current lodging situation. Instead of room service, champagne, and eight-hundred thread count sheets, I was surrounded by stained Berber-style carpet, a toilet that never stopped running, and moth-eaten orange and brown curtains that reeked of decades of mildew and a bad acid trip.

My plans, in disarray once more. All thanks to that insufferable redhead.

Outside the grime-covered window, someone laid on their horn. Three times. Four. By the fifth noxious screech, I leapt to my feet, my fingers twitching with the urge to slam the driver's head against the steering wheel until they stopped breathing. The threadbare floor shook as I stomped over to the door. By the time I reached for the knob, the honking ceased. Of course. Even this small joy was to be denied me.

Not that I could afford to be committing flagrant acts of violence right now anyway.

Also Ellie's fault.

My nostrils flared. I whirled, swiped the closest object off the scratched dresser, and flung it as hard as I could. The cheap ice bucket bounced off the wall and hit the floor. A fault line now cracked the plastic container down the middle.

How dare she rob me of my plans for Gabe? My taste for inflicting pain on that traitor hadn't come close to being satiated. If anything, the torture I'd had time to commit had served as a starter course. Merely whetting my appetite rather than satisfying the immense hunger churning inside me.

I returned to the bed, careful to avoid a suspicious stain near the far pillow, and sighed. Yes, I blamed Ellie, but to be fair, I also shouldered a portion of the responsibility. That wide-eyed cop never should have come so close to capturing me in the first place. Yet again, I'd underestimated her, and that failure was mine, and mine alone.

One thing I detested was a hypocrite. I demanded meticulousness from everyone who worked with me, so there was no excusing my own shortcomings in that department.

I crossed my arms behind my head and snorted. As exceptional as I was in many ways, I had to concede that in others, I was a bit of a cliché. The meticulousness, for instance. I'd picked my fastidiousness up in childhood, in the most yawn-worthy way. Via my indulgent but disinterested jet-setter parents. Between them flying off to foreign countries at the drop of the hat and providing me with little to no boundaries, it was almost to be expected that I'd grow up to become obsessed with details and routines.

I hadn't always been the masterful planner that I was now, though.

Nostalgia filled me as I reminisced back to the early days, when that dark curiosity I harbored inside me like a malignant tumor was only just starting to form. In fact, the first time I pinned a neighborhood cat in our backyard and smashed his tail until he howled, I was probably only looking for a reaction from my mom, who sunned by the pool a few yards away.

Like the behaviorists said, negative attention was still attention. But she hadn't even bothered to look up from her magazine to check.

Before long, I'd graduated to enjoy the way the animals struggled to get away, and the cries they'd made as I plucked their whiskers and sawed off their tails. Then came the day old Mrs. Dechert spotted me slamming a rock to her sweet little tabby cat's head. I remembered the horrified expression on her face. The way my body had filled with a mixture of fear and excitement. This time, my parents couldn't fail to react.

I shook my head at my naiveté. Yes, I'd been young, but truly, I should have known better. Having a juvenile delinquent shame the family simply wasn't tenable, so my mom and stepdad did what parents have been doing since the dawn of history. They dismissed the narrative they had no interest in hearing.

She must have been mistaken, they told the elderly woman. Their son would never dream of committing such a terrible act. By the time the police showed up, even poor Mrs. Dechert seemed almost convinced of my innocence.

The cops asked my parents and me a few half-hearted questions, but no charges were ever filed. Still, I'd learned a valuable lesson standing in our entryway before the two uniformed officers that day, sweat soaking my underarms as I pictured myself locked away in a nasty, cramped cell that reeked of body odor and urine.

The idea of jail held no appeal to me, so I learned to exert caution and cover my tracks.

And yet, I'd pushed my luck again when I'd kidnapped that mousy, gap-toothed girl from our abnormal psychology class as she stumbled home drunk from a campus bar, in order to test out a new toy. The delicious knowledge of the scars that must still mar her pale, creamy skin excited me. I'd dumped her half-conscious body in the early hours of the morning, in the dirt near the sidewalk where I'd found her.

The first time she'd returned to class after that had been two weeks later, and I could tell by the way her eyes landed on me and then skittered away that she had an inkling of who'd attacked her. At least subconsciously. But either she never breathed a word, or she did and the campus police laughed her out of the station.

Even then, when I was young and still rather foolish, I understood an important truth. In a world where middle and lower-class college athletes could sexually assault intoxicated women on camera without being charged, who would dare accuse me, now that my mother had remarried into wealth? The son of a couple who'd donated an entire wing to my university? A generous contribution that I often suspected had been made with the express goal of offsetting any sort of...indelicacies that might arise regarding their only son.

Someone knocked on a door a couple rooms down. Muscles coiled in my legs, preparing my body for a potential threat. I ceased breathing. Listened. Voices echoed, a man and a woman's, before the door slammed shut and the noise stopped.

Reassured that nothing was amiss, I returned to my

musings. I possessed little doubt that both my mother and stepfather grasped at least a rudimentary understanding of my nature by the time they sent me away to a high-priced boarding school, or the very least, college. They simply couldn't be bothered to care. They'd leave no stone unturned when it came to protecting the family reputation.

Unless, of course, one of those rocks was hiding a suggestion for mandatory family therapy, court hearings, or spending time with their odd son. No, they much preferred throwing money at any problems that arose for me, leaving them free to gamble in Monaco, or ride elephants while enjoying a five-star Kenyan safari.

Like all budding prodigies, I grew more accomplished with practice. By the time I'd moved on to grad school and murder, no one ever even looked my way when locals went missing. That was because I planned everything ahead of time, took no unnecessary risks, and followed my own set of rules.

Never the same location twice.

Limited transfer of victims so there was less trace evidence to worry about.

Wigs, sunglasses, changes of clothing and gait to alter my appearance.

And of course, gloves were a must. To add even an extra layer of safety, I'd abided by the philosophy that if I couldn't guarantee a successful cleanup after my little games, then I burned the entire crime scene to ash.

Which brought me back to Gabe. The mere thought of him dialed up the burner under my simmering anger, and I banged my skull against the headboard. Gabe knew how exacting my standards were, and yet I'd delivered a subpar performance for him. I'd planned to savor Gabe's death like one might a fine, barrel-aged Scotch, sipping at his pain over time so as to fully appreciate every delicious, fiery drop. The traitor had deserved no less.

After slamming my skull into the headboard once more, I glared into the crooked mirror beside the garage-sale TV. My reflection snarled back at me. Ellie had stolen my justice from me, an indignity for which she would pay. Dearly.

I sat up, calming myself by smoothing the wrinkles from my shirt. My little flame-haired puppet would pay soon enough, but she'd have to wait her turn. In the mirror, a wicked grin spread across my face. First, though, I had other priorities to tackle.

30

T he next two days were hectic, with Ellie's time divided between scouring Vancouver and the surrounding areas and meetings with the new Kingsley Task Force. She spent hours hashing out potential leads in the cramped, temporary headquarters set up in the Vancouver PD building, dissecting Kingsley's potential escape routes, and chasing down any people of interest.

By the time she and Clay returned to Portland to board their flight home, Ellie was running on fumes. She'd busted her butt in Vancouver. Despite that, after stowing her carry-on in the overhead bin and settling into her window seat, Ellie felt defeated.

All that work, for nothing. No sign of Kingsley anywhere. Once again, the Master had vanished, safe from facing justice for his heinous crimes.

As Clay settled into his spot on the aisle and snapped together his seat belt, Ellie pulled down the window shade and slumped. In-between hunting for clues and endless meetings, she'd attended Gabe's autopsy. Any lingering hope that she'd clung to over the charred remains on the medical examiner's table not belonging to Gabe died when his dental records arrived.

Comparing the X-rays provided by his old dentist in Florida to the body rescued from the burning car left no room for doubt. The man who'd spent his final moments screaming his pain from a trunk was Gabe. Burned to death by Kingsley, his former employer and a man he'd once respected above all others.

The memory of those anguished cries echoed in her mind, making Ellie wrap her arms around her chest and shiver. She fumbled with her phone and flipped on her playlist, turning up the volume until Gabe's screams were drowned out by bass and drums.

At first, all Ellie daydreamed about on the ride home from the airport was holing up in her apartment for days and catching up on sleep. She even dozed off in the car for a few minutes, her exhausted body lulled by the constant motion. She jolted awake when Clay turned a corner and slammed on his brakes.

"Sorry. Some idiot shoppers darted right into the street without looking. It's a zoo out here."

Clay hit the gas again while Ellie straightened in her seat and blinked out the windshield in disbelief. Clay hadn't been exaggerating. Downtown Charleston was packed.

Her jaw fell open at the sheer numbers of people out, scurrying along the sidewalks and crossing the streets toting colorful bags. Was there a festival or event that she didn't know about? "What's going on? Where did all these people come from?"

"Do you really not know?" Clay slid her an amused look before honking at the van that pulled out in front of them.

Ellie wrinkled her nose, about to tell Clay that she wouldn't have asked if she did, when she noticed the big red bows and green wreaths adorning the storefronts and streetlights. She checked her phone for the date and did a double take. December 23rd. Tomorrow was Christmas Eve? Yikes. How had that happened?

"I guess I didn't realize it was coming up so quickly." Ellie groaned and slouched lower in the seat. So much for her plan to hibernate for the next few days. She'd been so caught up in catching Kingsley that she hadn't shopped for a single gift yet, much less set up a Christmas tree or decorations.

"Looks like someone needs a little help getting into the holiday spirit."

She rested her cheek against the cool glass and ignored Clay's teasing. Dealing with the holidays right now sounded like so much work. Ellie had no idea how she'd find the energy, but she'd have to try. She couldn't show up at her family's annual holiday dinner empty-handed.

Holiday stress dominated her thoughts when Ellie entered her apartment. She took two steps inside and froze as the fresh, crisp scent of pine enveloped her like a warm embrace. "Oh, wow."

Her hand flew to her chest as she took everything in. Stockings dangled over the fireplace and garlands twinkling with white lights draped across the hallway and along the kitchen counter. Big red bows reminiscent of the ones strewn along the shops downtown adorned the walls. The pièce de résistance was in the living room, though. A nine-foot Christmas tree with a shiny gold star on top towered along the wall, all lit up and decked out in an array of colorful ornaments.

"Surprise!" Jillian beamed at her from the kitchen, but her smile faltered when Ellie didn't speak. "It's a good surprise, I hope?"

Ellie swallowed the knot in her throat and blinked away the tears. After all the crying yesterday, she was surprised she had any left.

"Are you kidding? This is the best surprise! Thank you so much. You have no idea how happy this makes me." Ellie rushed forward and threw her arms around her friend, wrapping her in a tight hug. Maybe a little too tight, because Jillian yelped. "Oops, sorry. Didn't mean to break my very own Christmas elf. I'm just so thankful."

Jillian rubbed Ellie's shoulders, and mock scowled. "I'm glad I could help, but let's dial the thankfulness down a few notches, okay? Us Christmas elves are more fragile than we look. Oh my god, you're not crying, are you? Why are you crying? This was supposed to make you happy, not sad."

Ellie blinked harder, but her eyes refused to stop leaking. She couldn't help it. She'd returned home feeling so down, only to open the door to an irrefutable reminder of how lucky she was. Her life was so full and rich now, with family and the best of friends. What a difference a few years could make.

She smiled through her tears. "I am happy! These are my happy tears, I swear. I'm just feeling emotional over how lucky I am to have all of you in my life." She turned a semi-circle so that her gaze could encompass Jillian, Jacob, and Clay.

"Woof! Woof!" Sam interrupted the moment by bounding over to Ellie and rubbing up against her legs. A ridiculous stuffed toy dangled from her mouth, and her thick tail whipped back and forth like a windshield wiper set for a downpour.

Everyone laughed, Ellie included. "Yes, I'm lucky to have you too, you big goober." Ellie scratched the dog's head, while from his bed in the corner, Duke rested his dark head on his paws and groaned. "And you! Even if you didn't greet me with," Ellie squinted closer at the toy drooping from Sam's mouth in confusion, "a jackalope wearing a Santa hat?"

Jillian shrugged. "It was on sale. Oh! And speaking of

sales, I took the liberty of doing some shopping for your family on your behalf. I know how busy you've been lately, and I figured this was one stress I could remove from your list."

Struck speechless by her roommate's thoughtfulness, all Ellie could do at first was gape.

Jillian fidgeted and began wringing her hands. "I'm sorry if I overstepped. I saved all the receipts, just in case, and nothing is wrapped yet. If you hate it, we can take everything back."

For the second time in five minutes, Ellie flung her arms around her roommate. This time, she made sure to resist the urge to squeeze. "You're the best, you know that?"

Ellie spied the relief that swept Jillian's features before her roommate flipped her blonde hair over her shoulder and rubbed her knuckles on her chest. "Oh, trust me, I know."

From the kitchen, Jacob snorted. "Trust me, she really does."

Jillian stuck her tongue out at him before tugging Ellie toward her bedroom. "Come on, I'll show you what I bought. If everything looks okay, I can start wrapping."

Of course, everything Jillian had picked out was perfect. Each gift, thoughtfully chosen. If she were being honest, probably better than Ellie could have done herself. Jillian hadn't stopped at shopping for Ellie's parents, either. She'd also selected gifts for Ellie's siblings. Perfect ones.

"If I'd known that all those Sunday dinners with my family would pay off like this, I would have started taking you sooner."

"Yeah, yeah, shoulda, coulda, woulda." Jillian huffed as she put a lid on the last box. "Please. Pretty sure I started attending dinners not very long after we became friends."

"Exactly. I needed you in my life sooner."

Jillian's eyes grew misty. "Hey, right back at you." She

cleared her throat. "Now, enough of this mushy stuff. Go grab some scissors and tape, and I'll get the wrapping paper. We need to get these suckers finished before family dinner tonight."

Ellie clapped her palm to her mouth. "Oh, crap!" How had she forgotten? Today was Sunday, and according to Kline house tradition, family dinners were always on Sundays. Impending holidays or not. "Let's get cracking."

With Clay and Jacob helping, the four of them made short work of wrapping the presents in the glittering silver and red paper that Jillian provided. Clay, Ellie, and Jillian finished wrapping two gifts each and then kicked back to watch Jacob painstakingly curl ribbon on the single present he'd been assigned. Ellie smothered a smile as her former partner smoothed the edges and fussed with the ribbon until the package met with his approval.

Clay whistled. "Jacob, buddy, you've been holding out. Why'd you never tell us about your stint in the North Pole as Santa's personal wrapper?"

Surprised, Jacob glanced at the other gifts strewn across the floor and winced. Ellie couldn't blame him. She'd patted herself on the back for pulling off a respectable wrapping job until she'd spied Jacob's work. In comparison, though…ouch.

Stacked up against Jacob's flawless execution, the rest of the presents looked like they'd been wrapped by Santa's reindeers. "No comment. Although, if I were going to comment, it'd be along the lines of, 'good thing it's the thought that counts.'"

Jillian poked him in the rib cage with the scissors' handle. "Hey, we can't all be Mr. Anal."

Ellie's gaze flew to Clay's. A moment later, they both busted out laughing. Jillian's eyes rounded before she dissolved into giggles too.

"All right, children, time to get your minds out of the

gutter and help me clean this up so that Ellie and Clay can shower and change clothes before we go." Jacob rolled his eyes, but even he couldn't hide a grin.

A short while later, the foursome parked in the circular driveway in front of the stately brick mansion where Ellie had grown up.

Eustace, the family butler and another staple of Ellie's formative years, greeted them at the door. She hugged him the same way she did every week, inhaling the familiar whiff of Old Spice. Of course, the second they walked inside, the delicious holiday aromas of Ellie's childhood enveloped them: spicy pumpkin, sweet apples, and savory turkey, all accented by fresh pine, courtesy of the glittering twelve-foot tree that looked like it belonged on the cover of a home magazine.

Soon, Ellie was surrounded by laughter and the warmth of her family's love. Even Dan and Blake, her stuffy older brothers, acted happy to spend time with her. She traded hugs with them while Wesley pulled faces at her from behind their backs. Ellie grinned.

Wesley was her favorite, and boy, did he know it. Her little brother, who now towered over her by a good five inches. Growing up, he'd been the only one who understood her need to buck their family's high-society expectations. In this moment, she realized how lucky she was to remain so close to him as they'd both grown.

By the time she'd finished catching up with Dan and Blake, Wesley had corralled Clay over by the kitchen. The FBI agent threw back his head and laughed at whatever Wesley said, making Ellie smile. The two of them together were the best kind of trouble.

She watched them until her mom pressed a champagne glass into Ellie's hand. "Merry Christmas, Eleanor dear."

Helen Kline looked exquisite with her flame-colored hair

piled on top of her head and emerald-cut diamonds flashing from her ears. Ellie and her mom hadn't always seen eye to eye about Ellie's job, but in the end, the Kline matron had come around.

"Merry Christmas. I love you, Mom."

"I love you too." Ellie's mother blinked before narrowing her eyes. "Wait, is something wrong?"

Ellie laughed. "No. Tonight, everything is just right."

Her mother's astute gaze studied Ellie for several more seconds before she nodded. "I agree. Or at least, everything will be all right once we corral these ruffians in the dining room. Shall we?"

Helen Kline held out her arm for Ellie to link hers through. Together, they led the group to the elegant dining table laden with holiday china and glittering crystal, while Ellie once again counted her blessings.

The last week had been tough, but now was the time for Ellie to let go of her cases and focus on all the wonderful things in her life. She settled into her chair, determined to do precisely that. As her gaze roved over each and every person at the table, her heart swelled and began to overflow.

Yes, Kingsley would have to wait. For the next few days, Ellie was going to count her blessings and draw from the well of good in her life.

After the holidays, she'd be back to sifting through evil soon enough.

31

Milos sat alone at a high-top table near the bar, sipping his IPA and pretending to read a newspaper. The scattered TVs were all tuned-in to college football. Most of the other patrons chatted and drank while keeping one eye on the nearest screen. Every once in a while, a cheer would go up when someone's favorite team carried the pigskin into the in-zone. The rowdiness of the celebrations increased as the sun beyond the tinted windows sank out of view.

"Yeah, baby! Way to go, Hurricanes!"

He surveyed the man who'd jumped to his feet to pump his arms in the air and perform an excited little dance. He wondered idly why the dancer was so excited about a team from a state that was over two thousand miles away, or if the man had ever even been to Miami before his gaze drifted back to the couple tucked away in a booth near the back.

The light hanging over that back booth was out. Whether a coincidence or by design, Milos wasn't sure. He only knew that the poor lighting made his job more difficult, especially since his perspective only gave him a view of the woman's profile. That was okay, though. Difficult didn't faze him. In that way, he was like a spider...he knew his patience would pay off.

As if he had all the time in the world on his hands, he sipped his beer and waited. Eventually, the man in the booth signaled a passing waitress over to them.

He leaned forward.

Sure enough, the dark-haired woman turned her face in his direction as she smiled at the waitress and placed her order.

He lifted his phone, zoomed in, and snapped a photo before scrolling to his gallery to compare. With the low lighting and distance, his shot wasn't perfect, but that was also okay. He wasn't here for his photography skills.

His assignment was clear: locate the woman in the picture his boss had provided. There was no longer any doubt in his mind that the woman he sought and the woman seated in the booth were one and the same.

A rare smile formed on a face that had been called everything from cadaverous to creepy.

Gotcha, Katarina Volkov.

An hour later, the couple closed out their tab and left the bar. He tossed enough cash on the table to cover the tab and a fifteen-percent tip. No more, no less. Always left fifteen percent because a run-of-the-mill tip meant not standing out. In his line of business, blending in was key. After waiting ten seconds, he followed the couple out.

The woman kissed the man from the booth before climbing into her car. As she reversed out of the parking spot, he surreptitiously snapped a photo of the license plate.

That task complete, he headed to his car and exited the parking lot in the same direction he'd watched the woman turn, allowing another car to pass first so that there was a buffer between them. He bided his time, always keeping at least eight car lengths between them.

Ten minutes later, Katarina Volkov pulled into a driveway.

He continued driving past until he reached the end of the street, where he turned left and cruised the neighborhood for exactly five minutes. When he was certain he'd given it enough time, he circled back around and headed down the woman's street from the opposite direction.

As he approached her address, he eased up on the gas, readying his phone in his right hand. Once his nondescript Ford rental drew even with the neat little house, he held his thumb down on the screen. The camera shutter clicked multiple times in rapid succession, snapping pictures as he passed.

He didn't stop or park. He knew better than to risk any unwanted attention. Besides, he had what he needed. For now.

He continued down the street and out of the neighborhood until he hit the main drag. A right turn and a mile later, he pulled into a drugstore parking lot. The only thing saving the squat brown building from ugliness was the sweeping view of mountains in the background.

After checking his rearview mirror to make sure he wasn't followed, he pulled up his pictures and texted several of them to his boss. Images of both the house and the woman's face.

Less than thirty seconds after he hit send, his phone dinged.

Good job. Wait for further instructions.

The reply made him smile as he tossed his phone to the passenger seat. That text might read like faint praise to most, but from his boss? The text qualified as effusive. Good job meant his boss was pleased with him, and in his mind, that was a fortuitous thing.

People who displeased Abel del Rey tended to wind up dead, and Milos planned to live for a very long time.

The End
To be continued...

Thank you for reading.
All of the Ellie Kline Series books can be found on Amazon.

ACKNOWLEDGMENTS

How does one properly thank everyone involved in taking a dream and making it a reality? Here goes.

In addition to our families, whose unending support provided the foundation for us to find the time and energy to put these thoughts on paper, we want to thank the editors who polished our words and made them shine.

Many thanks to our publisher for risking taking on two newbies and giving us the confidence to become bona fide authors.

More than anyone, we want to thank you, our readers, for clicking on a couple of nobodies and sharing your most important asset, your time, with this book. We hope with all our hearts we made it worthwhile.

Much love,
Mary & Donna

ABOUT THE AUTHOR

Mary Stone lives among the majestic Blue Ridge Mountains of East Tennessee with her two dogs, four cats, a couple of energetic boys, and a very patient husband.

As a young girl, she would go to bed every night, wondering what type of creature might be lurking underneath. It wasn't until she was older that she learned that the creatures she needed to most fear were human.

Today, she creates vivid stories with courageous, strong heroines and dastardly villains. She invites you to enter her world of serial killers, FBI agents but never damsels in distress. Her female characters can handle themselves, going toe-to-toe with any male character, protagonist or antagonist.

Discover more about Mary Stone on her website.
www.authormarystone.com

Donna Berdel

Raised as an Army brat, Donna has lived all over the world, but no place has given her as much peace as the home she lives in with her husband near Myrtle Beach. But while she now keeps her feet planted firmly in the sand, her mind goes back to those cities and the people she met and said goodbye to so many times.

With her two adopted cats fighting for lap space, she brings those she loved (and those she didn't) back as characters in her books. And yes, it's kind of fun to kill off anyone who was mean to her in the past. Mean clerk at the grocery store...beware!

Connect with Mary Online

facebook.com/authormarystone

goodreads.com/AuthorMaryStone

bookbub.com/profile/3378576590

pinterest.com/MaryStoneAuthor

instagram.com/marystone_author

Made in the USA
Middletown, DE
07 September 2021